About *The Feudist*

"A classic coming-of-age tale set amidst the violence and despair of the Arizona frontier. With authentic characters, fascinating situations, and spare prose, Dan Herman has delivered a wonderful western in the tradition of John Williams's *Butcher's Crossing*."

—John Mack Faragher, author of *Eternity Street: Violence and Justice in Frontier Los Angeles.*

"Like Kelton's *The Day the Cowboys Quit*, *The Feudist* evokes historical realism and vitality that move the reader beyond mere facts to the pathos, pain, and complexities of the time. You'll enjoy the ride."

—Richard W. Slatta, author of *Cowboys of the Americas*, *The Cowboy Encyclopedia*, and *Cowboy: The Illustrated History*, among other books.

"Herman's mastery of the story and splendid prose style (to say nothing of his uncanny ear for Western dialogue) make this an enormously satisfying read."

—Andrew Graybill, co-director, Clements Center for Southwest Studies, author of *The Red and the White: A Family Saga of the American West.*

"Daniel Herman's novel pulls the reader into a time and place we think we know, but don't. *The Feudist* is a love story, a coming-of-age story, and a vicious war story, all rolled into one. The story just sings . . . Herman's dialogue is absolutely amazing, infused with regional verbiage and historical colloquialisms."

—Melody Groves, author of *She Was Sheriff*; *Ropes, Reins, and Rawhide: All About Rodeo*; and the *Colton Brothers* series, among other books.

THE FEUDIST

Odysseus, after killing his wife's suitors:

As to the flocks that pack of wolves laid waste
They'll be replenished: scores I'll get on raids
. . . till all the folds are full again.

—HOMER, *The Odyssey*

THE

FEUDIST

A Novel of the Pleasant Valley War

⎯⎯◆⎯⎯

DANIEL JUSTIN HERMAN

Fort Worth, Texas

TCU Box 298300
Fort Worth, Texas 76129
817.257.7822
www.prs.tcu.edu
To order books: 1.800.826.8911

Design by David Timmons

To summer evenings with my father, listening to Dodgers games and gathering storms.

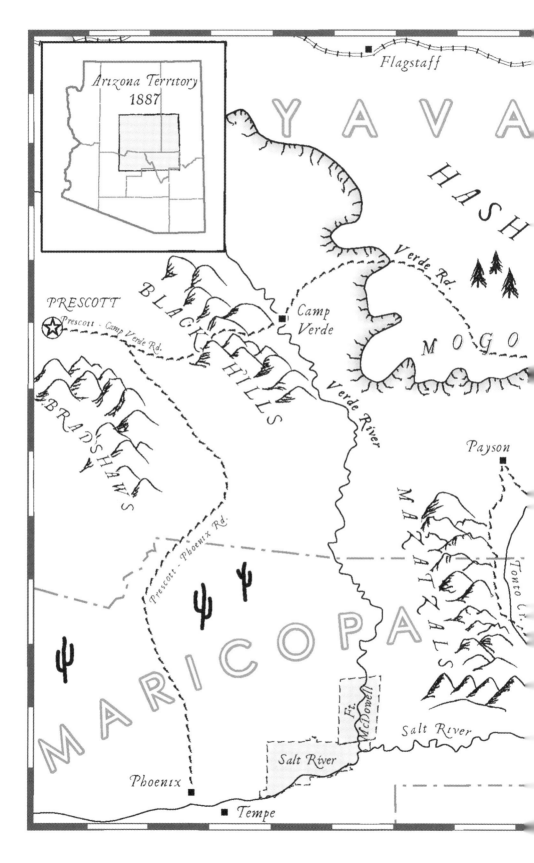

1.

When I was twelve years old, my father took me to a Baptist prayer meeting. We'd tried the Methodists and the Presbyterians, even the Mennonites, only my father couldn't settle on any of them. We got there after the preaching had started, forcing us to take an open pew up at the very front. We perched stiff as a pair of crows, watching the pastor as he paced the floor and halted. He finally stopped directly in front of us.

"I see Brother Holcomb has brought his son," he said as he fixed his eyes on me. "What's your name, lad?"

"Benjamin," I replied.

"And what brings you here? Did you come for the fellowship, or for the saving?"

I stayed silent a moment as I struggled to figure why he was asking. "Both, I reckon."

He strode across the floor again, boots thudding like the drum of a soldier. Then he stopped and looked out over his flock. "Well, if it's the saving you want," he said in his ringing pastor voice, "I can't give it to you. There's no preacher in the world that can." He paced the floor again and halted, locking eyes with me. "If perchance the Lord should come to your door some morning, it won't be at the invitation of any preacher. It won't even matter if you answer his knock. Either he turns the key and opens your heart, or he passes on his way to your neighbor. The truth is he's decided our fate from the moment he made eternity."

That was the last of the prayer meetings. My father never made another experiment. On Sundays, he'd share a Bible verse with us in the mornings, then we'd celebrate earthly life with bacon and biscuits. Whether that Baptist preacher was precisely right about predestination, he told us, was beyond his powers to judge. Alls he could say was that if God came knocking, it was just as well to be at home.

I guess I've followed my father's example. I never did become much of a churchgoer. There were times I prayed nightly and fervently for the Lord to find me, but no voice came to set me right. It's been fifty years now since I heard that Baptist preacher, but I still find myself pondering salvation. I don't know whether God damned my soul before he made the universe, but sure as creation he left me cursed.

———•———

I can't say precisely how the curse came to be, or when I became fully aware of it. Maybe it started the day my mother died. Or maybe it was the night my father administered the last of his tongue-lashings after I'd broken the yoke on his reaper. It wasn't the fiercest rebuke he'd ever inflicted, but his words gave me a final shove.

Before the sun rose the following day, I'd stuffed provisions in his ancient haversack. I stole out a window and made my way to the rail station, then hid in a muddy culvert. When the westbound freight came crawling by, I pulled myself into one of the boxcars. Two weeks later I reached a place called Tucson. I took a job in a lumber yard for fifty cents a day before hitching a ride with a creaking mule team destined for one of the boomtowns. Someone told me a man had found a ball of grayish silver that looked like Rand McNally's globe. They'd got President Grant to pry the place from the Indian reservation and gone directly to blasting holes. "Globe City," they'd declared it. The silver ledges had petered out by the time I got there, but the profits flowed from lanes of copper. Paid forty dollars a month to anyone strong enough to muck their mines.

I had in mind to toil as a mucker long enough to learn about stopes and ore bodies and the like, then strike out with a mule and grubstake. Most of the big finds had been made a decade or more before I got there, but men still scoured the hills for another bonanza. Only what I fell into weren't any wondrous glory hole. It was a pit of spite.

Not that I had anything to do with the digging of it. I just had the misfortune of arriving when the feud exploded. Looking back on it with the sorrow of experience, I can see the dominoes ripe to tumble. The Grahams had fallen out with the Tewksburys after they'd accused each other of rustling. They'd had some sort of trial in the town of Prescott, but the judge dismissed the case. The anger had cooled to embers, then flared again in the fights for range.

Part of the troubles came from Texas. Seemed like half the cattlemen in the Lone Star state headed to Arizona pastures to escape the tick fever. The worst was the swaggering Hashknife Outfit with its million acres. Not that it was a genuine Texas outfit. A bunch of New York millionaires had gone in together to buy the railroad land between Holbrook and Flagstaff. They'd brought in 30,000 head of Texas cattle, then told their cowboys to drive out any trespassers, mostly meaning Mormon settlers and some of the sheepherders who'd been running flocks in the grassy highlands.

It was like lobbing a mortar into a prairie dog town and watching the survivors scatter. The concussion rolled into Tonto Basin and all the way to Globe City. It was the Daggs brothers that got the worst of it, with their 50,000 sheep and the small army they'd hired to herd them. After the Hashknife cowboys drove them out of the Mogollons, they leased their sheep to men in the basin.

Of course I didn't know any of that on my arrival, and if I had, it wouldn't have mattered. I knew ciphering and simple geometry, and this and that about stars and planets. But the gravitational pull of human malice was an arithmetic beyond my grasp.

———•———

I set out from Tucson with boyish hope in my breast. It wasn't until I'd got a view of the place that my mind registered a twinge of doubt. The man they called "the captain" halted the mules for respite after we'd topped the last of the ridges. "That be your Globe City," he called to me as he peered into a sprawling basin. I followed the thread of trail that wound ahead. It descended through scrubby hopbushes and spiky mescals, then emptied into a jumble of clapboard and adobe brick pinched into a barren draw. Blocking the view to the north and westward was a wall of crowded hills. To the east lay a sea of desert. Bony ridges fringed with saguaro cactus stretched all the way to the Indian reservation. I've grown fonder of the country over the years but at the time it was desolation.

After I'd helped with the unloading and getting the mules fed, I took a stroll through my new surroundings. Smack in the middle of town loomed a theater and a sturdy bank like battleships in a fleet of sloops. On the other side of the street stood a couple hotels and an Odd Fellows hall along with a saddlery and a run of saloons. Accordion bursts spilled from the nearest of them along with muffled chortles from one of the customers.

The only other places worth the noticing were a druggist and couple restaurants along with a rambling mercantile called the Globe Commercial. The miners had taken up residence in shanties and boarding houses on the streets spoked from the row of businesses. What few had brought their families tucked themselves into peak-roofed cottages with iron fences.

I sweated that night in a boarding house as my mind swirled with scenes from home. I finally lit the lamp by the bedstead and scribbled in my diary. When dawn came I had my breakfast, then made my way to the mine office.

Only when I arrived I got a surprise. "Copper price took a dip," the foreman told me. "Won't be any hiring until the bosses raise production." I had a few shekels in my pocket, but not enough to wait it out. I marched back to the boarding house and asked for my rent back, then grabbed my haversack and went to wandering. Thought I'd drum up work at one of the ranches or maybe one of the farms on the banks of the Salt. I found a task here and there digging a well or a shallow privy. I earned enough to fill my belly but not a penny to spend for pleasure. Then there wasn't any work. Dried up like a summer puddle. When I finally tired of searching, I made my way to the Globe Commercial.

It was late afternoon when I got there. I took off my hat and slipped through the door. I remember the store like a photograph, but at the time it was a perfect welter. From the door you could see down a broad aisle ending at a counter where a man in a cravat glanced up from his newspaper. The rest of the floor was quilted with crates and bins and bloated tubs, with tables here and there crammed with mining gear and sets of crockery. I glanced around to get my bearings, then proceeded toward the man at the back.

"Looking for something in particular?" he asked.

"For an offer of gainful employment. I was hoping you might know of someone looking for a hand. I ain't much at stone masonry, but I can dig a hole good as the next man. That or help with carpentry or blacksmithing. Just about any chore suited to the son of a farmer."

"Not in a while," he answered as he closed his newspaper. "What's your name?"

"Benjamin Holcomb."

He looked me over carefully. "I don't believe I've seen you before. Are you new here?"

"Came over the Pinals six weeks ago. I've been wandering between the cow camps." I'd been in once to buy coffee and hardtack, but I guess I hadn't made much of an impression. "I'm lookin' for anything I can get. Anything that gets me fed."

He gave me another once over, then turned back to his newspaper. "I'll keep my ears peeled for you, Benjamin Holcomb. Stop back in a few days, and I'll let you know if I've heard anything." If he gave a damn about my desperation, he went out of his way to keep it hid.

I thanked him politely and made my exit. I stood holding my hat as I heard the door shut, searching the street for a fellow human. Drops of sweat crawled from my underarms. I finally settled myself on the porch stoop. If anyone showed to buy supplies, I got to thinking, I'd offer my services.

I sat for a time feeling the melancholy come spilling over me. A pair of horseflies hovered just out of reach, trading sallies for a patch of skin. From off in the distance came the plaints of a he-quail. A fading note, then a silence, like he was on a vigil for a lost companion.

I finally scooped a rock from the dust and gave it a lob. A pleasing thud registered from the side of a shed. I bent to scoop a couple more then stood to add some force. I was launching another when the door creaked. When I glanced back, I saw the clerk. He stood like a sentinel.

"Almost closing time," he called out, "and I'm nary a shilling richer." Then he walked out on the porch. "Judging from how hard those rocks are hitting yonder innocent shed, my intuition tells me something's troubling you."

I stooped my head and apologized. "I'm about hungry as a prize pig without a nickel to buy his supper."

He nodded silently and folded his arms. "Can you work a broom?"

I spun my rock into the dirt. "They ain't made the broom that's stumped me yet." Thought I was clever to answer with something flip.

"Well if you'd be willing to display your talents, I'd be willing to buy you a meal."

He told me his name was George Heard. He didn't own the entire operation but he was sure enough managing partner. He'd run away himself, I came to find out, back in '78. Soon as I'd finished sweeping, he did as he'd promised. Took me to a Chinaman's restaurant called the Irish Parlor that served the wateriest son-of-a-bitch stew under stars and stripes. We chewed shreds of gristle and sipped our coffee whilst swapping stories about riding the rails. Then he loaned me a little money so's I could sleep in a boarding house. Told me to hustle back the next day and he'd give me another chore. Pretty soon I was regular. Hired me as a stockboy. Paid twenty-two a month and sometimes a little bonus money.

2.

That was the first I'd had dependable pay since I'd quit the lumber yard. The wage wasn't any improvement, but the work was twice as easy. He gave me regular tutorings about inventory and overhead and every particular about the store business. When the mule teams came once a month was the only time I broke a sweat. I'd have thought myself a prince of commerce if it hadn't been for boredom.

Like many a lad in limbo, I had a taste for women and adventure. Not that I had any. George had warned me to stay away from mischief, and that's precisely what I'd tried to do. I'd come to work in the crisp of morning and spend the evening hours playing rounds of whist. I might have stayed on the path of virtue a little longer but for the live boys' merry evangelizing. They kept talking up the ecstasies of the chandelier chapels until finally I went to worship. I suppose you can guess the rest of it. Weren't any Jesus in it.

I'd done some gambling when I was hauling lumber, but I was too weary to make it habit. Now that I was a stockboy, I had steam enough to see the sun. I'd play the faro tables here and there, then try my luck at a hand of poker. By the eve of my eighteenth birthday, I'd got to fancying myself a practiced sharp. Between my cards winnings and a month of back rent, I'd scrounged the silver for half a pony. Alls I needed was a pot to match.

What I got was a bitter reckoning.

After they'd swept all my savings, I tumbled into the empty night. I guess someone saw me passed out in the dirt, else I'd have frozen like a lump of clay. I woke on the saloon floor next to the stove. I reached to grab a chair, then pulled myself to a standing position. I could see the dawn's glow through a grimy window. The taste of stomach bile came up in my throat, but I didn't have any hurt parts. Nothing but a bruise from when I fell and smears of dirt on my hips and legs. I walked outside and fought the vomit back. After I'd ducked behind the blacksmith's to drain myself, I started toward the boarding house.

It was one of those clear winter mornings that felt like Canada. A wave of goose bumps rolled up my back, then my teeth started chattering. I'd gone about fifty yards before I regretted it. I could see the mistress out in front of the place, beating dirt off a rug. She'd pass judgment on my appearance, then start dunning me to pay the bill. I stooped and fought the vomit again, then headed for the mercantile. I figured I'd play on George's sympathies to beg an advance.

I walked to the porch and paced fretfully, rubbing my shoulders and watching my breaths melt. It was twenty minutes before I spotted him ambling store-ward. He greeted me without emotion as he unlocked the door and ushered me in. "You look as if you've met a ditch," he clucked.

I looked down for a moment with my lips pinched. "I've got fresh clothes at the boarding house. Only I'm a little behind on paying my rent."

He gave a disgusted sniff as he pointed to a pile of work boots. "Go over and see which ones fit." I stood still for a moment, trying to fathom what he was getting at. "I imagine the fresh clothes won't be much cleaner than the ones you're wearing. I can hardly stand the sight of you. Now go over and pick some boots."

No sooner had I chosen than he confronted me with a pair of overalls. "You'll find they have ample pockets. From here out keep your wages in 'em. Soon as you can afford a suit, I'll introduce you to the Odd Fellows. Assuming you can lay off the drink." He stood there inspecting me, then waddled over to the till. "The clothes cost $7.50," he said gravely. "I'll take it from your pay." Then he handed me a couple greenbacks. "Now run over and pay the boarding house. And the next time you come crawling in like this, I'll fire you in half a blink."

If I'd been a wiser lad I've have heeded his scolding. He'd given me a job when I was hungry and tried his damnedest to teach me business. But my youthful obstinacy advised defiance. I wasn't particularly eager to quit him, but my mind began to stray. I'd come all that way from Ohio, I kept telling myself, and I was damned if I was going to be a gelded saint.

———•———

The bath of spring turned to scorching summer before the skies gave the earth a dousing. I waked one morn to tinkling spatters that gave announcement to a blasting din. Pinal Creek had shrunk to puddles and not a drop of it fit to drink. Smelt like a bucket of rotten eggs in the furnace of mid-July. But not that day. It swirled and thrashed like a flume in the Rockies as it scoured a year of filth.

After I'd pulled on my work clothes, I sauntered downstairs for bread and coffee. I found the house mistress seated by the door to the kitchen. She stooped over an open Bible nestled in the lap of her apron.

I wished her good morning as I seated myself with a couple miners. She nodded and repeated my words between spits and groans of thunder. Curving sheets of graying hair framed her face like a silken hood. She'd been forced to take in boarders after she'd lost her husband to silicosis. She mostly kept to herself except for church meetings and the Wednesday temperance league.

After I'd poured the dregs from the coffee pitcher, she disappeared into the kitchen. She came out carrying a second pitcher as a thunder blast shook the china. "The Lord stands in the thick of the storm," she announced as she took her seat again. "He unlimbers the cannons of judgment, and woe to them that fails to hear."

I felt my mood lift as I stepped into daylight. The thunder had passed to the south of us, leaving nothing but a cooling drizzle. I strolled down the street to the porch of the mercantile. I picked up the brush laid against the wall and rubbed the mud off my boots before I entered. George sat at his post in back. I said my hellos, then started my rounds. Our conversation bent to floods and tempests until we heard a customer rattling the door open. Before I could turn my head, George bellowed out a greeting. "The Honorable Edwin Tewksbury! Out of the storm and into harbor."

"Ain't heard such a pretty commotion since the legislature went on a drunk in Prescott," said Ed as he removed his slicker. "Goddamn hot in this thing." He was a dark-skinned, dark-haired man—half Indian, they told me, only he swore he was a white man when he came to trial later. He was the sort of feller that makes an impression. Slitted eyes and pencil mustache with the sturdy build of an Irish pugilist. I'd met him three or four times when he'd made his supply runs. He'd always show in his town clothes—checked vest over a linen shirt, or sometimes the vest was black. He wasn't especially partial to George but he'd joke with me like an elder brother.

Ed looked around the place and sniffed like he'd come for a plate of biscuits. "The delectable scent of Kendall's laundry powder," he called out. "Like flowers in the breeze of spring."

A second man came in behind him and hung his hat next to Ed's. He sported a pair of bushy side chops shaved flat at the sides of his chin. "This is Mr. Saxton Benton," announced Ed. "Helps with the cows now and again, on the off chance he takes a notion." That was the first I'd seen him. He was one of those prideful fellers that tuck their pants into their boots. You could tell the make from the fancy tooling: Coffeyvilles, shipped from Kansas state. Looked like ancient hieroglyphics with all the stars and moons and tumbling hearts. A year later I'd have the misfortune of getting to know him but at the time I felt a touch of envy.

"He knows damn well I don't go by goddamn 'Saxton,'" answered Side Chops. He gave us a cursory nod as he made his way to the bulk groceries. His voice trailed as he loosened a gunny sack. "If a feller don't want no quarrel with me, he'd do well to call me 'Sax.'"

"Got any sales going, George?" Ed asked teasingly, "or is it the usual scandalous markup?"

George gave a half smile. "Come now, Ed. Half of it gets barged across the Great Lakes and down the Mississippi before they even load it on a train. Then it winds its way to Tucson and gets muled up to Globe. If I charged less, I'd be a bankrupt."

"I imagine you're making out alright."

"Not as alright as I'd like. Not with the mines down. It'll come back soon enough. They can't string the telegraphs if they don't have the copper wire." He brushed a knuckle over his nose, then clasped his hands behind his head. "How's your herd coming, Ed? They tell me Vosburgh hired you on to run five hundred head."

Ed gave a wincing smile as he peeled off his tasseled gloves. "He got the cows, and I got the skill to work 'em. Just need the buyers."

"And your brother, John? I hear he's made a similar arrangement."

"Guess you heard about them Daggs brothers hiring him to run their sheep."

The lanky tabby cat George kept as a mouser ran her tail across Ed's ankles. He tucked his gloves behind his belt, then stooped to pick her up. She turned stiff on him, pushing her legs into his chest. He frowned and gently dropped her.

"I certainly did hear about your brother," George replied. He watched the tabby cat as she jogged behind a crate. "More than once. Your fellow cattlemen are none too pleased."

Ed shook his head grimly. "We ain't in business to please our neighbors.

Need the sheep money 'til cattle prices make a comeback. Vosburgh was gettin' twelve a head year before last. Now he's gettin' six."

"I want no part of the stock trade," answered George as he sat himself behind the counter. "Turns decent men into misanthropes."

"Misanthropes?" I asked dumbly.

"French for 'impeccable gentlemen,'" joked Ed.

"You confuse the word for its antonym," answered George. "Comes from the Greek. It refers to men who disparage their fellows. Whether the condition be entirely circumstantial or partly innate, I can't say, but either way it bodes ill for humanity."

Side Chops gave me a wink as he filled a bag with sugar. "I may be nothin' but an ignorant cowhand but I surely know a call to righteousness." He looked at George with his eyes asquint. "I been preachin' about the evils of missin' ropes since the day he hired me, only damn if he'll listen. Wasn't but last Wednesday when he come near to shootin' me after he couldn't find his favorite lariat. Stalked around in a perfect fury 'til he finally went and checked his saddlebags."

George shook his head with mild disgust. "I've been here long enough to make observations." He blinked a few times as he set aside some receipts. Then he straightened himself in his chair and pitched into his favorite lecture. "Every time the county court is in session, this town is mobbed with cowboys, all charging each other with rustling. What you ought do is precisely the opposite. Join forces. Make an agreement to sell your breeding stock so you can lower supply and drive the prices up. Then consolidate your animals for the drives to Holbrook. And lobby Congress. Tell 'em to go after the meatpacking monopolies and the railroads."

I'd about learnt that speech like a Sunday hymn.

Before Ed could reply we heard the door unlatch. Someone opened it a crack and peeked. We stood motionless as the freighting boss's daughter stumbled through the threshold. She couldn't have been more than eight or nine. I could see the hand of the friend who'd shoved her disappear behind the edge of the doorway. The girl looked around uncertainly then walked to the counter. "I wonder if you can bag a dozen lemon drops, Mr. Heard." She pronounced the words like a woman of twenty.

George smiled obligingly and made his way to the candy. "That's six cents for ordinary mortals but with a penny off for the grace of youth."

The girl made a show of searching her coin purse before making an address to Ed. "I'm afraid I'm a nickel short. Perhaps Mr. Tewksbury would be kind enough to pay the bill." She blushed crimson and fled for the door as the girl outside broke into a fit of giggles.

Ed shook his head and smirked as he fingered one of the canvas miner's hats. "I'll be damned if the little ones don't come all a-nibblin' whilst the keepers stay out from shore." He stood smiling bemusedly. "Put a dozen lemon drops on my bill, George. Give 'em to her and her friend next time they're in. Just don't tell 'em it was me that paid."

"I'll be goddamned," I could hear Side Chops muttering. "Can't even afford to buy me a whiskey but he can sure find the money to please a girl."

There was a long quiet after that as Side Chops finished bagging a load of barley. Ed went back to examining the canvas miner's hats, turning one of them in his hands. "Might do to keep the dust off," he commented. "Ain't apt to stop the boulders."

"That's what they shipped me," replied George, "I don't always choose my stock."

Ed placed the hat back on the shelf, carefully lining it up with all the others. "Had a man go and quit me a while back," he said as he turned to me. "If you know any young fellers lookin' for work, Ben, tell 'em I got an opening. Pay's twenty-five dollars a month with room and board into the bargain."

I was half eager to convey my interest.

"I'll put the word out," answered George.

Out of the corner of my eye I could see Side Chops sweeping cartridge boxes into a gunny sack. "You wantin' me to take 'em all?" he shouted.

"How many's in there?" asked Ed.

"Three hundred or so .45-90s and about half as many .58s. Damn bag feels like a load of rocks."

"Sweet Jesus," exclaimed George. "Are you outfitting an entire regiment?"

Ed pulled the gloves from his belt. "Need those .58 rounds to down the grizzlies. Seems like every time we kill one, a couple more waltz out of the mountains." Then he spoke again to Side Chops. "Go ahead and tumble 'em in."

"But why the .45-90s?" asked George.

"Ballast. We'd better be getting finished here, George. Got a hell of a long trip ahead of us."

3.

Ed's mention of a job wasn't the cause of my sickness, but it raised the fever another notch. I should have known better than to consider hiring on with a man in a quarrel, only I never imagined it would come to much. In fact, the gun stuff appealed to my fancy. I hadn't been any faithful son to a devoted father, but there was part of me that wanted to match him. He wasn't but a stripling teen when he'd marched with Sherman through the Carolinas. I'd somehow got to thinking I'd send him a portrait photograph of myself outfitted with a grizzly rifle.

Beyond all that lay a loftier vision: a 160-acre homestead in the grassy high country with a couple thousand head spread over the range and me as boss. If I'd known cattle prices would stay sunk into the '90s, I'd have thought different, only like most men, I was a pious optimist. The newspaper was talking up a big railroad project that would make the Tonto Basin into a cattle kingdom. Wasn't but six months later when that railroad laid off its construction crew and folded, only by then I was on my path.

I had somewhat dimmer visions of a woman to share it with. Not any delicate blossom of a girl-woman, but a sure-enough one who could ride the fences in a pinch and loosen her hair in the evenings. Not that I had immediate prospects.

What few women abided in Globe City were generally of a class that either avoided me or wanted money. Every now and then a married woman would venture into the store to order a harpsichord or a lady's writing desk. They'd sometimes deign to throw a maternal smile or a thanks my way, for which I felt more appreciative than I ought. Then there was the other end of things. The sporting ladies.

They fell into two sorts, generally speaking. The brothel gals were a younger set. Swedes and Mexicans and jet-eyed colored women and every shade and shape betwixt. Not a one of them but knew her art. They'd put a spell on a man to make him levitate until his wages jumped into their coin purses, only it was the pimps that got the lion's share.

The other set were the rheumy eyed laudanum drinkers who'd rent crib berths in the adobe tumbles on the trails to town. The ones that had lost their chance. I took my turns, I'll freely confess, but I never came away particularly cheered.

It wasn't that I lacked hope of abandoning bachelorhood. Some of the girls made their way to the grace of matrimony if they found a man with the right attainments, mostly meaning a proper avocation or a sizable herd and enough lip bloom to attest to gravity. Only often as not it didn't work like that. I knew a cowboy that paid a girl he favored for a week of her company. They strolled like a twosome. At the end of the week, she accepted his marriage proposal. He came near to putting an end to himself when he found she'd jumped for another town. He never did know whether she was dissembling to him or whether her pimp stole her. Wasn't but a year later when that cowboy got killed in a brothel. One of the whores shot him when he got belligerent.

I guess I was luckier. Or not so full of myself. I wasn't fool enough to think any woman would marry a penniless stock boy, though I had hopes to climb the grade. If I'd stayed with George for another decade, I'd have had the mustache to recommend myself. Likely he'd have made me store manager after he turned his attentions to politics. But like half the spikers in the territory, I'd got the idea of forging a shortcut. Figured I'd turn that ten years into five by way of homestead papers and a herd of cows.

————•————

It wasn't but another week or two after Ed's visit when I saw my chance. Landis Hooper came into the store that morning. He'd drifted into town a couple months earlier and taken a job at one of the liveries. You wouldn't have taken him for any ticket to a respectable future. He was a rope of a man with curling locks and a smile that could charm a snake in a pickle jar. You could generally find him in his leisure hours at a cheap saloon, offering to do a card trick for a dram of beer. I hadn't spent much time in his company, but I'd taken a liking to him all the same. He had a way of mocking folks' conceits that made me laugh like a mischievous schoolboy.

Not that he was joking that day. He'd come to buy a month's provisions. He told us his father had disappeared when he was hunting horses that had strayed from his pastures. Hooper was headed out to join the search.

"I'm sorry to hear about your misfortune," George said solemnly. "How long's he been gone?"

"Been ten days since my ma saw him last." He took a deep breath and swallowed. "I got a favor to ask. I'm about dead broke. I was hopin' you'd give me credit 'til I can sell my sorrel pony. She's worth forty easy, but I'm only askin' thirty. Soon as I sell her, I'll pay my bill and head out." The words came tumbling like he was desperate.

"You've tried the horse trader?"

"He ain't buyin' at present. Not unless it's brood stock. Thought I'd tack up a fer-sale ad on your wall if you'll allow it."

George put a hand on the back of his neck and rubbed. "Go ahead and pick out your provisions. As for the ad, tack it to the front door. That way no one will miss it." George didn't make any big show of his generosity but he'd help anyone that was down.

"You think your pa's alive?" I asked.

"Not likely," Hooper answered. He ran an open palm along his temple and forehead.

"What d'ya reckon happened to him?"

He gave a grunt and went silent. Then he cleared his throat and answered. "Maybe thrown from his horse and busted a leg. There's a hundred ways to get hurt out there and not a single man you can hail fer help. Not if you're riding alone."

Hooper shuffled around after that, avoiding our glances. The pall of quiet turned the store hollow. He finally uttered a cheerless thanks after he'd gathered his provisions.

"That's a damn shame," said George as we watched him trudge into the street. He didn't speculate on it being a bushwhack though I guess both of us had it in the back of our minds.

I went back to my regular chores, only I kept thinking about the pony. I hated to take advantage of a man's misfortune, but for a saddle horse, I'd make an exception. He needed the money pretty bad, I figured, and sure as heaven I couldn't afford any horse trader. I'd had my eye on a sturdy roan, but my meager savings fell shy of the mark.

When the work slowed that afternoon, I went over to George and asked permission to leave early. "Thought I'd see Hooper about his horse," I explained sheepishly. "I been thinking I might ride up to the Tewksbury place and see if he still needs a hand." I didn't figure he'd be all that surprised at my announcement. I'd been making noises about hiring on as a cowboy. Besides which, it wouldn't put him out much. There'd be a dozen men lining up to replace me, what with the mines down. I half figured he'd be glad to be quit of me.

"And if he doesn't?"

"Then I'll ride around 'til I find someone who does, I reckon."

He tapped his pencil as he stared at me. "Bard Henry was in here the other day when I had you out making grocery deliveries. You know who I'm talking about, don't you?"

"The Atkinsons' foreman." It was hard to forget him. He was a slim-built Texan with a face ridged like the shell of a walnut. His real name was Bartholomew Hollister Henry, only they called him Bard on account of his stories. Wore a close-trimmed little Van Dyke beard that had long since turned to white. He'd plod around town like a gouty box turtle, but he could sit a horse like a bantam jockey.

"Exactly the one. He said Luett's looking for a hired man. I told him I'd mention it to you, but I got distracted with the bookkeeping. The pay would be the same as Ed offered. Twenty-five a month. They'll raise it if you show ability."

Luett Atkinson was George's fiancé. At least that was George's hope. Only they didn't hardly see each other except for Christmases and Fourth of Julys. She'd come riding in with Mr. Henry and her father, Colonel Atkinson, leading a string of ponies to sell. Then the men would find a saloon while George escorted her to a theatrical or a costume party.

"You reckon they'll still take me?"

"Well if they don't, they'd at least feed you before sending you on. I'd feel a hell of a lot better about all this if I knew you were somewhere safe. Of course, you're free to do as you please."

———•———

Ten minutes later I was squeezing myself through the livery door. "Looking for Mr. Hooper," I shouted. Threads of sunlight shone through the roof slats, but most of the place was like a cavern.

"Over here," he called. I saw an arm waving over a row of horse stalls. "Just finishing up some shoein'."

"I come to see you about your sorrel," I explained as I walked toward him. The tang of hay and horse urine hung like vinegar in the stagnant air.

"Well you come none too quick. She ain't gonna be fer sale long. Not fer the price I'm askin'." His voice had a peculiar tinny pitch like he was talking through the top of his mouth. "Come on over and I'll show her." He put down his shoeing tools, then walked to a stall. "She looks like an old ragbag, but she's strong enough." He stroked her neck, then slipped a rope halter over her head and walked her out.

"How come you want the horse?" he asked nervously as we came into daylight. "You fixin' to quit Heard?"

"Ridin' up to Payson. Got a job as a hand." I stared at the horse and let a sigh out. I wouldn't have rated her the sorriest-looking specimen I'd seen since I'd left Ohio, but she surely merited consideration.

He gave me a once-over then nodded his approval. "Who ya workin' fer?"

"Luett Atkinson," I said sheepishly. I bent and checked her hooves and legs, then stood back a few paces and gave her a survey. She stood low like an Indian pony. Her chest showed she had lungs enough but she wasn't any overfed.

Hooper shifted his weight and squinted toward the desert. "I guess that gal about runs the place. Ain't never met her, but my brother was over there a while back. Says that old man of hers lets her do it."

"I reckon."

"They say she's got a sweet tooth for Mr. Heard."

I let a snicker escape my throat. "They sure enough trade the letters."

"Well if I had a couple tits, I'd make the dust fly to put my claim on him. Makes more money than a train robber. I hear they're talking him up fer legislature."

I didn't answer him. Just ran my hand across the sorrel's flanks, touching the scarred patches where the hair grew white. I figured she might faunch at the touch of a stranger but she was calm as a Sunday eve.

Hooper grimaced and sniffed. "That white stuff's healed saddle sores. Some hellion rode her to tatters before I bought her up in Holbrook. I gave her some doctorin'. She ain't a young 'un, but she's got some vim."

I led her around the livery once, then asked him to saddle her. He went back inside for a few minutes, then came marching out with a California rig. Looked like some ancient vaquero's hand-me-down from the war with Mexico. The horn jutted like a cavalry saber from a pommel of corroding rawhide. He tightened the cinches and adjusted the stirrups, then I climbed aboard and gave her a nudge. She didn't falter any; sailed easy as a canoe on a rippling pond. I rode her to the far end of town and back, putting her into a steady canter.

"You're askin' thirty?" I inquired after I'd dismounted.

He kicked at the dirt, then folded his arms. "Long as it's lady liberties. I ain't lookin' for any barters."

"Give ya twenty." She didn't have an ounce of ornery in her, but I wasn't any too encouraged about her frame. "That's the best I can do."

He shook his head from side to side. "That's too low."

"Twenty's all I got." If I hadn't felt a tad of sympathy for her, I wouldn't have offered that.

He stuck his thumbs behind his suspenders and sighed disgustedly. "Twenty-five or nothin'."

I thanked him for showing her, then started to turn.

"Hell's bells. I'll take it. Ain't got time to wait around."

I turned back and gave her another look over. I was cursing myself for not offering less. "What are you gonna ride if you're sellin' the sorrel?"

His dour countenance turned to grin. "Oh, I got somethin' to ride. Don't you worry. Got me a regular queen bee in the stable. Pretty as a señorita in a San Antone whorehouse. Got a new Mexican saddle to put on her. She'll be jinglin' when she prances, with all them silver fittin's."

"You're sure this old gal's gonna get me to Payson?"

"Might look a little rough, but she knows her business. Only I'll need that forty dollars." He went over and unbuckled the California rig, then set it down against the wall of the livery.

I stood motionless trying to read him. "That's ten more than you asked in the first place."

"You got a saddle or are you ridin' bareback?"

"Wouldn't make much sense to buy the saddle before the horse," I answered curtly.

He pulled an index finger out from behind his suspenders and pointed at the saddle. "If you want that ol' California rig, it'll run ya forty. Saddle, bridle, and bit with a decent nag to throw it on."

I ran my hands over her scarred patches. "I ain't exactly a sultan, Hooper. I'll take the horse, alright, but you can keep the other stuff."

"You takin' the stage road to Payson?"

"I reckon."

"Might be better off to ride with me. I could use the company. I'll be takin' the Jerked Beef Trail up to Dutch Louis's old place, then cross the

Sierry Anchies. I can point you to the Payson cutoff. It'll take ya through the Hellsgate gorge, then straight to the Atkinsons'."

"I thank you for the offer, Hooper, but I can't afford no forty dollars."

He grimaced and scanned the hills, then took out a pouch of tobacco. "You go ahead and ride with me and I'll make it thirty-five for the whole caboodle."

———————

After meeting with Hooper, I walked back to the store. I found George sitting in the back room, bent over his oaken desk.

"I bought the horse," I reported.

"How much did it run you?"

I hesitated a moment. "He wants twenty for her."

He raised his brows with mild surprise. "What'll you do for a saddle?"

"Plus fifteen for the paraphernalia. Gave me the saddle blanket free."

He nodded his approval. "You've struck an agreement that redounds to your benefit." He'd have thought different if he'd seen the merchandise.

"Hooper asked if I wanted to ride with him. Says he can take me to the Payson cutoff."

He took off his glasses and rubbed his eyes. "In which case you'll be leaving immediately."

"Tomorrow morning. If you'll give permission." I explained about Hooper lowering the price a few dollars if I agreed to tag along. I half expected flat refusal.

His chest rose with a powerful breath, then shrank with a longish sigh. "I'd have preferred a little more notice, but I suppose two men riding is safer than one." He rocked back in his chair and folded his arms. "You're a grown man, Ben. You can make your own decisions. But I do have some sage advice. Men are feuding out there. Stay out of it. What they desperately need is a peace treaty, but they're too hot to negotiate."

After that he stayed at his station while I gave the place a final sweep. At closing time, he called me into the back again. He walked to his desk and picked up a pair of envelopes. "I took the liberty of writing you a recommendation letter. The other one is a personal note for Luett. See that she gets it."

He held them in the air with his crooked arm as he waited for me to take them. He'd splintered it years before in a fall from a barn roof.

Always looked odd to me. Stiff as a cane of hickory, but it didn't slow him in the least.

I answered, "Yes sir," as I reached for them.

He pressed his lips into a rigid seam as he shook his head with disapproval. "Do whatever Luett requires of you and refrain from your wonted cheek." He stared to get his point across. "I'll be damned if I won't miss you. You're a decent boy with a worthy future. Your only want is prudence."

I bowed my head toward the floor. "Except maybe there's another thing."

"And what other thing might that be?"

"A shooting iron, I reckon. I'd buy one from the gunsmith, except I'm altogether busted." George didn't generally deal in firearms but he'd taken a few on consignment.

He gave a smirk, then walked to the front room. He came shambling back with a holster on a gun belt and two boxes of bullets. Then he went back and fetched a revolver. "Smith and Wesson," he muttered as he laid it carefully on the table. "Model 3, .44 caliber. Fired not half a dozen times by the previous owner. Just promise you won't use it. Not unless you're forced." He looked at me expectantly.

"No sir, I won't. How much do I owe for it? I'll pay soon as I have it." I might not cut much of a figure on the pony, but I'd have gun enough to court respect.

"No need," he answered gravely. "Consider it a gift. You can repay me by avoiding the booze." Then he went back to his desk and retrieved a book. He rolled a thumb across the pages then held it aloft. "Homer's *Odyssey*," he announced. "Composed two thousand years ago by the original bard of ancient Greece, not to be confused with any withered cowhands from Albany, Texas. It's about a warrior captain who sails for home but ends up lost in a sea of troubles." He paused for a moment, then handed it to me. "I'd like for you to have it."

I reached out to take hold of it, then turned it in my hands. It was thick as a Baptist hymnal, with pebbled leather and gilded stamping.

"My mother gave it to me when I was about the same age as you are. I suppose she already had an inkling that my path would be circuitous. I'd hoped to study law, as I've told you. My father being a drunk, we didn't have the money." He was quiet for a second, then gave a wistful grin. "So I saved a few dollars and fled the farm with only the *Odyssey* for map and guide. Three years later I landed here. Wasn't the course I'd charted, but it's where the gales finally swept me." He paused again to catch my eye, then tilted down his chin. "Now they're sweeping you. Don't fight 'em, Ben. Just drift. Hold tight to your moral compass and you'll end where you belong."

4.

Landis Hooper was a two-faced man. I don't mean he was a liar, though he did his share of that. I mean he was his own travelling theatrical troupe. He'd wake full of jokes and laughter and by midmorning he'd be in the gloom of tragedy. Then all of a sudden he'd wheel to his jokes again, like all the world was lark and mischief. I guess the gloom came when he remembered about his father disappearing. Only I've met men that knew him before any of that who said the hot-and-cold ran in his blood.

Not that I was the best of traveling companions. The farther we rode into the mountains, the more I sank into the wash of melancholy. Partly it was the dread you get to feeling when you've left a familiar place to take a gamble. Another part was plain old soreness. I hadn't ridden much since I'd left Ohio. When I eased out of the saddle on the third day of riding, I felt my back seize in a ball of pain. I'd got so stiff I could hardly walk. I woke next morning feeling spryer until I reconnoitered what we were up against. A few miles to the north sprawled the Naegelin Rim like the Great Wall of bloody China. It was a shadowy snake of a mountain capped with a black forest of ponderosas.

We rode slow as we approached it, letting the horses pick their way. "We'll head east to skirt the cliff," called out Hooper. "Just follow the drainage into the hills, then cross the ridge to the next one over. We'll come out at the edge of a gap at the top end of Canyon Creek. The homestead sits in the middle of it."

George had warned me to ride with Hooper only partway, then beeline for the Atkinsons'. Only between Hooper's jokes and flattery and his gloomy spells, I lost my resolution. I guess that two-faced business had its effect. When he'd go into his dark spells, I'd think I'd said something to dampen his spirits. Then I'd feel extra eager to bring him out of it, which caused me to say things I came to regret. I finally heard myself offering to look for his father. Hooper speculated he'd been attacked by a grizzly or struck by lightning or bit by a rattlesnake. Then he hunched down in his saddle and went into one of his silences.

The season was the peak of summer in the sourest year of my twisting life. That's when the rains fall in the mountain country that turn the bunch grasses into clumps of green. Roiling thunderheads roll in like regular freight trains from July to mid-September. Except for in the dry stretches, which we'd had for a couple years. Wasn't a speck of grass on most of the lower ranges, just withered-up gangs of cattle crowded round the seeps. Nearly all of it was unclaimed federal land—free range—meaning anyone could run their stock on it. Hadn't no one brought a single cow there until they'd evicted the Apaches a decade earlier. Only now it was trampled by scrawny heifers and littered with whitened bones.

There I was anyways, a-climbing the Rim, hell-bent to be an apprentice cowboy on the heels of a wicked drought. Only I'll be damned if a corps of thunderheads didn't square up straight in front of us. Not two weeks since the tempest in Globe City and now here came the spitting twin. We didn't know it at the time, but the droughty spell had reached its end. All the furies that exploded that summer came crashing with the summer storms.

"Pa calls that 'bitter rain,'" called out Hooper. "Comes at ya with a grudge and leaves with a lie."

"How's that?"

He craned his neck upward and watched the skies. "Damn theater clouds flood the creeks and get everyone to thinkin' the drought's over. Then nothin' happens fer a whole 'nother year. Just makes everyone bitter."

"You reckon it'll hit us?" I called out as I ducked my head against the wind.

"Hell no. Just make a little noise."

No sooner had he spoken than my hat went flying behind me. I had to fetch it up a couple times before I finally stuffed it in my saddlebags. Then here came the jabbing lightning and the angry thunder in booming volleys. I felt like a Union man at Spotsylvania when Ulysses Grant made his useless charges. Like to make us deaf and blind and wretched cold when the rain came in drenching sheets. "Get off and lead her!" Hooper yelled back as he jumped off his horse. "Ain't you got a slicker?" he added as he struggled with his own. He was already soaked by the time he'd got his arms through.

"Hell no!" I answered as I searched desperately for shelter. We finally found a copse of junipers that gave us a little protection. We must have huddled twenty minutes before it softened. Only just as we mounted, we heard the report of something worse. Like a string of thunderclaps without the rumble. "You hear gunshots?" I shouted.

"Don't goddamn yell! Keep your voice down. Let's ride up the ridge and get a look."

Soon as we'd topped out at a clear spot, Hooper swung off his horse and fetched some field glasses. He had me tie the horses while he walked to a ledge. He dropped flat so no one could see him, then scanned across the hills. "Don't see nothin'" he muttered. He'd just started to walk back to me when we heard a couple shots. He jogged to another lookout and got flat again, turning his glasses toward where the shots had come. He settled his focus on the draw to the north, then lifted a hand to wave me over.

"Keep low," he ordered as I crawled beside him. "I can make out four or five of 'em. Goddamn injuns. Looks like they've cornered a couple of white fellers in the boulders at the head of the draw." He handed me the glasses and told me to look.

I didn't see anything at first. Then I caught sight of a bare-legged man. He dodged behind a fallen ponderosa, then propped his rifle on it and fired. I saw puffs of smoke come from some trees above him as his friends chimed in. "Jesus Christ," I whispered. The only Indians I'd seen were the friendly ones that worked the mine tailings and sold us squash.

"Blasted goddamn renegades," cursed Hooper as he pulled his gun and inspected the chamber. "Better jump in and help them boys or they'll sure get fogged up. Can't hit nothin' with pistols but we'll give 'em a righteous scare." He ordered me to walk halfway down to a rocky shelf while he dashed across the draw. He didn't wait for an answer. Just took off at a jog down the side of the ridge, sliding in the scree here and there and dodging the manzanita.

No sooner had I got myself situated than I heard the report from his muzzle. I began to fire, too, but it was like shooting at a cloud of flies. I got to shaking so bad I couldn't hold the gun straight. That Smith and Wesson that George had given me may as well have been a wriggling snake.

Just then one of the Indians jumped out of cover and made a run in our direction. I guess he'd thought to flush us. One of the white men popped his head up and fired his rifle, hitting the man in the ribcage. He fell on some rocks and went to tumbling. When he got to the bottom, the white man shot him up some more. That's when I saw a blue soldier come trotting out of nowhere astride a mule. "Cease your fire!" he shouted at the white men as he waved his hand in the air. He rode in close to the wounded Indian, then reached down to pull him on. I'd figured the Indian for a dead man, but he sure enough swung over the mule. Strangest thing I ever saw, a blue soldier rescuing a renegade, and everyone all a-watching it like they'd smoked a bowl of opium.

Then the blue soldier turned his mount and made for a line of scrub oaks at the crest of the ridge. When he'd got about halfway up, one of the Indians yelled a command. The rest jumped from their hiding places and scrambled toward the blue soldier while the two white men plugged away at 'em. I'd never seen men move like that—straight up like they were floating. Like hawks on a draft of wind. Only they weren't fast enough to avoid the lead.

I saw a man stumble like he'd been hit in the thigh, then struggle to make the summit. It got quiet a few minutes after they reached the scrub oaks. I could see blurs of movement behind the foliage, then here they came on their mounts. One of them yelled down at us in his Indian language, then they galloped out of sight. I figured they were hightailing it.

It was a hell of an ugly mess I'd got into, but for the moment I was happily ignorant.

———•———

Not ten minutes after the battle ended, the sun came out to toast us. We waited half an hour to make sure the Indians were gone, then Hooper slogged back over to me. The men that shot the Indian had retreated to a bouldered stretch at the top of the ridge. One of them climbed out onto a rock and waved a bandanna to get our attention. We retrieved our mounts from where I'd tethered them, then set a course through the chaparral.

"Son of a bitch!" called out Hooper as we came zigzagging into their aerie, "if it ain't Sheriff Lafayette Marcus McGowan!" I was taken aback they knew each other. Wasn't the last surprise I'd get.

After we'd tied the horses to a juniper, Hooper slapped my back and introduced me.

"Pleased to meet you, Ben Holcomb," said McGowan as he nodded in my direction. "I'll be damned if you two ain't the blessed testament, ridin' right into the shadow of death. Almost makes me believe in Jesus." He was a tidy-built man in his thirties with reddish hair that draped his shoulders. I guess you'd say he had sort of a Wild Bill Hickok look, like some Western sheriff out of a dime book. Sported a glossy pair of leathern chaps with two rows of shiny conchos. I took him for a sure-enough law-and-order warrior, but I soon came to a new opinion.

"My sidekick here's called Jeremy Houck," continued McGowan as he motioned toward his partner. "Those Hashknife bullionaires tried to hire him to chase the Mormons off their range, only they barely paid enough to keep him liquored. I told him there's more money in catchin' bad fellers."

"Pleasure," said Hooper as he nodded at the deputy. "You sure got a fittin' name. 'Jeremiah' sounds about right for a lawman."

"Jeremy. If it was Jeremiah, I'd be a preacher." His leaden eyes looked like balls from a musket. When he gazed at me, I felt a chill. It was like he was looking through me. Like he saw a shadow instead of a person. "I ain't nothin' but the hired help," he added dryly. "Lafayette's the man in charge."

"Don't I know it!" blurted Hooper. "Sheriff-General of Apache County!" He cocked his head like a rascal jay. "Tell Ben here how you come by the name."

McGowan gave a sniff. "Named me after my father and named my father after General Marquis de Lafayette. Helped Mr. Washington whip the Britishers. If they'd given me any say in it, I'd have asked for somethin' smaller."

"Rather have a splash of a name than a sprinkle," I chimed in a little too boldly.

"Well I'd say you've got plenty of splash in ya judging from that fray," answered McGowan. "Thought you were old Stonewall Jackson charging in on the flank."

"Just shootin' blind. It was your rifle got that Indian." I didn't mention about getting the shakes.

McGowan smiled broadly. "Not 'til you two got him in a crossfire. Didn't have a chance to aim good 'til you drew him out of cover. I imagine he'll be good and sore." He walked off into the trees to where they had their horses hidden, then came back holding a whiskey bottle.

"I imagine that man'll be sore sure enough," said Hooper as he looked at McGowan, "leastways 'til he dies." He spat a sprawling wad of chewed tobacco to ready his mouth for liquor. "I'd sure like to know what that was all about. I ain't seen the like. A damn blue soldier rescuing a renegade! What the hell was he, some kinda deserter?"

McGowan winched his head around as he scanned across the hills. "Goddamn horse thieves. Navajos. Been taking horses from Mormons and herding 'em up toward Fort Defiance. Me and Jeremy get paid a little extra to fetch 'em back. Only goddamn if they didn't track us."

"But what the hell was a soldier doin' with 'em?"

McGowan twisted his mouth and snorted. "Reckon he's an assistant agent at Defiance. He was wearing a lieutenant stripe. Likely trying to drag 'em back to the rez."

"Well it sure seems strange for 'em to come all the way down here. Must be a hundred miles from that blasted reservation."

"No point worrying over it," replied McGowan as he placed himself on a rock and uncorked the bottle. "They'll be taking those hurt men back to the rez for some witch doctoring. I don't reckon we'll be seeing 'em again. Just needed a little discouragement."

———•———

After we'd passed around the whiskey, we stripped our wet clothes and laid them out, then we sat there a-gabbing 'til the hills had turned to shadow. Just four cowboys white as fish bellies, crouched atop some rocks. If any Indians had come upon us, they'd have been laughing too hard to shoot. Then we huddled up by a thread of fire and passed around the syrup. After we'd pulled on our dry things, we went to joking and telling tales again. We finally stamped out our thread of fire and buried ourselves in our soogans. Every couple hours we'd trade off the guard duty. Now and again I fell off into fretful dreaming, but mostly I lay awake.

Soon as it was light out, we scanned the hills for signs of the Navajos. We packed our soogans onto the backs of our horses then huddled around our little fire again to share some hardtack. Hooper chewed his ration listlessly, staring into the flicker. He'd gone into one of his glooms again.

"I sure hope you find your pa," McGowan suddenly said. "If he'd disappeared in Apache County, I'd help you look. But it sounds like he was headed west. That's Yavapai. Ain't my jurisdiction."

"You's in Yavapai right now," Hooper quietly replied.

"Not on official business, exactly. We're meeting up with some fellers. It's a private matter, Hooper. Did you notify Sheriff Mulvenon over in Prescott?"

He was silent for a moment. "Not yet."

"Well, if you figure it for a bushwhack you'd better tell Mulvenon."

"Not 'til we're sure what happened. Me and my brothers figure we'll hunt around before we fetch law."

"Well, I'm sorry I can't help. Godspeed to your search."

"Godspeed?" repeated Hooper as he looked up from the fire. "Godspeed? That's sure a new one. How about 'God, can ya please speed some more a that whiskey down my maw'?" All the worry in his countenance disappeared in a blooming grin.

McGowan scanned the hills again. "I'd happily oblige under other circumstances, Hooper, but we'd best be gettin' a move on."

"Hell's fire, Lafayette, you shot one of them fellers to shreds and a second one in the back of his leg. I don't reckon the three that's healthy gonna come back for a dose of lead."

McGowan gave a throaty laugh, then glanced at his saddlebags. "I guess it won't hurt to start the day with some elixir." He arched his back and yawned, then walked to his horse.

"Hey, Lafayette," called out Hooper as McGowan came walking back. "What's the chances you'd make me deputy? I'm at loose ends at the moment. Besides which, I reckon you owe me. I was politickin' for you right along 'til I rode down to Globe City."

McGowan shook his head in the negative as he handed over the bottle. "If you were doin' any politickin', they'd have chased me half to China."

Hooper sat himself on a rock before taking a swig. "I guess I'm fibbin' a little. But I'll tell ya square. Surprised the hell out a me you was runnin' fer sheriff. Just the thought of it had me tickled. All them grim-faced Mormon polygamist fellers, standing in line to vote fer some dead hero from days of yore."

"You wobble your mouth too much, Hooper."

I was silently agreeing with him as I sat myself across from Hooper, then reached to scratch my ankle. Felt like the chiggers had called a fiddle dance when I'd had my feet stuck out from my bedroll.

"I got the right to speak my mind," answered Hooper. "You ought to be protecting it! You's the sheriff, ain'tcha?"

"Just don't go making insinuations about what I done in the hoary past."

Hooper leaned forward to drop a twig in the fire. "Ain't no hoary past that's like to trouble you, Lafayette. It's the present. You just shot an Injun that was ridin' with a blue soldier." A little smile came over his face as the twig burst into flames. "Wing of owl and tongue of bat, lizard's foot and tail of cat, by the powers of Satan tell us plain, what's like to happen to them that's vain."

I started to get nervous about then. I could see Hooper was tweaking him. Only it wasn't just the tweaking that worried me. It dawned on me it wasn't renegades we were shooting at. It was a posse of genuine Indian police with a soldier riding at the head of 'em.

"You're dumber than a tub of slop," burst out McGowan. "We took back what they stole. If they hadn't goddamn tracked us, they'd be slurpin' firewater in their wigwams."

"I believe they call 'em 'hogans,'" answered Hooper. His mouth flickered with a trace of smirk. "I somehow got a wild hunch them fellers was Navajo policemen. In which case they ain't apt to be dippin' into the whiskey. More likely dumpin' it in the dirt. Only here's what's got me puzzled. If you was fetchin' back stolen horses, where in hell they at?"

McGowan looked at his deputy and rubbed his thigh. Neither one of them said anything for a time. They looked like a couple of school truants. "We put 'em in with Jayzee Mott's animals," McGowan finally stammered. "Damn fool lets anybody use his land. Got four or five brands mixed together."

The name Mott rolled around in the back of my head until it hit me. I'd seen him in Globe City a few months back when I was out of work. I was passing an afternoon at the courthouse when they'd arraigned him for stealing a horse.

"Well you ain't got no string," continued Hooper, "and you's a hella ways from home."

"Like I told you, Hooper, we're meeting some fellers," grumbled McGowan as he reached into his shirt pockets and pulled out some cartridges. "It's none of your concern." He rubbed the cartridges against his pant leg, then fitted them on his belt.

Hooper let out a chuckle mixed with snort. "Well you wouldn't be the first to put horses on Mott's range. Me and my brothers left some ponies there a while back. Tried to pay him in whiskey and he turned us down flat! Said he'd voted fer a prohibitionist fer US president. Recommended we do likewise." I got the impression he was softening the blow he'd landed.

"That's the hen preachin' to the foxes," answered Houck as he seated himself on a boulder. He pulled a handkerchief from his pocket and stretched it on the ground, then lay his pistol atop it like it was some delicate morsel.

"I told him he'd have us cowboys to thank if that prohibitionist ever won."

"How's that?" I asked Hooper as he handed me the whiskey bottle. I'd promised George I'd forego the spirits, but the scrape of circumstance had loosed my vow. I never was much for temperance oaths. Not in the flame of youth.

Hooper made a chortling in the back of his throat. "Landis Hooper's law of politics. Everyone says they're votin' fer principles, only that ain't the case. A man votes against the ones he hates."

"I don't follow," I said.

"If us cowpokes wasn't drinkin' and raisin' hell, wouldn't no prohibitionist stand a chance."

"Ain't that the devil's truth!" chuckled Houck as he picked up his pistol again and examined the chamber. "That Mott feller sure is a peculiar gink. Don't touch a drop and talks like a prissy schoolmarm, but he sure pals up with that Hashknife trash. They use him like a doormat. Run stolen stock through his range, and he don't even know it."

"He's sure a strange one," I heard myself reply. "I was sittin' in the back of the Globe courthouse a while back when they brought him up on a charge of horse theft. Said he'd come all the ways from Massachusetts state so's he could call hisself a bally cowboy. He made a pretty speech about his innocence and sure enough, they let him go." It was like listening to another man steal my voice and utter a slander. I had nothing against Mott except he'd put his words into perfect marching order. The truth was the judge had lectured the plaintiff about bringing a criminal charge instead of filing a simple replevin.

"I don't take him for any horse thief, but sure enough he talks persnickety," said Hooper. "Don't make any sense for a man like that to come all the way out here to start a horse ranch." He pulled the corner of his mouth up in a puzzled grimace. "Maybe his daddy made him leave. Like them English chaps. Get in trouble fer some damn thing and their family makes 'em leave. Sends 'em money so's they stay away. I hear Mott's old man is rich as cream. Owns a cotton mill."

"Prob'ly runnin' from all those Yankee women," joked Houck. "Those Holbrook whores say he's so pretty they'd give it free. Only he won't give it back. They tell me he prefers the gents."

His words took me aback. Never occurred to me that Mott was a man-lover. I'd heard whispers about that stuff when I was riding the rails. Some of the rail tramps had their beaus. No one paid much attention to it.

Hooper pushed his boot heels into the gravel as he picked up another kindling stick. He turned it in his hands and studied it. "Don't matter to me one way or the other. Whatever a man does in darkness ain't grounds to lay a judgment."

"I don't care whether he buggers porcupines," said McGowan. "Fair warning, Hooper. Tell those Hashknife pals of yours not to put no stolen stock on his land or he'll surely pay a wicked price. That includes you and your brothers. Since you got me out of a jam, I won't take you just now. But if I catch you in town, I'll sure as hell be coming. I don't care what name you use. Hooper. Johnson. Jakes. Hell, I don't care if you call yourself Davy Crockett. I got a special room with an iron door reserved for a gent by the name of Blevins."

Hooper threw the stick in the fire. "I aim to lie low! You'll not see me in your county, Lafayette! No sir! Not 'til I run fer sheriff."

McGowan gave a snort then picked at his teeth. Then everything got quiet. I watched a daddy long legs make its way over my boot, then dash under a rock. *Son of a bitch,* I got to thinking, *I'm riding with an outlaw with a blasted alias.*

I wanted to ask about the warrant, but decided to stay my tongue.

"Y'all look like Presbyterians at a church meetin'," chuckled Hooper. "I got an idea," he blurted as he groped in his shirt pocket, then pulled out a card deck. "I'll show you a card trick. Might even tell your fortune if you ask me extra nice."

5.

We took our leave when the sun came over the treetops. I had half a mind to turn for Globe City, but I was too fearful to ride without a companion. I didn't have to admire Hooper's morals to trust his qualities as a seasoned scout. He knew those hills and canyons like a fox knows a patch of woods.

An hour later we ascended a ridge called the Valentine. I couldn't see much romance in it. Nothing but brambly switchbacks thick with tree roots and loosened rock. Hooper charted our course along the deer traces that paralleled the Black Canyon Trail. We'd have stuck to the regular thoroughfare, only we were shy of meeting the Indian police. We'd got our fill of sociability.

It must have been about noon when we stopped at a beaver pond fringed with willows and birches. Hooper got off his horse and tumbled toward the creek. He bathed his face in it, then turned on his back and lay spread-eagle.

"You reckon we should stay here and let the horses get some rest?" I asked him. My raggedy sorrel acted like she had another thirty miles in her, but that stocky quarter horse of his had begun to labor. Made me smile to think I had the better mount. I'd taken to calling her Dorothea Dix after the gritty old lady that ran the Union army nurses.

"That's a fine idea, Ben. I could use some rest m'self." He got to his feet slowly and stretched his arms out, then went to unstrapping that fancy Mexican saddle. "We'll be cuttin' back onto the Black Canyon Trail just around the bend up there. We'll make my pa's place about supper. May as well have a siesta."

"Jesus, Hoop," I blurted as I swung my saddle off the sorrel. "You sure got a mouth."

He lay his saddle against a birch trunk then came back over to fetch the blanket off her. "Reckon I did get a little saucy. But it was all in sport. Lafayette takes hisself too damn serious. Always has. I rode with him a spell. I know him plenty. There's a lot I wish I didn't know. I don't wanna think about it."

It got quiet after that as we spread our saddle blankets on a grassy spot. I pulled my boots off and lay on my side for a time listening to the murmuring creek. I finally began to relax a little, but I couldn't fall asleep. "Landis?" I finally said. "You awake?"

"Hell's bells, tryin' not to be. And call me Landy from here out. Every time I hear 'Landis' I think some schoolteacher's come to cuff me."

"I'm sorry. Just my mind's all cockeyed."

"What's that mean?"

"Just got jangly nerves."

"Then sit up and smoke a quirly."

I lay quiet for a time, ignoring his advice. "You suppose you can teach me some a them card tricks?"

He rolled over to face me and shot me a little smile. "Yes sir! You let me rest up here. I'll show ya how it's done."

"I'd prob'ly just forgit. Don't have no card deck to practice on."

"Heard woulda given you one if you'd a asked."

"Just never thought about it." Heard's store suddenly seemed half a world away. "Had in mind to get a bicycle," I added wistfully. "George said he'd let me have one on credit. Said I could work it off a little at a time."

He looked at me through slitted eyes then propped himself on his elbows. "A bicycle? I'd a lot rather have a good horse than a useless bicycle."

"George don't sell horses."

"Well you're lucky I sold ya mine, else you wouldn't be here."

"How am I lucky? After what we just come through, I don't see no luck in it."

"Jesus Christ," he replied as he sat himself fully upright. "You wasn't but a shadow back there in Globe."

I looked at him blankly, "You reckon he really stole horses from them Indians?"

"Who—Lafayette?"

"Yeah, him."

"Likely. I imagine he was tellin' truth and some fib along with it."

"What's that mean?"

"Prob'ly did go up to the rez to fetch back Mormon horses. Might a took a few extras while he was at it."

"But he's the damn sheriff. Why would he go to stealin' horses?"

He turned his head and grinned at me. "Just the way it works. Them Navajos take our ponies, and we go and take 'em back. Take the extras to pay the interest."

"Oh."

"Only that Indian agent is like to give him trouble. If they ever find out it was Lafayette that fogged that Navajo, they're apt to put a warrant on him."

I flicked a tick off my wrist. "They'd put a warrant on a sheriff?"

"Thinks he's king of the range, but he'll sure find out otherwise." He gave a little yawn then reclined on his saddle blanket. "I'm about tired as Methuselah," he muttered. "Let's get some sleep."

I watched him a moment, then sprawled myself out. Got quiet after that as we squirmed to get comfortable.

"Landy?" I finally said.

"Hell's fire, Ben. What now?"

"Nothin', I guess." I rubbed my eyes and pulled my knees up. "How come the law's after you?"

"Oh, hell. Why don't you turn over there and getcha some sleep."

"Sorry, Landy."

"I didn't do nothin' but what Lafayette and that deputy did. A bunch of Navajo thieves took our horses last year and my brothers and me fetched 'em back. Couldn't find the ones the ones they stole exactly, so we took some other ones to make the deal even. Ain't a court in the territory gonna convict us of anything and Lafayette goddamn knows it."

"Then how come you changed your name?"

He kept his eyes shut like he was sleeping. "Woman troubles," he said quietly. "Got on good with a pretty little gal in Llano, only her husband didn't like it. Had to hightail it. Figured I'd take an alias in case he come a-lookin'."

"And that man that disppeared is your genuine pa?"

"He's my pa alright. Raised me from a button. Switched me about every time I blinked, if ya wanna know the honest truth."

I slept light for a time, waking every now and then just enough to remember where I was. Almost felt like I'd entered some other world. Nothing but breezes and soft waters and dappled sunlight on my eyelids. Only half an hour later my head filled with worry. If George had known about Hooper's hjinks, he'd have forbidden me to ride with him. Then again, I reflected, Hoop was altogether right. I'd been a ghost back in Globe. And besides which, I got to thinking, I was doing what George had told me. I was letting the winds sweep me across tossing seas to whatever shore I was meant to find.

After we'd rested an hour or so, Hooper walked out to inspect the fork onto the Black Canyon Trail. I followed behind him until he stopped at a damp stretch. Didn't look like much to me, just a mess of muddy horse tracks. I watched him walk back and forth with his head stooped.

"I guess those Navajos are halfway home by now," I offered.

He put his hands on his hips and glanced at me. "Prob'ly so judgin' from the tracks, but that ain't what I'm lookin' at." Said he'd found the tracks of a barrel chested gelding his brother rode. Couldn't mistake the splay of the gait. He stooped his neck again and walked along the trail for a stretch, then shook his head. "Looks like he come through a couple hours ago headed down to the Graham place. Got half a dozen men in tow. I reckon we'd better catch him."

We spent the rest of the afternoon descending the hills we'd climbed, only we took a dodge here and there to keep away from McGowan. That was the first I'd taken stock of that whole upper sweep of country. Long grassy pastures bright with poppies and sunflowers and late-blooming lupines, with little creeks here and there to sluice away the rain. Even two years of drought hadn't turned it sour. It was the best range in the territory as far as I could see. We rode along in silence, listening to the warblers and flitting mockingbirds. Must have been about four o'clock when we came into a meadow. A couple hogs scurried as we rode into it.

"What in the hell's that?" I called back to Hooper. I pointed to where the hogs had been.

"Ain't pretty," he answered.

"Dead calf?" I asked as my sorrel tossed her head.

"Not unless calves wear woolen pants."

We rode carefully toward it, like its bones could cause us harm. I heard the words "Jesus Christ" come out of my mouth, then disappear into the shadowed stillness. Looked like they'd dug him from his sandy grave so's they could play tug-of-war with the torn remains.

"Mexican or Indian from the look of his rags," muttered Hooper. "Sure ain't my pa." The arms and legs were chewed to bone, and the head was entirely missing. There were slashes on the neck bones like someone had chopped it off. Hooper rode in little circles looking at the ground.

"I think I see his head," I called out, my gaze fixed on a puddle. I rode closer to have a look at it. Sure enough, it was a head, face up in the murky water. Looked almost like he was alive with all the hair and leathery flesh. Except for the nose and eyes. Nothing but hollowed sockets.

Hooper rode up beside me and grimaced. "I believe he's winkin' at ya, Ben. Go ahead and throw him a nickel. That ain't somethin' ya see every day. A man talented with his head like that deserves to get some pay."

I felt my stomach give a heave just then. I turned my head away from Dorothea Dix as I splattered on the ground.

Hooper raked his eyes across all the horizons, then glanced back at the puddle. "I reckon he's one a them Mexican herders that the Tewksburys brought in. Been lyin' here a while, judging from his bones. Them hogs musta dug him out a couple months ago and circled back for his boot leather."

Jesus Christ, I got to thinking, *that mighta been the hired man that Ed said had quit him.* "Who you reckon killed him?"

He kept staring at the head. "Apaches most likely. Wouldn't be the first time they killed a man and cut his head off. They say it blinds the soul."

"You reckon they're a-watchin' us?" I felt myself getting sick again.

"They scurry pretty quick else they'd be hognip sure as this man. Probably drove his sheep back to the rez and had 'em a square dance."

I gazed at the head again, then turned back to Hooper. "Maybe we oughta bury him."

"Hell no! Leave him where he lays. Let them Tewksburys put him back. Ain't none of our affair."

———◆———

Hearing Hooper mock that dead man was when I should have known to ride the other direction. Never dawned on me at the time that Hooper

was the one that killed him. Shot him in the lambing season, they told me
later, then rode on into Globe City. But I've heard others tell it different.
Some say it was another man, only Hooper got the blame. Only ones
that know the truth lie a-moldering in stony graves. But I wasn't nothing
but a wayward boy and a bollixed atop of that. A man sticks with his
cursed range pals 'til they prove themselves entirely false.

That evening we rode up to a little stone house built like a fortress.
Had tiny slitted windows that looked about like gun loops. In fact they
were gun loops, Hooper told me, meant so a couple men inside could
hold off a couple dozen. They'd built it a few years earlier to fend off the
Apaches, but there were new dangers once they'd left.

As we got closer we espied some cowboys. Three or four seemed to be
playing a card game while another one tended a coffee pot. One of the
card players stood up with a pair of field glasses and gave us a careful
inspection. He called something to the other ones, then came trotting out
to meet us.

"Goddamn if it ain't brother Landis!" he yelled out as he stood
bright-eyed at Hooper's stirrup. He was a stick of a red-head with a face
near as wide as brother's was skinny. Hooper leaped off his horse and
gave his brother an embrace.

"Champ goddamn Blevins!" Hooper blurted, "you must a growed
half a foot since I seen you last!" Hooper paused a moment, then
laughed. "Hey, Champ, I got me a new card deck from George Heard's
store. I'll show ya some cleverish tricks." He pulled the cards from his
shirt pocket and held them in the air. Seemed like he'd forgotten all about
his pa being lost.

"I got some new tricks to sh-sh-show you, too, big brother, after all
this h-hell is over."

"Don't stutter, little brother. Ain't no one but me."

Just then the man tending the coffee pot got up and walked over to
us. The rest of the crew followed. "Good to see ya, Hooper!" he called
out in a hard Scottish burr. "Put yoor hawrrses in the trap and get some
coffee. Not enough daylight to do any riding. If the heavens decide to
piss on us, we'll crowd inside the fawrtress." He walked a little closer
and flashed a grin. "We've hung a porker in the smookhouse. She awaits
a rendezvous with Texas gentlemen."

After we unstrapped our tired horses, we turned them out in a handsome pasture. Then we gathered with the other fellers as they stood around a lick of fire. "This is Ben Holcomb," said Hooper as he tilted his head in my direction. "He's got him a job workin' fer that little she-cowboy over to Payson. Figures he can help with the search before he heads over."

"I hope she's paying a handsome wage," answered the Scotsman. "Misery enoough to work for a Mistress Do-Good, let alone one with a tyrant father."

"We're obliged for all the help we can get," cut in Champ. He gave me a glance, then turned to address his brother. "Met up with these Hashknifes yesterday when I was ridin' down from Dry Lake. We f-f-figure it's about time to call on them Tewksburys. Ain't nothin' personal to these fellers—just hate the sh-sh-sheepers s-same as us."

"That's a damn lie!" yelled a man in a bowler hat. "Love 'em all to pieces when we half get the chance!" He followed his joke with a curdled laugh.

"This here's John Payne," said Champ, nodding toward the man in the bowler. "One minute he's a-workin' me to become a M-M-Methodist. Next minute I see him gallop off to p-p-pistol-whip some p-poor Mormon that's crossed onto the Hashknife." He went silent and swallowed hard, like he was struggling to find his words. Then his face lit up. "'The Lord smiteth them wicked polygamists,' he shouted out to me as he come lopin' with his righteous grin." He'd somehow lost his stutter.

A couple of the others laughed quietly as Bowler Hat made a scowl. "Not no more I ain't smilin'. Do your job the best ya can and what the hell happens? Boss calls us all together yesterday, tells us to stop goin' after the Mormons. 'Well I'll be damned,' says I. Here I thought we was doin' just what the company wanted, runnin' off all them Mormon trespassers. Company wants you to lay off, says he, or quit right now." He tucked his thumbs under his suspenders as he pursed his lips and shook his head. "'Well gosh all Friday,' says I, 'I already quit three weeks ago. Rather picnic with Champ anyways.'"

"Picnic?" I asked.

"Yes sir!" replied Bowler Hat with a big moon of a smile. "Didn't you know we's on a picnic? Brung quite a spread, cowboy. Fried chicken and corn on the cob and some a the choicest pie that ever darkened your gums."

I looked back with a puzzled expression. "Thought you gents come to look for a lost man."

"You's a green 'n, ain't ya, cowboy?" he winked. "But you'll get some pie! Best recipe in the world! Sugar and butter and four pints black 'Tewks berries'!"

I felt a chill curl up my spine. I was willing to help them search, but I wasn't attacking no Tewksburys.

"What about Pa?" scolded Hooper as he squatted and rolled a cigarette, then reclined against a scaly juniper. "We're supposed to be lookin' fer him."

"We'll f-find him," replied Champ, "dead or alive. If he's dead, I'm gonna make a bonfire and roast some sh-sheepers."

"You don't reckon an Apache got him?" I asked quietly. There was silence for a moment, then they went on like they hadn't heard.

"Ease off, little brother," said Hooper as he whisked out a match and fired his quirly. "You're gonna get that mouthy face a yours shot full of holes. Then you won't be able to kiss that sweetheart under the nose no more."

"Under the nose?" asked Bowler Hat.

"Yeah, under the nose," retorted Champ. "Ain't polite to say 'lips.'"

"Well, nose, lips, it don't matter," continued Hooper. "Won't be kissin' no girl if you get yourself shot."

"I'll kiss her sure enough if they don't marry her off to no dirty polygamist. And if you don't s-s-scare her away. She never heerd anyone curse her people the way you done. She don't care for ya, big brother."

"You cursed 'em, too, before you got to likin' that girl. Don't you lay it all to me!"

"Well I ain't plannin' romance. Gonna call on Mr. Ed Tewksbury. Won't be no social call." He'd lost his stutter again.

"Slow down a little, Champ," said a tall man with sleepy eyes. "If you march over and show your six-gun, we're like to have a war."

No one answered right away. Off in the distance, I could see a couple of blackbirds on the tail of a hawk. I must have seen them do that a thousand times. You'd think that ol' hawk would loop around and grab 'em, but they stay on his tail 'til he quits the game. Them little birds keep a-swooping and diving, trying to catch a claw in the big ones' eyes.

"Sounds about right," Bowler Hat finally answered as he shifted his weight from one foot to the other, then tilted back his hat and crossed his arms. "Look what they done to you. First they run out old man Stinson. Y'all went and testified they was rustlin' his herd and look at what happened. Them lyin' Tewksburys damn near got ya put in the hoosegow for perjury. Poor ol' Stinson had to goddamn sell his whole herd and then *vamoose*. And now it's your turn. You think it's bad they brought a few hundred woolies? Well lemme tell ya, cowboy, there's plenty more a-comin'. Them Daggs brothers gonna send 'em all. They have to. Got fifty-thousand sheep and nowheres else to put 'em."

You'd have thought they were holding a funeral from all the grim faces bending downward.

"You and that goddamn Hashknife Outfit are as much to blame as they are," said the man with the sleepy eyes. "Bally cattle barons buy a goddamn million acres and run out the sheep barons, only it's small fry like us that has to pay the price. I lay it to you, Payne. You and your Hashknife friends. Might as well be rounding up the sheep yourselves and driving 'em down here."

"Just doin' my job, Tom. Anyways, I don't work for the Hashknife no more. I'm here to help y'all clean up this mess. Don't matter how it happened, we got to clean it up. If we shoot a few, they'll leave. Believe me, they will."

"No goddamn shooting!" yelled the Scotsman. "They steal our cows and we roon off their sheep. Bad enoogh the way it is."

I felt myself shaking as I tried to ante up my courage. "Might could go and talk to 'em," I called out. "Ed Tewksbury ain't half as bad as you make him out. He ain't the one herdin' sheep anyway. It's his brother doin' that." The force of my words loosed the spit in my mouth.

"And in Gawd's name who are you?" replied the Scotsman.

"Hooper told ya. I'm Ben Holcomb. Been stockin' shelves for George Heard. I'm on my way to work for Luett Atkinson."

"And I am John Graham," he replied loudly. "I suppose you've heard of me. It seems I've become notorious in certain precincts to the south."

I swallowed hard to keep the spit from flying. "Heard you and your brother are into it with the Tewksburys."

"Brothers. Two of them, for worse or better. To my right is Thomas." He gestured toward the tall, sleepy-eyed man who'd spoken earlier. "And that winsome lad to the right of him is Baby Billy. Celebrated his sixteenth birthday in Des Moines a month ago, then volunteered to join our army." A pretty blond boy with beardless cheeks gave a nod. "Here we be, Master Holcomb," went on the Scotsman as he doffed his hat and bowed. "The infamous brothers Graham. Knights of bloody cattledom. Defenders of the blasted realm."

You'd have thought them cowboys were regular stage players with all their puffed-up bluff and swagger. Every time they met a stranger, they felt obliged to give a show. It was like they were trying to make you fearful, except they wanted you for a friend. One minute they'd be banty cocks and the next they'd sidle up.

"May I speak fer us?" asked the Scotsman, looking at his brothers.

"Ain't no one stopped you yet, Johnny," replied Tom. "Just privately wishing you'd speak American."

"Being raised among the Yankees," laughed the Scotsman, "my brothers falter in their elocutions."

"Well, at least we got the looks," joked Billy.

"Hear me oot, young Holcomb," continued the Scotsman. "My brothers and I are not quite so unconscionable as you've been led to believe."

"No one said ya was."

"I rawther suspect they did, Globe City being a Tewksbury bastion. Even your contemptible newspaper proclaims its fidelity to cursed Ed."

"Might take a fancy to you, too, if you'd bring that editor turkeys the way Ed does."

"Which we very well might, were it nawt a Tewksbury town." He glanced around at the other men as he spoke.

"Alright."

"But it is a Tewksbury town, which makes us a wee bit shy to go there."

"I heard ya."

"Well how do you suppose we can fix this, young Holcomb?"

"George Heard says you need to talk to each other. Negotiate a treaty." I expected to hear my voice falter, but somehow I was calm. I know it probably sounds strange, but I'd got to feeling my own importance. Here I was friends with Tewksbury—or so I fancied—and parleying with the Grahams. Like a missionary to the rebellious heathens that thinks he'll convert 'em with righteous words.

"Negotiate a blasted treaty?" growled the Scotsman as he rolled his eyes and pursed his lips. "If they want peace, tell 'em to send the sheep back to the Daggs brothers. It's not just Tewksburys who've caused this mess; it's those bloody damned sheep barons."

"Hell's fire, maybe this boy is right," cut in Tom Graham. "Maybe Ed'll talk."

The man in the bowler hat made a sucking noise then spat off to the side. "They're sending y'all death threats and you think they're gonna talk?"

"Death threats?" I asked.

"Yeah. Notes that say 'GO.' Written in blood."

"Are they signed?" I finally asked.

"Are they signed?" shot back the Scotsman as he paced back and forth with his arms folded. "Why in Gawd's name would they sign 'em? So they can get themselves arrested?"

"You're sure it's Tewksburys?"

"Who the hell else?"

I thrust my hands inside my pockets and stooped my shoulders. I felt the puff come draining out of me. "Hell if I know," I answered quietly. "Maybe someone wants to rile the both of you so's they can take this pretty range."

"Ye shoorly are a green sprig, Master Holcomb. But I won't hawld it against ya. I'll give ya this much satisfaction: my brothers and I will give it time." He hesitated a moment, then looked at Champ. "We'll be glad to help ya search for your pa, Champ. But we don't want any shooting."

Hooper walked up behind me just then and planted his hand on my back. "Champ," he called out, "I agree with Mr. Graham. Don't go to shootin'. Not just yet. Take these boys and ride over there and ask 'em polite if they seen Pa. If they say no, just turn yourself around. We'll meet here in two days and palaver on what to do. If it's war they're a-hungerin' for, we'll serve 'em soon enough."

"You ain't a-c-c-comin'?" cried Champ. His stutter had come back.

"I'm headed up the Rim with Ben. Gonna poke around near that little stock pond he used to camp at when he was huntin' deer."

———•———

At the first peek of rosy dawn me and Hooper headed out. We rode under a cloudless azure as we proceeded toward Naegelin Rim. He pointed out a homestead here and there as we slowly wound our way. Then he halted without a word at a cutoff that headed west. "There she is," he called out, "that's the Hellsgate cutoff to Payson." He nodded toward a narrow path that wound through pretty pastures and up the slopes. "Just take the left fork every time 'til you cross the gorge. It'll take you down through the hills to a big meadow called Little Green Valley. If you take the first right fork at the meadow you'll come straight to the Atkinsons'. Got his cabin tucked against the Rim at a place called Myrtle Point. It's up and down through broken ridges, but the trail ain't hard to follow. You'll do alright."

"Thought we were gonna look for your pa."

"You got no stake in this fight, Ben. Go on and get your job. My brother and them are fixin' to make trouble. I don't want you involved."

"Told you I'd help search."

"You sure did, Ben, and I'm grateful. But the searchin's about over. I'll look up at the stock pond, but he ain't gonna be there. He's lyin' dead somewheres, killed by a bullet. Now go on. I don't want you in this."

I half thought he wanted to be rid of me on account of I'd slow him down, but another half of me was glad for the discharge. I remembered George's words about staying out of the feuding, though it was like everything else George commanded. His words frayed on the trail. If it hadn't been for Hooper cutting me loose like that, I'd have jumped straight into his yawning hell. Looking back on it, I guess I'm thankful. Hooper wasn't any model of Christian charity, but he had his decency all the same.

Only in the moment I didn't see all that. What I felt most was the fear of riding alone. I looked up the trail, then glanced back at Hooper. "You reckon them Indians killed your pa?" Between the Navajo police and the dead sheepherder, I'd gotten my nerves rattled. I hadn't slept hardly a wink at the Graham place. Hooper had spent the evening regaling them with the tale of our Indian scrape, only he'd doubled their numbers from five to ten.

"Didn't no Indian get him," Hooper called back to me. "My brother woulda seen the sign. He's got the tracking gift same as I do."

"You don't figure they're a-hidin' along the trail?" I kept seeing that dead sheepherder with his bones all helter skelter.

"If you're so worried about blasted Indians, might as well go back to Globe City."

I gave him a fretful look, then glanced at the cutoff. "Guess I'll go on then."

"Yessir," he replied as he reached to shake my hand. "You go on. You're gonna be one hell of a cowboy once you learn the ropes. Just don't go and tell Colonel Atkinson you rode with Landis Hooper."

"Why wouldn't I?"

"On account of he's got it in for me. Got it in for all of us. Me and my brothers and the Grahams. Goddamn Tewksburys been tellin' him we're stealin' horses."

"Jesus Christ," I muttered as I stared at the hills. "Are they right?"

"Good Lord, Ben. You take me for a thief? If there's anyone stealin', it's apt to be the Tewksburys. They're the worst thieves in the territory. Won't no one be mourning if they get run out tomorrow."

"I apologize," I said as I bowed my head.

"I don't need no apology, but I sure can use a favor."

"What's that?"

"Wanna borrow that haversack of yours. Prob'ly do some scoutin' afoot. Can't see the sign good from the back of a horse."

I pulled my haversack from my saddlebags and handed it over. "Guess you'll owe me double."

"Owe ya double?" he asked confusedly.

"Said you'd show me how to do some card tricks."

He grinned like a scrawny jack-o-lantern. "Teach you a dozen of 'em when this hell eases up."

6.

Hooper said to take the left forks, but somehow I took an extra. I got lost in the hills for half the day before I found where I'd gone astray. Every time I came around a bend, I half expected to see a band of Apaches. I finally camped on the lip of the Hellsgate.

Wasn't 'til the next morning that Dorothea Dix and I wound our way into the gorge. Looking down into it, I thought I'd found an Eden. All quiet waters and shadows and a canopy of shimmering green.

When we got to the bottom of it, we slaked our thirst in Tonto Creek. Then I realized we were boxed. I rode up and down the canyon, searching for a sign of a trail. Upstream lay a quiet pool between blackened cliffs that ran to sky. Haigler Creek trickled in through a little side canyon, threading through a bed of boulders. The far side was nothing but tangle. Broken sycamore logs lay heaped like battlements guarding thickets of box elders and spindly willows twined with tendrils of wild rose. I sat grim-faced atop my skinny sorrel, squinting into the thicket.

Finally I saw a little chute leading up the far wall behind the trees. I had to laugh as I studied it. Couldn't figure how a horse and rider could make the grade without a ladder. I got down and led Dorothea Dix through the knot of tangles, pulling thorn branches away to protect her eyes. Five steps into it, we were sunk half to the knees. The storms had made a swamp of it. Just when we came out on a bed of talus, I tripped over a loosened root.

"Goddamn it!" I yelled as loud as my lungs could muster. My curse went bounding across the cliffs, then came circling back like a frighted dog. Blood came oozing from a ragged tear on my hand. Then we walked along the talus 'til we finally reached a slide of rocks. I turned upwards toward the chute and cursed again, then did my best to lead her. Half an hour later I came huffing to a sandy ledge.

It was getting near evening when I came trotting to the Atkinsons'. I followed the trail through a row of apple saplings, then came to a big pole corral that caged half a dozen horses. Just behind the corral stood a palisaded wall. Looked about like an army fortress, except they'd left the gate completely open.

Soon as I came through it, I was swarmed by a pack of hounds. A hatchet-faced, balding man stood up from a log, casting his long stooping shadow between giant hides tacked to the barn. I thought they were cow hides, but it turned out I was wrong. They were the first grizzlies I'd laid eyes on. Right beside him stood a skinny young woman holding a horseshoe. She shot me a glance, then tossed it at a peg.

"I think you've got me whipped, Papa," she called out to the bald man. Then she turned towards the dogs with her hands on her hips. "Jezebel! Scoundrel! Loafer! Let that man pass!" She stood with her lips pursed until the barking petered out. "I believe you're Mr. Holcomb," she called out.

"Yes ma'am. Mr. Heard says you have a job for me."

"We have plenty of work for you alright, if you're keen to learn the trade." The dogs kept running in circles like it was some kind of big event.

"Goddamn right," chimed in the old man as he took a tug on his pipe. "The thieves took the Mormons for thirty horses last month. They're like to take my whole herd, too, if I ain't got men to guard 'em. If you're an honest man come for work, we'll happily oblige you." He whistled at the dogs, causing them to slink away.

"These are for you, Miss Luett," I said timidly as I got off my horse and handed her George's letters. "They're from Mr. Heard. I reckon that skinny one's a letter recommending me."

I watched nervously as she turned them in her hands. "Our man, Mr. Henry, came from Globe ahead of you," she said matter-of-factly as she opened Heard's recommendation. "George told him you might be coming. Thought we'd see you long before now."

"He forgot to tell me about it right away. Got lost in his bookkeeping."

"Didn't come by way of Hellsgate did ya?" asked the colonel.

"Yes sir," I answered. "I rode with a feller from Globe who was headed up the Rim." I didn't tell him it was Landis Hooper.

"Well, I wouldn't go that way again if I was you. Better stick to the stage road. Someone's apt to take you for a spy, what with this feud going on. Mr. Henry tells us they had some kind of gun fight yesterday. Heard it straight from Ed Tewksbury." His pipe smoke came out in little bursts as he talked.

"Was any of 'em killed?" I inquired nervously.

His throat bobbed with a quiet chuckling. "A couple of 'em got their heads shot off. Good riddance is what I say."

I wanted to ask who was killed, but I was quiet as a rabbit.

"Papa!" cried Luett, her face set in a grimace. "They're the Lord's people same as us."

Atkinson opened his eyes wide in mock surprise, then shook his head with resignation. "Ben, you reckon you can kill a grizzly if one comes a-chargin'?" His eyes glowed down in their sockets like embers from a campfire.

"Reckon if I had to."

"Well, you might have to. There's quite a few in these parts."

"I can see that," I answered as I stared at his bear skins. "You appear to be quite a huntsman, Colonel Atkinson."

"Pa's a huntsman, alright. Takes his dogs out after grizzlies when he oughta be working."

"It is work! Can't just leave them bears to make hash outta my cows. Anyway, Mr. Holcomb, consider yourself hired."

"He knows he's hired, Papa. George Heard already told him."

"George Heard told him? Well no one asked me!"

"No need. Mr. Heard says he was the best stock boy he's ever had." I didn't bother to explain that he'd only had the one.

"Stock boy?" the colonel called out in feigned anger. "We need a cowboy!"

"I'll teach him. And so will you."

"I imagine I'll have to. I take orders from my daughter here, Ben. She hires and fires my men and forbids me to drink, curse, and gamble." He blew out another puff of pipe smoke that hid his face, then dissolved.

"I can't forbid, Papa. I can only counsel."

"She forbids, Ben. In fact she was just lecturing afore you arrived. But she can't forbid me all the time! Why don't you go install yourself yonder at the bunkhouse. Unpack your things and put 'em away. Bard's over there now. He'll show you around. I'll swing by later. Me and Bard get together every so often for a game. Luett ain't invited."

———•———

Later that evening I tucked into a feast. Mr. Henry boiled up frijole beans and fried some pork chops in a pond of lard. After my tormented ride with Hooper, I felt myself begin to settle. Mr. Henry asked how much cowboying I'd done just to size me up, then regaled me with stories of bear hunts. He was about to make a pot of coffee when the colonel came busting in.

"Ben Holcomb!" called out the colonel as he pulled up a chair. "You look cowboy enough to me! I'm glad you escaped from that storekeeper in Globe. He's bad as Luett, always after everyone to stop drinkin' and playin' poker."

"Yes sir. I surely hated to quit him, but I ain't suited for a stock boy. Figured I'd do better at snappin' broncs if I could find a man to hire me."

He smiled and shook his head as he gave me a close appraisal. "Not just yet, Ben, not just yet! Takes a special man to snap the broncs. Can't just bust 'em and ride away. Got to school 'em. Teach 'em to stop, go, stand still, lift their hooves for shoein', go fast, go slow, hold the rope tight when you got a calf on the other end. A horse might buck ya off more than once before he learns all that. Ain't that right, Bard?" Atkinson nudged Bard Henry as he spoke. "Bard's busted a few broncs in his time, only they've busted him a deal worse."

"Yessir, I'm an old man before my time. Ain't much use for anything 'cept takin' the colonel's money in these poker games."

Just then Atkinson pulled a bottle of whiskey from the shelf and poured us each a tumbler. "You like whiskey, Ben? Best medicine in the world for turnin' peach fuzz into a set of whiskers." He winked at me as he talked.

"I reckon I could stand a drop."

After we each took a drink, Bard shuffled the deck and dealt a hand. They frowned like a couple fence lizards after I won five hands in a row. "You'll make an even better cowboy than I thought you would," said Atkinson, "judgin' from the way you play poker. Too bad we ain't playin' for high stakes. Reckon you'd own my ranch before the night's over."

"Well, if luck's with me, it'd be a first. Or maybe a second, countin' when George Heard took me on. Hadn't had a scrap of food for two days before that."

"I count that bad luck! Not just the bein' hungry part, but the part about Heard takin' you under his wing. Like a preacher rearin' a bear cub. Don't matter how much Sunday school the bear gets; it's got to grow up to be a regular bear. Now have another drink." He poured my tumbler full.

The whiskey had already worked its way to my head. I felt warm inside and I was beginning to feel feisty. There was something I liked about Colonel Atkinson. He wasn't like George at all. The colonel was tall as a poplar and whippet thin, whereas George was like a pony with stubby limbs and sagging gut. In fact they were altogether opposites, as different as a firebrand and a block of ice. The colonel was easy to be around, always wry and full of jokes. George was friendly, too, for the most part, but reserved and a little sharp.

I drank my second whiskey with the same gusto as the first. I felt that little fire kindle in my gut, then spread into my arms and chest. I lost a round, then won three, causing Bard and Colonel Atkinson to grouse in a friendly way. Then I got reckless. Instead of folding when I had bad hands, I kept raising the stakes. By the time midnight rolled around, the colonel owned my gun. I was oiled enough by then that I bet my sorrel to get it back.

"That's alright," the colonel chuckled after he beat me with a pair of jacks. "Ain't takin' your possessions. That sorrel's too skinny for a workin' horse anyway." He rose from his chair and grabbed the whiskey bottle, then turned it to his lips and drank the dregs. "We'll put her in the barn and fatten her," he continued as he set the bottle on the table. "You won't need her on the range. You'll be ridin' some a mine. And as for that gun, reckon I'd just have to give it back. You might have need of it here before long."

He didn't say nothing else about the gun, and I didn't ask. Just lay myself on a bunk like a dead man and fell into the fog of sleep.

———•———

The sizzle of bacon brought me awake. Wasn't yet full dawn, and I was still a little drunk. I could walk without holding on to something, but I felt pretty shaky. That and my right shoulder ached like sin. Reckon I'd been too drunk to remember to roll over.

It was Bard who was frying the bacon. He shot me a friendly grin as

I pulled up a chair to warm myself. "Figured you'd come to if you got a whiff a this. How you feelin'?"

"Sick."

"Can you get down some bacon?"

"I think I can, Mr. Henry. I ain't never turned down a slice of bacon yet."

"You ain't used to the whiskey," he continued as he carefully tipped the skillet to pour the grease into a jar. He'd erred a little in his judgment, but I was loathe to enter a protest.

"I ain't used to that hard bed, either. Ain't you got mattresses?"

"Had to burn 'em when the vermin got bad. Atkinson's been promising us new ones, but he's so damn far in debt he can't afford it."

"In debt?"

"Up to his eyeballs. It's been one damn catastrophe after another. First his cattle started dyin' from the tick fever. Then the nesters started cuttin' his fences. After that it was a sleet storm. He brung his herd here to recoup his losses, but he lost half of it on the way."

"But they tell me he's an up-and-comer," I said as I poured myself some coffee from a pot on the stove.

"Oh, he is that. He works like a devil on the range. He's one a the best cattlemen I ever knowed. He'll get square with his debt in a year or two or three. Soon as cattle prices come back. 'Course he's got Luett to keep his books. She don't miss a trick when it comes to doin' business. She cowboys for him, too, when he needs her."

"I reckon she likes it."

"Why you reckon that?" he asked as he forked some bacon and biscuits on a couple of plates, then handed one to me.

"On account of she's here when she coulda married up."

"She wants to marry alright. She's in love with your old boss. I told the colonel to let her go, but damned if he'll listen."

"Mr. Heard told me the colonel's a hard man."

He raised his eyebrows then shook his head. "The colonel ain't hard. Hell—he's downright sociable."

"Reckon I like him."

He reached over to the pan and forked out another piece of bacon, then dropped it on my plate. "That's why he's the colonel. Whenever riders come through, the colonel makes 'em sit down to a good meal and a friendly game of cards. They start out calling him 'Mr. Atkinson' 'til they come to see his inner man. By the time they're a-ridin' out they address him as the colonel."

"Didn't he fight for the Confederates? That's what George Heard told me."

"Texas cavalry," he grinned, "same as me. But he wasn't no colonel. We were the orneriest buck privates in Joe Johnston's army."

"Musta seen plenty of hell in that war." Didn't tell him that my pa had fought on the other side.

"More than I care to remember. But I surely learned one thing. The colonel, he's a gamecock. He ain't one for surrender."

"Reckon he can't if he's that far in debt."

"Sure he can. Some men just scamper. Not this one." He broke off a piece of biscuit and dipped it in his coffee. "The cattlemen around here tried to run him out just as soon as he come. He took the four-hundred head he had left and wintered 'em right on Tonto Creek. Them ranchers over there told him to be gone. Said the range was overstocked. No water and no feed for any more cattle. Said they'd kill him if he stayed. Well he stayed alright, and they sure didn't kill him. In fact they's mostly friends."

"Meaning some ain't?"

"Some."

"Is he in this feud?" I sipped my coffee and looked around. The dawn's light filtered through the windowpane over the table. Every inch of the far wall was covered with hooks and paraphernalia.

"Not much," answered Bard as he grabbed for his coffee cup. He gulped down half of it, then turned back to me with his jaw clenched. "He don't hold any love for sheepers, but it's the thieves he hates the worst."

"Meaning who?"

"Grahams. Blevinses. Hashknifes. There's others, too."

"That don't sound like 'some.' Sounds like half the valley plus more on the Rim." A wave of nausea came over me as I swallowed a bite of biscuit. I'd been mulling over telling them about that cursed ride with Hooper.

"Not a good man among 'em," he muttered as he took a dirty rag and wiped the dregs from his plate, then walked across the room and put it on a shelf.

"Then who's the colonel friends with?"

"Oh, lots of 'em! Jake Lauffer and the Colcord brothers and John Rhodes. And Sam Haught and Bill Vorhis and Bill McFadden, and Glenn Reynolds, and there's others. Some of 'em came with us from Texas. The colonel barbecues a hog now and then and invites 'em to play cards. Then you'll see the whiskey flow."

I went over to my bunk and located my bandana where I'd tucked it in a corner. I wiped my mouth on it, then thrust it into my pocket. Then I sat back down again. "What about the Tewksburys?"

"Ain't against 'em, but he ain't friends with 'em. Figures they won't be here long anyways. We hear them Grahams been sendin' 'em death letters. I reckon they mean it, too." He shook his head with disapproval. "A bunch of 'em rode over to the Middleton cabin day before yesterday thinking they'd drive out the blasted sheepherders. Only they got more than they bargained for. The Tewksburys shot four of 'em off their horses before the rest of 'em skedaddled. Killed that stuttering Champ Blevins and his pal by the name of Payne. 'Course it won't take 'em long 'til they regroup and ride back. I imagine it's gonna be a war. Best thing to do is stay the hell out of that valley. It'll sort itself out. Just need to give it time."

"Jesus Christ," I muttered as I bent my eyes toward the floor. The goddamn Grahams were sending death letters to the Tewksburys same as what the Tewksburys were sending them. And now Hooper's brother was a dead man along with the man in the bowler hat. I wanted to ask more about it only I was too fretful to say a word. Just clammed up like a deaf-mute 'til I heard the barn door clanking shut.

"Ben Holcomb!" yelled Luett from somewhere outside. When I glanced out the window, I saw her marching a handsome black toward the bunkhouse. I opened the door and watched silently as she tied the horse to the hitching post. "This gelding is for you," she called out as she stepped up on the porch. "That old sorrel is worn out. My father says she needs a rest."

"Thank you, Miss Luett," I replied haltingly. "That's a strong animal by the look of him." I'd become partial to my raggedy sorrel but I wasn't eager to dispute my boss. Somewhere in the murk of my thinking I knew Dorothea Dix had earned her pension.

"His name's Percival. Don't jerk on his reins or you'll sure wish you hadn't. But don't go thanking me until you hear me out."

I looked at her with an open mouth, like I was about to ask a question.

"You can have him. He's yours. But if you get drunk again around here I'm taking him back."

"But the colonel poured the whiskey."

"Papa promised he'll stop his drinking. That's the bargain. I stay here and take care of this damn ranch and he corks his bottle. The booze makes him mean. Makes him stubborn, too. I understand he won your sorrel and your gun last night. You're lucky he let you keep them. I wish some of his betting partners had been that generous to him. He's lost a lot more than a horse and gun in his poker games. I won't allow it. Not anymore."

"I work for you, Miss Luett. I will do as you say."

Bard sniffed and went silent.

"You see to it you do," she said. "Else I'll send you straight back to Globe City."

7.

I got to liking that Atkinson place, even despite Luett's threat to fire me. 'Course I never quite knew who was boss: the colonel or Luett. Both of them fired off the orders and they weren't always the identical same. Not that I particularly minded so long as they treated me good. Fortunately, the colonel didn't invite me to no more card games, and I didn't have money for whiskey even if there'd been somewhere to buy it. Not that I'd have wanted it anyway after my latest bout of drunken foolishness.

I learned all about cowboying from the three of them. Bard taught me the arts of horsemanship whilst the colonel explained the trade. Some days Luett rode with us; other days she worked his ledgers. She did more than her share of the sewing and cooking, too. She had her mother and her sister to help, though the sister couldn't do as much on account of her crippled leg. All the other sisters were married except the two young ones. He'd packed them off to Santa Fe for boarding school. Somehow he'd found the money. Just the mother and the lame sister stayed home, and an eight-year-old boy. He had an older boy, too, only he wasn't around.

Only Atkinsons I did see were the colonel and Luett. At first I figured Luett's mother and sister and her little brother must be sick. No one talked about them, at least not to me. Since I ate in the bunkhouse, didn't figure I'd see them much. Still it was odd that they didn't once show their faces. When I finally asked Bard about it he shook his head and gave a chuckle. "The missus don't live here," he confided.

"Don't live here?" I asked as I stared out the window. The last threads of sunlight turned the hilltops to golden lanterns.

"Not now. Got mad at the colonel. Took the lame daughter, Enna, and the boy and rode over to Payson. She stays with his sister over there. But he sends her letters regular. Sends her a beef cow now and then, too. Some a the boys in Payson slaughter the cow and save the best cuts for

Mrs. Atkinson. Then they sell the meat and hide and give the proceeds to her, too."

"Well it's none of my business."

"It ain't. But you work here. Hell, you're almost family." He lit one of the lamps, then grabbed up some rawhide strings from a hook on the wall and began to braid them. Wasn't hardly a spare moment that he wasn't braiding something. Bridles and hat bands or sometimes a quirt.

"You hear that tinkling piano?" he went on.

"I do."

"That's Luett's revenge."

"Revenge?"

"The colonel got her that damn piano back in Texas after he had to take her outta school and put her to work. We all thought she'd play some sprightly tunes. But hell no. Plays nothin' but dirges." He rolled his eyes toward the house. Then he went to clinching his hands and stretching them out, trying to straighten his knotty fingers.

"What's she playin' now?" I asked.

He sucked his lips in and shook his head, then started singing in a mournful voice.

Weep no more, my lady.
Oh, weep no more, today.
We will sing one song for the old Kentucky home.
For the old Kentucky home far away.

"I love her like my own daughter," continued Bard, "but I'm about sick to death of that song."

"Don't you reckon she's missing Texas?"

"Not unless it's that convent school they had her in. She didn't like Texas no more than she likes it here. Just wants the rest of us to miss Texas. Particularly the colonel."

I studied him silently. "What prompted him to cast his eye toward Arizona?"

"Same as what prompted all of 'em. Heard tell of grass high as a horse's belly. Found a patch, too, after we done a little scoutin'. Right out yonder." Bard nodded toward the pasture. "Soon as we got here the drought killed it back. That's when things got bad in that house. The colonel gets testy when it don't rain." He didn't look at me while he talked. Just went on with his braiding.

"How come Mrs. Atkinson to get so mad at him? Can't just be the drought."

"If I tried to explain, it'd be like riding through mesquite. Nothing but thorns and tangles."

"How come I ain't seen the older son? He ain't in Payson, is he?"

"That's another story entirely," he said, finally glancing up. "He's around. He's off on one of his wanders. Might be off at the Tewksbury ranch one day and the Haught place the next. Helps the colonel with the cattle some, but he mostly stays away."

"Guess I won't ask you to explain that one, either."

"You'll meet him. You'll meet 'em all. It'll all unfold. No point in worryin' about it."

———◆———

It was about two weeks later that the colonel took me out to survey the range. "Just the two of us," he grinned as he saddled up, "so's we can get better acquainted." He jimmied the horn around to make sure it was good and tight. "Besides, I got a lot to show ya. You're doin' okay, but you don't know the land. Wanna show ya some waterholes where the cattle hole up. We'll ride toward Houston Mesa and give the grass an inspection."

Three hours later we arrived at a little canyon. We picked our way down the side of it 'til we came to a crystal pond walled by slabs of rock. Looked like one of them Roman ruins with broken columns strewn around. From the far side came a splashing sound where the pond emptied through the boulders. "That's our swimmin' hole," said the colonel as we pulled up to let the horses drink. "I take 'em all out here once in a while when the house gets too hot. You'll get your chance, Ben. Can ya swim?"

"Yes sir. Had a regular lake near our farm in Ohio. Musta been a hundred times as big as this pond."

"We're just lucky to have what we got," he went on as he leaned forward over his horse's neck, then spat some tobacco. "Ain't a critter in a dozen miles that don't come here to drink. 'Course the catamounts come, too. They hide in them rocks and wait for the fawns. I seen a she-cat tear half the buttocks off one of our colts right down by the water. Thought that colt was gonna die, but damn if he didn't heal."

"I reckon these waters got miraculous powers."

He straightened up in his saddle and gave his horse a little prod. "I was afraid it'd dry up, what with this drought. Didn't get no rain at all this winter, but we're sure gettin' summer storms."

From the pond we continued west, toward the east fork of the Verde. The whole valley looked green from a distance. Needle grass with rye and grama, the colonel told me, but it looked sparse as a dog's belly when you got right up to it. Every now and then, we'd see a few scraggly horses, their midsections like parched rawhide stretched tight across bony staves. "Mares didn't foal," said Atkinson, "and the ones that did lost their colts."

"I see one yonder," I replied, pointing to a mare under a sycamore, nursing her colt.

"Hell and tarnation! Told Bard to get that mare into the barn before she dropped her colt. If we leave her out here, we're apt to lose 'em both."

"I can bring 'em in. She ain't on her last legs."

He kept his gaze on the mare, almost like he hadn't heard me. "I seen 'em just stand over their dead colts like they're guardin' 'em."

"That colt looks plenty lively, Colonel."

"Leave 'em out another week and they'll look like that one there." He gestured toward the base of a hill where a yearling heifer was lying dead. Scavengers had ripped her flesh off. "Get so weak they can't get away from the wolves and cougars. Hell, I seen coyotes get 'em when they're that weak."

"I'll bring 'em in," I repeated.

"No need. Do it myself soon as I get a chance."

As we continued riding, I noticed our shadows had got behind us. The sun was sloping toward the western mountains. My belly was getting restless, but the colonel refused to stop. "Payson's a couple miles south," he finally said. "Let's mosey over. May as well introduce you to the 16-to-1."

—•—

The 16-to-1 was a two-story plank building at the edge of town. A couple horses stood listlessly at the hitching post. From inside came the sound of a man harrumphing, followed by the tinny laugh of a woman. A freckled man with deep lines on his face swung open the bat doors, then stood there with a broom in his hands. "I come out to sweep and find a surprise!" he called out. "How come I ain't seen you in so long, Jass?" he said thickly as he set his broom against the wall. "Didn't come down with this influenza that's been goin' around, did ya?" He wheezed a little, like he'd been sick himself.

"Just on a hackamore. My daughter don't let me go far these days, Billy."

"Then you'll have to make up for lost time."

"This here is my new hand, Ben Holcomb. Ben, this is William Pendergast. Known as Billy Thundergas to all us regulars. Runs the finest drinking establishment in the metropolis of Payson. Of course there ain't but one."

"Pleased to meet you, Ben," chuckled Pendergast as he motioned us in. "I guess you figured out by now that you've made a hell of a mistake hiring on with old Colonel 'Jass You Lissen.' If he ain't bragging about whippin' Yankees he's a-riding grizzlies bareback."

I smiled and took my hat off, then stepped inside as the colonel held the door. Smelled like juniper smoke mixed with beer and sour tobacco. Along one wall ran a long wooden counter with three or four empty stools. Against the back wall sat a cast-iron stove with a steaming pot atop it. Off to one side was a pool table and on the other a splintered staircase. A trio of cowboys played cards at a circular table in front of the stove. A couple of painted women sat at their sides.

"How come they call it the 16-to-1?" I asked the colonel as we took seats at a table up front.

The answer was windier than I'd expected. It seemed the cattlemen were bitter on account of cattle prices took a tumble, and the miners were mad because silver prices stayed low. But if the government would open the sluice gates and mint more silver coin, cattle prices and miners' wages would both make a jump. The more silver in people's pockets, the more they'd pay for beef. Then the colonel and Billy Pendergast could get rich and move to Dallas. Only it depended on Congress pegging the worth of silver at sixteen troy ounces to a single ounce of gold, else they could mine all the silver in creation and it would just be worth the less. "Sometimes there's a drunk Republican that makes bold to argue the contrary," concluded the colonel. "Apt to lose a molar if he gets extra zealous."

After the colonel finished his pedagogy, he turned his head toward the counter. "Give us whatever you got cookin', Billy. Two orders. One for me and one for Ben. And some beer. Two glasses for each of us. Gotta wash down the dust."

One of the girls raised herself from her chair and studied us. Then she walked behind the counter and drew our beers, as though Pendergast had asked her to do it. She silently smiled as she set the beers in front of us. Had pretty white teeth only a front one was busted off.

"Howdy Claretta," said the colonel. "This here's Ben Holcomb. I reckon he'll be regular."

"Glad to make your acquaintance, Ben." She gave me a half smile, then walked back to the men playing cards.

"You better treat her good," said the colonel in a low voice. "She's a first-class woman. I won't tolerate no roughness."

"Ain't in me to treat a woman rough," I mumbled. She was near as skinny as the mare we'd seen earlier. Had a narrow mouth on a longish chin, with big emerald eyes that shimmered like a rippling lake. She wasn't any Cleopatra but I sure enough felt her tug.

When I turned my head again, I saw Billy Pendergast bringing two steaming bowls of beef stew. He set them down on the table along with a big spoon for each of us. Didn't give us any napkins; we made do with our dirty sleeves. "You sure you boys gonna be hungry after you drink all them beers and eat that stew?" asked Pendergast as he raised his eyebrows and gave a smile.

"I know what you're askin', Billy, but I got my wife to answer to. Believe I'll refrain from sinning just to keep the peace. But I want Ben here to have his fill."

Pendergast winked at me then walked back to the counter. I felt myself blush.

"Drink up!" laughed Atkinson. "I seen the way you looked that girl over. Don't call her Clare. She don't like that. Goes by Claretta. Don't be shame-faced. When a man feels an itch, why he'd better get to scratching."

"Ain't denyin' she's got my attention."

"Well, she'll get more of it shortly. Now drink them beers. George Heard ain't made you into some kinda teetotaling schoolboy, has he?"

I put the glass to my lips to shut him up. The sensation was more pleasing than I'd expected. I hadn't eaten since dawn. My stomach welcomed beer like a fire welcomes kindling. Wasn't half a minute before I felt it reach my head.

As I relaxed into my chair, I felt a smile cross my lips. Atkinson smiled back as he drank his beer and ate his stew. Then he turned serious. "Eat up and have a good time," he said matter-of-factly. "Just remember there's saddle horses and there's thor-a-breds."

For a second I thought the colonel might be fixing to make a wager. Bard told me they raced ponies right there on the street. They'd draft skinny cowboys to be the jockeys then fire a shot to start the race. Somewheres in my head I thought I might fit the bill.

"My daughter, for example," said the colonel.

"Oh," I replied as a jolt of chagrin ran through me.

He pushed his beer off to the side a little and looked me in the eye. "You're a fine lookin' young feller, Ben. Ain't full of yourself, either, unlike a certain storekeeper whose name I'll forebear to mention."

"Reckon not," I answered nervously.

"Well do you cotton to Luett?"

"I like her fine."

"But do you cotton to her? Do you think about her?"

"Can't say."

"Sure you can say. Either you do or you don't. I'll put it to you straight. I think she cottons to you. If you showed an inclination, I believe she'd do likewise."

I took another sip of beer, then looked off toward the bat doors. "Reckon I have thought of her once or twice, Colonel Atkinson, but Mr. Heard has her claimed." On the outside I was playing the honorable cowboy but on the inside I felt a tingle. My blurred imaginings of matrimony suddenly came into perfect focus.

"He don't have no one claimed," he said disgustedly. "She needs a man who can help with the ranch. Heard ain't gonna do it. Got that gimpy arm, for one thing, and he's gimpy in the guts, for another, if ya get my drift."

"Might be a little full of hisself like ya say, but he sure helped me out when I was down." I kept remembering one of my father's sayings. When your hopes come a-boiling pull the pot off the heat. He wasn't much of an optimist.

"Well she sure as hell ain't gonna marry him. I told her to break off that bally letter writing, but damned if she'll listen. She's torturing him slow."

"That may be the case, Colonel, but I barely have a nickel. A woman would be a fool to marry a broke feller like me."

"Well that might change, Ben, that might change." He gave a half smile then sucked down the last of his beer. "We'll have to see." I felt the hopes come boiling again. I could see a homestead application and a starter herd. That and a woman to share it.

Off behind him I saw Claretta slinking upstairs with a cowboy.

"You can go next," said the colonel. "I won't tell Luett. Whatever you do here ain't no one else's business." Either he had eyes in the back of his head or he'd recognized the creak of the stairs.

"No sir. I don't believe I want to go next." The truth is he had me flummoxed. It occurred to me he was giving his test. Any man that showed enthusiasm for a saloon whore wasn't apt to show marital fidelity. Only the more I've reflected on it, the more I think it was entirely opposite. Wasn't any pious morals that he respected. He was taking stock of my suitability for membership in his ancient lodge. Only it weren't any Odd Fellows or Ancient Hibernians. It was the Fraternal Order of Manly Sin.

"You ain't too good to poke a whore, are ya?" he asked as he glanced at the stairway.

"No sir."

He tilted his head a little as he looked at me. "Alright, I ain't makin' you. But think about what I said. The more time you and Luett spend together, the more you'll come to see her qualities. I wouldn't let no George Heard stand between me and a good woman."

Just then, one of the cowboys from the other end of the room called out to us.

"Join us for a game?" he drawled.

"I reckon not," answered the colonel. "I don't mean to be unsociable, but this man and me got business to discuss."

"Well at least let me buy you two a round a drinks. Billy, drinks for those boys and another round for me and my friends here. Whiskey, not beer."

While Pendergast ambled toward the bar, Atkinson leaned close and whispered. "That's George Gladden. He's real friendly when he's in his cups. Makes good money stealin' horses."

The colonel got quiet as Pendergast set two whiskey glasses in front of me. "Why in hell you givin' 'em to Ben?" asked the colonel in a mock surly tone.

"I don't want you to get in trouble with your daughter. I reckon this young man can hold his liquor better than you."

"Hell's fire, there's got to be at least one pleasure left to an old man."

Pendergast chuckled as he moved a glass toward the colonel, then walked back to the counter.

Before we could lift our glasses, we heard boot steps on the porch. A man leaned in over the bat doors and swiveled his head around. His face showed like a shadow against the sun behind him, but his tasseled gloves sparked my wick of memory. He pushed his way cautiously through the bat doors, then aimed himself toward our table. "Damned if it ain't the colonel," he called out. "And Ben Holcomb to boot! Last I saw, you was dustin' shelves!"

"The infamous Mr. Edwin Tewksbury!" called out the colonel. "Big as life and thrice as high!" I watched the colonel raise his glass in a friendly toast, then followed his example.

No sooner had Ed seated himself by the side of us than the man named Gladden gave an angry shout. "Billy, I'm buyin' another round. Give us each another whiskey. But none for that darky. Here's where I draw the line. I won't drink with no black man."

Ed stared hard at Gladden, then rose from his chair.

"Ed, set back down," blurted the colonel. "Got business to discuss."

"Be back lickety split," said Ed as he pulled off his gloves and walked to Gladden's table.

"Didn't hurt your feelin's, did I?" spat Gladden.

Ed made no reply, just bent down a little, then slapped him hard across the cheek.

"Give me an iron!" shouted Gladden as he lurched from his seat and desperately looked around. "I'll kill this man right now." The room was silent. Then he paced toward the bat doors and flung them open. We followed at a distance. "I'll be back for ya soon enough," he called out to Ed as he walked down the street. "Left my sidearm with the gunsmith." His spurs jingled like a pair of tambourines as his boots stirred puffs of dust.

I could feel my back shiver from a wave of fear as I watched Gladden disappear behind the blacksmith's place. The man who'd been playing cards with him swung over his horse just then and trotted away. When I glanced at the colonel, I saw his lips clenched into a smirk. "Ed, come on in and drink a whiskey," he said quietly. "If he comes back, we'll be here."

"Not drinkin' no whiskey. I'll fight him sober."

"One whiskey won't do nothin'. Besides which, I got things to discuss." He called out to Pendergast to pour Ed a round.

We all filed back in and sat at the table we'd just vacated. "That son of a bitch is a horse thief," said the colonel as Pendergast set Ed's whiskey down.

"You're tellin' me?" replied Ed.

"Well I wouldn't gunfight him. A man don't need to gunfight no thief. They ain't worth it."

"I got no choice. I'll be damned if I'll be insulted at the only saloon in fifty miles."

"I reckon not. But hear me out."

"Hear you out about what?" Ed shifted in his seat a little, then glanced around the room.

"About this thievin'. It's got to stop. And I want you to help me stop it."

"I'll start by killin' Gladden."

"That ain't necessary. He'll meet his end soon enough."

"What's that mean?"

"There's people looking for him. Only they ain't lookin' for no gunfight."

"Meaning they're gettin' up a lynchin' bee?" asked Ed as he pulled his gun out and inspected it.

I drained my whiskey and sat silently, trying to still my shaking hands. Ed kept looking right and left like he was afraid someone would sneak behind him.

"That's not the word I'd use," said the colonel. "There's law that's lookin' for him. He'll get a trial, I imagine."

"Not if he comes back here." Ed flared his nostrils a little and flexed his fingers. "He's one of the ones settin' fire to the sheepherders' cabins. I reckon I'll put some fire into his insides and see just how well it suits him." That was the first I'd heard mention of any cabin burning since they'd tried a man for arson when I was back in Globe.

"Well, Ed, I reckon you'll shoot him down sure enough if he comes back. I know you're good with that Colt. But I want you to think about somethin'."

"Think about what, Colonel? I'm a little out of sorts. Don't mean to be rude, but this ain't the time to talk."

"I don't see ya often, Ed. Anyways, I just want us to get square. There's some talk that you and your brothers stole a lot a stock from Old Man Stinson. Drove him out of the valley, some say."

"Well, talk is talk," Ed said under his breath. "I can't shut their mouths. Not unless I hear 'em." He kept his face down as he spoke like he was too angry to look at us.

The colonel stooped his head a little and cleared his throat. "I know that, Ed. I ain't sayin' ya did it. And even if ya did, I understand how it works. Hell, I learned the trade in Texas. If a man wasn't a little free with a running iron, why, he weren't gonna build no thunderous herd."

"What's your point, Colonel?"

"Well, I figure we got to stop this rustlin'. I mean all of it. No more of this takin' a calf from another man's herd and callin' it a maverick. A real maverick's one thing; that's fair game. But if a calf's with its mother, it ain't no maverick."

"That's right."

"I just want us to be clear. I won't take no calves from your herd, and you won't take no calves from mine. Or heifers, or steers, or bulls, or horses. None of it."

"I hear ya, Colonel," replied Ed as he pushed back his chair and crossed his arms. "But the only ones doin' that stuff are the Grahams and Blevinses and some a them Hashknifes. Them and that goddamn Gladden. He's in tight with 'em. I hear he run off some Mormons up in the Mogollons and claim jumped their farm. He has a wife and a babe, but you sure wouldn't know it the way he come lookin' for a fight."

Ed lurched out of his seat when we heard boot steps on the porch. Suddenly a boy poked his head through the door. "Gladden hightailed it," he said breathlessly. "Says his shooter's busted, but he'll come a-lookin' for you soon as she's fixed."

—•—

"Don't you get mixed up with sheepers," the colonel warned solemnly as we rode away.

"Reckon I see your point," I replied, remembering my ride with Hooper.

"If the Grahams hadn't tried to drive 'em out in the first place, they wouldn't a done that." He looked at me sternly, then readjusted himself in the saddle. "Had their backs to the wall and here come the damn Daggs brothers, offering guns and bags of money. Only thing required was to run the blasted woolies." He leaned over and spat tobacco. "Ain't easy to be a breed. Sold their souls to save their skins."

"Ed seems like a decent feller," I said quietly.

"He's a capital feller when he ain't rustlin' cattle. Got more sand than most white men. I just don't want you gettin' mixed up with him."

"I don't aim to. Not after what happened back there."

"Well that dumb Gladden's like to get his head punctured. If Ed Tewksbury don't do it, someone else will. But Ed ought not get hot like that. A man can't gunfight every fool with a lip."

"Ain't you been in no gunfights?"

"Never. Figured I might have to gunfight the ones that went to cuttin' my fences in Texas, but what good would it a done? If I'd gone and killed one, another one would come after me. Or his brother or his uncle or God knows. I got a family, Ben. I don't aim to get killed in no gunfight. There's better ways to earn respect."

"Reckon I'm lucky I ended up with you for a teacher."

"Oh, I'll teach you alright," he said with a snort.

Then our conversation drifted to horses and grizzlies and his doings in the war. He got so excited about his war stories that he showed me a cavalry charge. He hung a rag on a tree branch and galloped hard at it, ducking down low and leveling his rifle. Except he didn't duck low enough and the branch knocked his hat off. "Nothin' but a pride wound," he called back to me. "It'll heal." It was all I could do to keep from laughing, though I guess he'd have laughed as loud.

By the time we reached the swimming hole, the weather had gotten cool and breezy and the sun was completely hid. The clouds towered ahead of us, swirling north and dark as dusk. Crooked flashes lit the Rim, then left it veiled in ashy blackness. "Drought's sure broke," commented Atkinson. "Now we're like to get Noah's flood."

"I sure love a good rain. Just as long as it ain't overhead." Said like a cowboy, I thought with smug congratulation. I was beginning to feel almost giddy . . . like we'd dodged the devil back in Payson and those black clouds didn't amount to nothing. Up ahead was the glimmer of my future. A regular homestead ranch at the foot of the Rim and a hive queen to share the honey.

The colonel replied in a low voice. "That rider's bringing trouble."

"What rider?"

He pointed to the top of a ridge about a quarter mile distant. "It's a young woman, I believe, wearin' a black hat and ridin' a bay with a white star on the muzzle."

I strained to see the rider. Finally, I could make out a shape.

"How do you know it's a woman?"

"I seen that sight before. It's Luett come to fetch me from the 16-to-1. Now you know what I have to put up with. Luett's her mother's deputy. She comes after me when I've broke the law."

"Is she deputy or is she sheriff?"

Atkinson gave a guffaw. "Sheriff! And she's a hella lot tougher than the one we elected!"

When I looked back at the tiny figure riding toward us, I could see she'd spurred her horse into a lope. She was in a hurry.

"She seen us," said the colonel. "She's comin' fast. Must be some kinda trouble."

Both of us sped up to meet her.

"Bard's dead!" she gasped when she reached us.

"Bard's dead?" replied Atkinson with a puzzled look.

"Yes, Papa, dead! He didn't get up this morning, so I went to check on him. He wasn't breathing."

"There weren't no shootin'? No one come lookin' for him?"

"No, Papa. I looked him over careful. No wounds. Just dead."

I could see Luett's eyes glisten. When I turned to the colonel, he looked away. "He wasn't gonna last forever," Atkinson muttered as he turned back to us. "Lived a hard life, that one."

"Papa, we got to fetch the coroner. I want him to certify that it was a natural death. Otherwise the rumors will fly, what with this feuding."

"Reckon I'll load him on a horse and drag him to Payson. They can look at him all they want. Least he ain't got no relatives. His brothers died in the war and his worthless sister married a Yankee."

As the three of us rode back I kept glancing at Luett, sizing her up. George was right; she was handsome. Wasn't her looks that done it. It was her poise. She rode that little bay horse like she was commanding a whole brigade. George or no George, I got to wondering whether she'd have me.

8.

We wrapped Bard's stiff body in a blanket that evening, then set him on his bed. When darkness fell, I reclined on my bunk. I lay awake for a time and stared at the rafters. I kept picturing the two of us walking noiselessly through the glow of night. We didn't have any destination; I just followed his steps through the curving hills. I finally pushed my blankets off to cool myself, then groped for a path to sleep. Only I couldn't. First the coyotes got to yipping in unison, then the lobos had a lengthy go. No sooner did they fall into silence than a couple of bulls began a war of bellowing. Guess I fell asleep somewhere in the storm of noises, but then I heard something else. It was Bard. He kept calling out for me in desperation like he'd been thrown from a bucking horse. I woke with a start as I struggled to find him. The fading blackness was turning pink. I glanced over at Bard's silent body to make sure he was where we'd left him. Then I fell into a fitful sleep again 'til Atkinson broke the calm of morn.

"Let's dress him in his Sunday clothes, Ben, if he ain't got the rigor mortis."

I felt myself flinch with surprise. He'd made his entrance without my noticing.

"We'll strap him to a pack horse," continued Atkinson. "I want you to stay here and help Luett with the chores. I'll be back tomorrow, most likely. Don't forget what we talked about at the saloon. Don't settle for any saddle horses."

"Yes sir," I heard myself answering as I lifted myself into a sitting position.

An hour later Luett showed up with a Bible. We'd dressed Bard in his Sunday clothes, then laid him out again atop his bunk. "This isn't a fit way to say goodbye," she announced, "but it's the best we can do under the circumstances. Come over here and stand around him." As we did so, she rested her hand on his shoulder.

"He was my best friend," said the colonel as he fetched out a match to light his pipe. "Reckon I loved him."

"I picked out a Bible verse, Papa. Put that pipe down and be quiet."

Atkinson put the pipe in his shirt pocket, then closed his eyes and bowed his head.

"*Though I speak with the tongues of men and of angels, and have not charity,*" Luett went on, "*I am become as sounding brass, or a tinkling cymbal.*"

"First Corinthians," muttered Colonel Atkinson. "Luett's favorite verse."

"Quiet, Papa." She read another passage, then continued from memory. Her voice got soft as she finished.

For now we see through a glass, darkly, but then face to face. Now I know in part; but then shall I know even as also I am known. And now abideth faith, hope, charity, these three; but the greatest is charity.

"That's pretty, Luett," said the colonel as he stood there with his head bowed and his hands tucked behind his back. "I know it ain't just for Bard."

"Papa, I've given up sending you messages. It's your good fortune that Jesus won't do likewise. Bard's probably up there now whispering in Jesus's ear, trying to get him to have a talk with you."

The colonel gave a little snort, then looked over at me. "If Bard's whispering to Jesus," he confided, "he's a-tellin' him about all these priggish females I got to put up with." I gulped hard and looked down trying to fight off a chuckle. Somehow the colonel's voice made the whole thing seem droll.

"Bard's telling him that you're a good man who does bad things," said Luett. "And as far as charity goes, he gave up a lot to work for you."

"I reckon he worked for me on account of I paid him," replied the colonel, his brows dancing on his forehead.

"Other way around. Gave up half his salary after you went broke. He forgave you every time you couldn't come up with what you owed. I believe that's called charity."

"I reckon so, dear child. He was a good man and an inspiration. But right now I got to ride. I'm gonna fetch back your mother and your sister and little brother, if I can."

"What if they won't?"

"Then they won't. But your mother's gonna have to get over bein' mad sooner or later. They can't stay with my sister forever. She can't afford to keep 'em, and I ain't gonna send no more beef over there just so my wife can go on with her protest."

Half an hour later, the colonel headed out on a stocky buckskin. Had a little pack mule right behind him with Bard's corpse across her back.

———•———

"Won't be the same without him," I said to Luett as the colonel rode away. "Didn't know Bard that well, but he sure made me feel at home."

"No, it won't be the same," replied Luett as she held the Bible against her chest. "I can't count the times he helped me carry Papa to bed when he was inebriated. Bard tried to keep him from the bottle, but he finally gave up. Truth is they both liked their spirits." She gave a little frown, then bowed her head toward the ground.

"I guess that's got somethin' to do with why your mama and sister are in Payson, but it ain't my business."

She watched silently as the colonel and Bard disappeared in the distance. "It isn't your business," she finally answered, "but yes, the drinking's got something to do with it. I don't mind him enjoying his beers at the 16-to-1. He's a cattleman. He's got to relax now and then. But I do mind the whiskey. Sometimes it makes him extra friendly and solicitous. But sometimes it works the other way. It's like he's got the hydrophoby. Starts barking and snarling—and sometimes it's worse."

She stood there looking round like she wasn't sure what to do, then she walked in the house and put away her Bible. When she came back out, she was carrying some halters. She handed a couple to me, then told me to follow. She went straight to the horse corral and had me swing open the gate. Once she'd got inside, she slung halters over a couple horses, then walked them to the barn. "We got work to do," she shouted as she came marching back. "Get in there with your halters and pick out your mounts. Be sure to get tame ones. You ain't ready for the broncs." Stung like an insult, but I knew it was true.

"Make up your mind!" she called out as I tried to find a tame one. I singled out a roan and led her to the barn, then returned with my other halter and laid it on Percival. By the time I'd reached the barn I saw Luett coming with a saddle. Must have weighed fifty pounds, but she handled it deftly, slinging it over Percival's back.

"I want you to use this Texas saddle, Ben. That full-rig California saddle of yours is just gonna get in your way. Percival's like to toss you across his neck if you stop him too quick. Probably catch your manhood on that spike of a horn and make you sing a pretty opera. I'm gonna teach you Texas riding and roping. Now hitch up this double-rig and I'll make sure you do it right. We'll bring these extra horses so we can change mounts. It isn't right to run a horse ragged the way you did that poor sorrel you rode in on. We'll ride one horse half a day, then change to another."

"You sure are green," she commented as I fumbled with the straps.

After I'd finished, we rode out in silence. It was like I'd all of a sudden forgot my words. I thought she'd make conversation but she reciprocated with an awkward chill. When we reached a little cattle pen near Atkinson Creek, she reined up and turned to me. "I need to talk to you. I've been dreading this but we have to get some things straight. I know Papa's been encouraging you to get friendly with me. You know what I mean."

I stared at her with a stony face, unsure what to say.

"He's been saying the same to me," she continued. "He likes you, and he thinks I should, too."

I was too embarrassed to say anything back. Didn't want her to think I was disloyal to George. But mostly I just didn't want her to know that I'd been thinking about her.

"I like you," she stammered. She seemed nervous. It occurred to me that maybe I'd made a better impression than I thought. Then my hopes fell. "You're a handsome man, Ben. Don't get the idea I haven't noticed. You've got good manners, too. I like a man who isn't full of himself. But you're damn near three years younger than me and you're poor as a Methodist pack rat. There, now I said it."

"Begging your pardon, Miss Luett. Did I do somethin' to make you think I was makin' a play for you?" I felt the disappointment bite my insides, but I refused to let it show.

"No, Ben, you didn't. I just want us to be square, so we can work together. I don't want any doubt about what our relationship is. You're a hired man, and I'm your boss."

I didn't answer. Just kept watching her, stony-faced.

"Papa's not much of a matchmaker, but I'll say one thing in his defense. He values loyalty and so do I. I mean that as a compliment. I expect you had the decency to keep your hands to yourself on account of you're loyal to George."

"Yes ma'am, I reckon I am." She wasn't entirely off the mark but she wasn't completely on it. I wasn't eager to set her straight in the matter.

"He isn't much to look at," she muttered as she took her hat off and tied her hair back. "Got that crooked arm and he's lost most of his hair, and sits heavy on a horse. I keep telling him to lay off the biscuits. But he's set himself against wickedness, Ben. He's determined to get into the legislature and make this territory a fit place to live. Before you come along, Papa was after me to marry one of these man-boys around here." She glanced at me with her lips set. "Well I won't. I don't want any cowboy. I love George. It'll be him if I marry."

I turned my head away, then looked back at her. "Then how come you ain't married him already?" I shouldn't have asked it but somehow I couldn't stop myself.

She sighed loud and shook her head a little, then she got quiet. "It's none of your business," she finally said, "but since you're asking I'll tell you. When we had an Apache scare last year, George didn't do a thing but send a fancy rifle and warn me about treacherous redskins. If he'd have rushed here to stand guard, I imagine Papa would have given me permission to marry him." She pushed a wisp of hair behind her ear as she looked off toward the Rim. "Papa says he's the biggest coward that ever lived, and there are times I think he's right." Then she turned back to me. "If he's ever going to fix this territory, he'll have to screw up his courage. Don't you dare tell him I said that! But it's the God's truth."

"Well I guess I'll have to give the colonel back half his kingdom," I replied with mock earnestness. "He offered it as a dowry." I thought she would laugh, but she only gave a half smile.

"I don't think he'd give you any dowry even if he had it. And besides, once you get to know me better, you might not like me so good. I'm too much like Papa. And I'm not talking about his friendly side."

"Well I ain't seen you frothing, Miss Luett." In the midst of my disappointment I somehow felt my heart lighten. It was like I had two different souls hitched to my insides and they were pulling in opposite directions.

Finally she let out a laugh. "Then I'll have to show you some. We'll ride together down along the creek this morning and do some range branding. Then we'll come back about noon and get our fresh horses and work up toward the Rim. You know how to use a running iron?"

"Reckon I don't."

"Well it's not like a regular branding iron. I'll show you how to use it. When we find any calves, we'll light a fire and paint our brand on 'em. I'll show you how to cut their ears, too—and bob their balls. You ready?"

"Yes ma'am!"

We worked the rest of the day catching calves and yearlings and then branding and castrating. It was plenty hard work but it had its excitements. About half an hour after we started, I managed to rope a calf. Then I got off my horse and walked over to him so's I could throw him on the ground. Only before I could do it, he began to bawl piteously. Then here came old mama cow, loping like an angry bull. I didn't waste a second; took a detour up an oak tree. Luett threw her head back and laughed like a banshee.

"I believe you show promise, Ben," she said wryly as her knife flashed across the calf's testicles. "You sure looked fine shinnying up there in those tooled boots and silver spurs. You might could compete at that event in a cowboy tournament if you practice." She dropped the testicles into a little bag and smiled. "I'll roll 'em in batter and put 'em in a skillet this evening. No point in wasting."

———•———

The sun dropped low as we rode, turning the clouds all orange and pink. The bright colors strung out across the eastern skies like stained glass in a fancy church. Only the northern view was something else. Nothing but roiling blackness, like some evil spirit come to swallow us. We hurried toward the ranch with the storm behind us. We were soaked and shivering by the time we arrived.

After we got the horses in the barn and took off our boots, we went straight inside. Luett hung her hat on a nail, then stripped to her camisole. When she saw me looking, I blurted an apology.

"Just got to get those wet things off," she responded. "I'd advise you to do likewise. Run over to the bunkhouse and get your dry things then come on back for supper. It'll take me a few minutes to get changed anyway."

I nodded to show I'd heard, then stepped outside, closing the door carefully to keep it from banging. Three steps later I realized my situation. Every stitch I had in the bunkhouse was sagging from the clothes line. I hadn't had time to fetch them before the storm came. Figured I'd have to shiver until I could cozy up to a stove. Only when I entered the bunkhouse, I saw something queer. Someone had gone and laid Bard's clothes out neatly on his bed. I saw something else strange, too. There was a man about my age hunched over the little card table. "Figured you'd get a bath out there," he muttered. "Might as well wear those. Bard won't mind."

I was too taken aback to answer. He had a narrow face like Luett's, only with thicker brows and a wad of hair swept over his forehead. He seemed more slim than lanky but with a voice that doubled his size. It dawned on me he was Atkinson's older son, the one they called Jeany.

"I reckon you've heerd about me," he said with a kind of offhanded conceit. "Used to live in that poisoned house 'til I got smart enough to keep away."

I gathered up my wits and offered my hand. He got up and shook it weakly then plopped himself on my bunk. "I imagine we'll be riding together," he commented as he rolled a cigarette, "if you're gonna stay, that is."

"Imagine so."

"Well while you're imagining, you might wanna go ahead and get in them clothes," he went on. "Better that than catchin' your death of cold."

"I imagine I'll just do that," I answered, pulling off my boots.

"I guess you know about all the trouble around here."

"I heard this and that. Rumors, mostly. Bard told me the colonel ain't in the feud, though." I played ignorant lest I make him suspicious.

"He ain't. But he ain't exactly clean of it."

"What's that mean?"

"I mean he's trying to put an end to it. It's got out of hand. He don't care if they kill each other, but he ain't gonna put up with 'em stealin' stock. Started out stealin' from one another, but they been castin' a wider net here lately. I imagine some boys will hang."

"I want no part of it," I answered quietly as I pulled on Bard's jeans.

"Well you probably will be. And I will be, too. Pa wants me to see a lynching. Says that might happen to me if I don't mend my ways." He scratched at his armpit then stood up and looked out the window.

"Why would he tell you that?" I got the idea he was trying to make me uncomfortable.

"On account of I'm his slave."

"You don't look like one."

He shook his head and clucked his tongue, like I'd said something rude. "Well I guess I take it back," he continued. "If I was his slave, he'd give me some work. Told him I'd do all the cowboying he needed, but what the hell did he do? Went and hired you anyway. Why you suppose him to do that? On account of he don't credit me for bein' a man."

"You look man enough. And it wasn't him that hired me. It was your sister."

"I am man enough, for you or anyone else. And as far as my sister goes, she's his goddamn foreman. She does the hiring 'cause he told her to do it."

Just then Luett knocked at the door. She opened it slow and stuck her head in.

"We're gettin' acquainted without your help," Jeany snapped.

"If you two want to talk, I'm not gonna stop ya. I'm fixing to eat supper. I guess you two aren't hungry."

"Hungry as a bear in April," I responded as I turned to the door.

Jeany followed at a distance, then took a seat at the head of the table, where the colonel usually sat. After Luett set the food down, she pulled a book from her apron pocket and went to reading in the dusky light.

"What book is that?" I asked as I picked at my food.

"*A Tale of Two Cities* by a man named Charles Dickens," she answered without looking up.

"Hell, Luett," piped up Jeany, "how many times you suppose you're gonna read that one?"

"Until George Heard sends another. There's a man in this book you would do well to emulate, Jeany. His name is Sydney Carton. He makes a mess of his life until he antes up with something noble."

"What's he do that's noble?"

"If I tell you it'll give away the plot. It's about the French Revolution and how the people became vengeful. I recommend you both read it. Papa, too. It would certainly be instructive."

"Is he bringin' Mama and Enna and the cub back from Payson?" asked Jeany, oblivious to what she'd said, "or is he just gonna drop Bard in the dirt and turn right around?"

"He's having the coroner certify that Bard died of natural causes, then he's going to try to talk Mama and Enna into riding back with him. I don't think Mama will come. Maybe Enna will."

"Is that your crippled sister?" I asked meekly. I hadn't ever met Enna, but I'd heard she had a limp.

"She doesn't like being called 'crippled.' She's more able than Jeany is, at least in regard to keeping up this dusty house and keeping Papa from his bottle." Then she turned back to her book.

Jeany gave a sniff as helped himself to beans and spuds.

After supper I retired to the bunkhouse. Jeany stayed in the house, much to my relief. I lit the lamp to read the part about the Cyclops in the book that Heard had given me. "*Strangers*," he calls out when he sees Odysseus and his crew, "*who are you? And where from? What brings you here by sea ways—a fair traffic? Or be you wandering rogues, who cast your lives like dice, and ravage other folk by sea?*" I pondered it a while, trying to conjure up a moral. It's Odysseus that's the hero but poor Cyclops was in the right. They were fixin' to steal his cheese. Only it wasn't justice that Cyclops cared about; he was hungering for their man-flesh.

When I finally drifted off, I kept dreaming of scenes from the book. I could see men approaching with spears and shields from way in the distance, their forms bobbing and sinking like ships on a heaving sea. Me and Hooper rode cautiously to meet them, unsure whether they were friend or foe. Only we found ourselves in a shadowy cave staring face-to-face with a wrathful grizzly.

Next morning I lay with my eyes shut, trying to fight the sun's relentless glare. It was already eight o'clock when I finally put my clothes on. I figured I'd run into Jeany on the way to breakfast, only he'd gone and disappeared.

"Claims he's going out to hunt strays," Luett said disgustedly, "only he'll stay away for weeks. I suppose I blame Papa. Too soft on Jeany when he was little and too hard when he was older. Papa's been trying to make up to him, but it sure hasn't helped. Jeany's angry inside. Spoiled and angry. Lets it rule him. We hear he goes and visits people and plays cards and drinks, when he can get liquor. Helps 'em steal a cow or a horse now and then. Mostly to embarrass us."

"Maybe your dad ain't the only one that was hard on him."

"I'd be nicer if he'd quit acting like a truant."

"He'll grow up. I imagine he'll inherit this ranch someday. Prob'ly run it better than the colonel."

"Well he hasn't shown any sign of it yet." She let out a sigh, then looked at me slit-eyed. "It was Jeany that caused Mama to go to Payson, in case you didn't know. Well, Jeany and Papa both. Jeany came home on a new horse a few weeks ago. Mama asked how he'd paid for it, since he's got no money. Jeany said he'd traded one of our milk cows. Papa heard him through the screen door and came charging out. Punched Jeany square on the mouth. Mama tried to step between 'em, but she fell when Papa pushed her. He was drinking, of course."

"Sorry to hear it. I like the colonel plenty, but treating Mrs. Atkinson that way is wrong." He wouldn't allow roughness with the whores but he'd shove his own wife. Somehow I couldn't square it.

"It's happened before," she continued glumly. "She gets mad and goes to Payson. But she always comes back. She's got nowhere else to go. And besides which, she loves him. I guess it sounds strange, the way he treats her."

Hearing about the colonel's family squabbles put me in a spot. He was my boss, after all, and I was in no position to judge. But there was something else that bothered me more. My feelings were tangled. I'd taken a shine to the colonel. In fact I idolized him. On the other hand, he treated his wife and son a lot like my own father had treated me. I didn't care for Jeany, but I could sympathize. Not being the colonel's real son gave me an advantage. He didn't yet know me well enough to make me feel small.

I was like a knight riding to help a king, I reflected, except the knight didn't know the king, and the king didn't know the knight. I hadn't known about his drinking and his temper, and he still didn't know that I'd rode with Landy Hooper. If he did know, he might banish me. The colonel put the Grahams and the Blevinses in the same category with the Hashknifes. He despised them. Of course I hadn't really sided with them, much less gone to thieving. But the colonel wasn't the sort to make kindly allowances.

———■———

As it turned out, the colonel stayed in Payson longer than expected. Didn't get back 'til Sunday afternoon, a week after he'd left. When he rode through the gate of the palisade, he had Enna on the saddle behind him. Mrs. Atkinson was on the pack horse that had carried Bard's body. She had one arm looped around a little boy that sat in front of her in the saddle. Atkinson halted just outside the barn door, dismounted, then carefully helped Enna down. There was a tenderness in him I hadn't seen before. Once Enna was on the ground, he helped Mrs. Atkinson and the boy dismount, too. She was slim as Luett, but with eyes gray as storm clouds. Once she and the boy were on the ground, the colonel took the saddles off the horses and walked them to the barn.

While we waited for the Colonel, Enna ambled over with a jerking gait. One of her feet seemed to be a little sideways. "You must be Ben," she said as she approached. "I'm glad to finally meet you. Papa thinks you'll make a fine cowboy once you get some experience. You can just call me Enna, by the way."

"Glad to make your acquaintance, Miss Enna," I replied, tipping my hat. I noticed her mother hadn't moved an inch. Didn't talk to no one, either. "Glad to meet you, too, Mrs. Atkinson," I said sheepishly, tipping my hat to the old lady.

Instead of answering, she took the boy's hand and marched him to the house. Enna looked puzzled for a second, then gave a little frown. "Mr. Holcomb, it was a pleasure, but I'm afraid I'm needed inside." She started to walk toward the house, then turned back around. "By the way, I used to ask Mr. Henry to save me all the labels from his Arbuckles coffee. And any stars or horseshoes on his chewing tobacco. If I get enough of 'em, I can send 'em in for prizes. Would you mind saving yours, now that he's gone?"

"I'll sure save them Arbuckles labels but I ain't chewed much tobacco."

"Well don't start on my account. But if you do, save the stars and the horseshoes."

9.

Iconfess I put myself into some fancy messes in my younger days. When I was ten years old I sloshed half a bottle of kerosene into the hearth to avoid the bother of loading kindling. The ball of flame that exploded took most of my hair off along with the whiskers of one of the dogs. My father knocked me down like a bowling pin and rolled the fire out of my shirt. I wasn't hurt anything awful but I suffered for weeks with puckering blisters. Not that my backside was any happier than my front after my father whipped me with a stick of wood.

If I'd been a quicker study I'd have learned a lesson. Just when you think you got it figured, the world spits a ball of flame. Then no sooner do you get on your feet in dazed confusion than some son-of-a-bitch gives you a thrashing.

I was sitting atop my bunk the evening my life exploded again. After Bard died, I'd taken to supping in the house with the Atkinsons. I'd stripped my boots off and went to massaging my ankle while I waited for Luett to holler for me. I'd twisted it in a stirrup when I'd tried to dismount with a kind of spin and jump maneuver. I'd seen Landy Hooper do it a dozen times, only I was too awkward to repeat the performance.

I kept rubbing my ankle 'til I heard a pair of voices. I could tell it was the colonel and Jeany, but I couldn't make out their words. Not thirty seconds later the door swung open.

"Get up off that bunk," ordered the colonel as he set a whiskey bottle on the card table. "We come to have a parley." I stepped down to the floor and put my boots on, then squeezed myself into one of the chairs. The colonel hauled out some glasses and poured us drinks. I put the whiskey to my mouth and pretended to sip, then set it back on the table. Luett had taken to looking in every now and then to keep me honest. If she'd seen them strolling over to the bunkhouse, I figured she was apt to follow.

After the two of them gulped down their liquor, the colonel filled their glasses again. He took another swallow then set his glass down with a ringing thump. "Got special duties tonight," he announced.

"Goin' after thieves," said Jeany excitedly. "We got word that they come in here last week and shot a man named Jake Lauffer from ambush. A couple fellers tracked 'em up toward the Rim only their tracks washed out. We ain't puttin' up with it."

I stared at my whiskey and pretended to sip again. "Am I goin' with you?" I asked sheepishly.

"You bet you are," replied the colonel.

I felt my hands quiver. "Then I'd better ask what we'll be doin'. We gonna join a posse or are we goin' on a lynching?" I had half a mind to turn them down on account of my ankle, only it wasn't bad enough to cause a limp. If I ventured some sorry excuse I'd only double the colonel's scorn.

"Don't talk like that," said the colonel. "First because what I tell you to do is what you're gonna do. You work for me. I command you. You hear me?"

"Yes sir, I hear you."

"And second because this is gonna be strictly legal. We're meetin' one of Lafayette's deputies up on the Rim. We'll be his posse. Us and some other men from around here. That satisfy you?"

"Yes sir. I reckon it does. I guess I'd better saddle Percival." I considered asking who the deputy was, then decided against it. I'd figured it might be the feller Hooper and I had saved from the Navajos, Jeremy Houck. Only there was just as much chance it was someone else. From what Bard had told me, Sheriff Lafayette McGowan had a dozen deputies spread out across the whole of the county.

"We'll be on our way directly after supper. Gonna have us a night ride. Oughta have a good bright moon if the clouds stay away." The colonel threw back his drink and flashed a smile. "We'll join up with a few other boys on the trail. Likely won't be back until late tomorrow."

No sooner had he spoken than the door burst open again. Luett stood there still clutching the knob, her face dark in the evening shadow. "Papa," she cried angrily, "you're gonna be in trouble if you go out and kill somebody."

"Damn it, Luett, already told you. Ain't gonna be no lynchin'! We're gonna ride with one of McGowan's deputies. Gonna arrest some men and turn 'em over to him. That's all there is to it."

She gave a disgusted sniff then stepped into the room and faced me. "Ben, don't you go with him! He's drinking and he's gonna get in trouble."

"Don't make Ben your handmaid!"

"Father, go home! Go now! Mama's waiting on you with supper. You have the gall to go off and drink yourself stupid while Mama tries to keep your meal warm. Damn you!"

Atkinson had a blank look. His gaze turned from Luett to the floor, then back to Luett. Then he turned to me. "You be ready after supper. We'll be meetin' a few boys on the trail here in the valley, then we'll go on up the Rim to meet some Mormon boys. We'll be riding with them, too." Then he walked out of the bunkhouse, leaving us alone with Luett.

"Well, you chased him off," snapped Jeany, "but you ain't changed his mind."

"Stay out of it, Jeany."

"I aim to."

"Ben, I'd like to have a word with you. Outside. Alone."

"Alright," I stammered as I rose from my chair. "I didn't have nothin' to drink, Miss Luett. You can see it for yourself. The glass he poured is still settin' on the table. I didn't touch it."

She paused for a moment, then picked up the glass and hurled it at the floor. It popped like a balloon, hurling little glass shards all over the room. The splattered whiskey dappled Jeany's pant legs. He gave her a hard look, then got up and stalked out. She looked around the room like she was searching for another bottle, then she wheeled and followed him.

As I stepped out behind her, I saw Jeany shambling toward the house while Luett headed to the barn. I decided to follow her out there but I wasn't in any hurry. When I got inside, she shut the barn door with a bang. She turned her back on me and walked to Percival, bending over him as she gave him a rubdown.

"What's the matter?" I asked.

"Don't say a goddamn word!" I could hear her quietly sobbing. I stood silent for a time, waiting for her to continue. When she turned back to me, the anger was gone. "I suppose I should be glad he wants you to go. You might be able to help. They've drunk half a bottle, in case you can't tell. I try to hide the whiskey, but I've been too busy to keep watch."

CHAPTER 9

I looked at her with my brows raised. "Beg your pardon, Miss Luett, but you can't police your father. Ain't no woman can control a man like that. Judging from what George says, it's him policing you." I walked over to a straw bale and sat myself atop it. "He's made you nothin' but a servant and a cowhand," I muttered. "Or maybe that's what you want."

I regretted those words before they even left my lips. Luett pulled back as if she'd been struck. There was silence for a moment as she collected her thoughts, a little crease in her brow. Finally she shook her head and answered. "Ben, I'll be honest. Some women love it out here because they can ride and rope cows and show the men how it's done. Well that isn't me. I loathe these wild hills. But if I run away to George, I'll be running from sacred duty. Papa would drink all our money and Mama would leave him. It would destroy everything we've worked for." Then she set the brush aside and rubbed her hands together, shaking her head in consternation. "Keep my father out of trouble. Please, Ben!"

"He ain't gonna listen to no boy from George Heard's mercantile. If you're wantin' to stop him, you'd better ride yourself."

"He won't let me ride with his vigilantes, and I won't do it anyway. Mr. Heard sent you here so you could help me keep the old man from doing mischief. Papa likes you, Ben. He'll listen to you. Sees himself as a kind of father to you, if ya wanna know the truth."

"I don't know about that."

"Well I do. He's training you up. Showing you what's what. Now he's taking you for your test. You're not just going to arrest cattle thieves. He's taking you to a lynching. You know that as well as I do."

I pushed myself upright and stared at her. "I know that? Begging your pardon, but how would I know?"

"On account of Jeany told you, same as he told me. He can't keep his mouth shut."

I looked down at my boots. "Who are they goin' after?" I finally replied. I was hoping she wouldn't say Landis Hooper.

"It's a man named Jayzee Mott. He's got a horse ranch on the Rim."

"Jayzee Mott," I whispered. That teetotaler Yankee with the handsome words. The one they'd tried for horse theft. The man-lover, or so they said. I never did know whether he was or not. I didn't give much of a damn.

"My father is a fighter, Ben. Thinks he's got to clean things up. He and his men are telling people they think are stealing that they can

81

either leave or be killed. Most of 'em are leaving. Just not all of them, unfortunately."

"Ain't bargained for no lynchings."

"No, but Papa has made that bargain for you," she answered as she picked up the brush again and went back to Percival. "He thinks it'll make a man of you. The same way he became a man. He wasn't but sixteen when he tagged along with one of the vigilante crews to lynch Comanches. After that, they strung up a couple Negroes. And more than a few white men over the years, if you wanna know the ugly truth."

I got up from the straw bale and walked toward the saddles. "Then I'll ride right now. I'll go back to Mr. Heard and tell him what's happened. He'll send the law and put a stop to this."

"No! You can't get to Globe before Papa rides out and George can't do anything anyway. He's in the wrong county. And besides, the last thing I want is to land Papa in jail."

"Then what in hell do you expect? I can't go with him and I can't get the law."

"You *can* go with him. You have to. He wants to be a big man in your eyes. Don't let him. Make sure he knows you don't approve."

I walked back toward the straw bales, eyes cast toward the ground. "He won't listen to me. Ain't but a boy next to him."

"You won't be no boy if you stand up to him. What matters is you'll witness. He'll try to convince you to participate. Don't you listen! Keep talking sense to him. Make sure it's an arrest."

"What if he refuses?"

"I don't think it'll come to that. He's riding with some Mormons. They aren't big on lynching. And that deputy is going, too. Papa won't lynch anyone unless the others all approve."

I grimaced and sat down again, shaking my head. "You know as well as I do what happens to witnesses that talk against 'em."

"Pff! If you're so scared of him, tell him I put you up to it. But for godsakes don't refuse me!"

———◆———

Not ten minutes later, I sat down to the bleakest supper I ever ate. No one spoke. Finally Jeany looked up from his plate with a smirk. "Where's my pistol, Luett? Did you hide my gun?"

"You're not going."

"Like hell he's not," the colonel yelled back. "You go fetch his pistol, Luett. We ain't got time for a lot a nonsense."

Before Jeany could answer Mrs. Atkinson shot out of her seat and slammed her plate to the floor. "Jeany is not going!" she shouted at the colonel. "I know what you're up to. You're going on a lynching. I won't have my son involved in it. You hear me! Goddamn you!"

"Yes I am goin', Mama!" shouted Jeany. "And I mean right now. Soon as I find my damn gun."

Jeany lurched from his chair but Mrs. Atkinson was already standing over him. She put her hands on his chest and pushed him down. "You won't go one step," she commanded. He was twice her size, but somehow it didn't matter. She was like a mother cat growling at a kitten. He was paralyzed.

"Ain't got time to wait," the colonel shouted at Jeany. "If you want to be your mama's boy, then go right ahead."

Jeany looked back at him with a dazed expression. Then his face changed to a scowl. "Go to hell!" he shot back. "Go on your little lynching spree if you want, Papa. I know some a them men you wanna kill. They're better men than you are." He jerked up from his chair and headed for the door.

"Where you goin'?" demanded the colonel.

"I'm riding out. None a your damn business where I'm goin'."

"Well this is sure a scene from a Shakespeare theatrical," called out the colonel. "I've had enough of supper. Ben, go get your horse. It's time to ride." Then he got up and stalked out.

I turned back to Luett, unsure what to do.

"Take Percival and follow him. He won't lynch anyone if he thinks you're gonna report back. He knows I won't tolerate it. I need you to do this, Ben. Make sure it's an arrest."

10.

I'd like to say I still had some missionary in me—some spark of decency, or at least some puffed-up idea that I could save the colonel from his sins. But my meeting with the Grahams and Blevinses had washed out my illusions. Thought I'd talked them back from wrath but they'd rode ahead regardless. Wasn't a damn thing I could say to make them turn the other cheek.

I wanted desperately to refuse her but somehow I couldn't say it. I still had a drop of hope that the colonel was on the square. If a deputy was riding with us, wasn't like to be a lynching. But mostly what I kept remembering was George's solemn warning. He'd told me to steer clear of all their feuding and take my orders from Luett.

It was like Luett told me when she'd set me straight about her feelings. I guess I hadn't made any outright play for her on account of I wasn't good enough. Or at least so I thought. But there was also a part of me that was loyal to George Heard. Though I didn't want to work for him, I still thought of him like a father. Odd as it sounds, though, I thought the same about the colonel.

Now that I look back on it, I'm ashamed. But the truth is the colonel mesmerized me. I was proud as punch to be his hand and double eager to hear his praise. On the other hand, I felt resentful that he'd put me to an awful test. It was like the saloon deal. Like he was making me do something sinful just to prove I was worthy of his fraternal order. Only this time it weren't any venal sin. It was mortal as bally Judas.

I mutely followed him into the darkness, blinded with a haze of doubt. He led on a handsome gelding with a couple of his tame mounts trailing behind. We traveled up the slope of the valley, moving north-northeast 'til we came to a clearing. Then he stopped and cocked his head like he thought he'd heard a voice. "We'll have to wait a little," he said. He wiped his nose with his cuff then reached into his saddlebags for a bottle and handed it to me. "Go ahead and take a swallow."

I tipped it up and sipped a little, then handed it back to him.

"I'm sorry you had to hear all that. You'd think my women were Yankee suffragists the way they get puffed up with their preaching." He wiped his nose again and looked around. "This here is a frontier country," he said as he studied the shadows. "No different than West Texas a couple decades back. Every excuse for a man rushes to get his land. Then pretty soon someone steals a horse. Then his neighbor, well, he steals a couple heifers to get revenge. Next thing you know, it's a goddamn rustling circus."

I leaned against my saddle horn. "Mr. Heard says they need a peace treaty."

I could see the colonel smirk through the cloud of darkness. "Ain't no treaty gonna stop it. It's a goddamn war. Just like every frontier country since the first white men came over the ocean. They chase out the blasted Indians then they get to fightin' with one another. Nothing but a goddamn war, Ben. Someone's got to win it." Just then Atkinson cocked his head again. "Here they come," he said.

I could hear men on horses way in the distance. When they got closer, Atkinson hailed them. "Y'all ready for this?" he shouted.

"If it's for you, Colonel, we're ready for hell itself," answered a cowboy with a Texas drawl.

In the moonlight, I could make out six of them, plus another man trailing behind. They'd tied his hands in front of him and roped his feet to his stirrups. Once they reached us, they stopped talking. Atkinson took the lead as we ascended the Rim, then headed east on the road General Crook made back during the wars with the Apaches. It was getting toward morning when we descended into the big bowl at the head of Canyon Creek. Wasn't but a few miles from there that I'd had that run-in with the Navajos.

As we rode along in silence, one of the cowboys pulled alongside me. "You snap any wild fillies yet, kid?" he asked in a teasing voice.

I squinted in the darkness trying to make out his features. Finally it occurred to me. He was one of the bronc peelers I'd met when I was wandering between ranches. Tom Horn was his name. He'd gotten to be one of the best rodeo men in the territory before he'd hired himself out as a man-killer. I didn't find out 'til a few months later that the cattlemen had made him what they called a stock detective. Fifteen years afterwards, he got himself hanged for killing a boy. Some son-of-a-bitch cattle baron in Wyoming hired him as his private assassin.

"No sir," I replied quietly. "They ain't found one mean enough."

He nodded his approval. "Well we'll meet some plenty mean ones on this trip. There won't be any buckin' fillies but we'll sure bust a couple stallions."

I replied with a fake laugh then sped up to catch the colonel.

Half an hour later we rode up to a little stock pond. I could see another bunch of horsemen milling in the moon shadows. "We're your saintly *comitatus*," called out one of them as we approached. I stared at him as I reined up. He was a stooping anvil of a man anchored atop a plow horse. Weighed twenty stone if he was a single ounce. He sat like a regular cyclops between smaller men on either flank.

"And we be your Texas devils," laughed Atkinson as his horse dipped down to drink. "We make a hell of a posse." Then he turned back toward the rest of us. "Let your horses get a little water, boys, but make it a quick one. Gotta be there by daybreak." He swiveled himself toward Horn and broke into a broad smile. "Too bad them Blevinses sold their place or we'd clean out both dens."

Hadn't even occurred to me we'd be riding past Landy Hooper's pa's ranch. I was still pretty ignorant about where the trails led. *Goddamn*, I got to thinking. *If we'd have gone after Hooper, I'd have been in a pickle. I'd have to tell the colonel I'd rode with him else Hooper would tell it first.* I bent my head and plodded forward.

After that there was silence as we wended through the pines. Must have rode for a couple hours when we saw a red glow. When we got up closer I could see it was a bonfire. It crackled and spat like a cornered bobcat, casting lurching shadows. Atkinson made for it straightaway with me following right behind.

"Deputy Houck!" shouted Atkinson, "what are you doin' out here, tryin' to burn down the forest?" I felt my heart flap like a frighted bird. I searched for an excuse about why I'd failed to report my ride with Hooper. Sure as hell Houck would recognize me just soon as the Colonel introduced us. I cursed myself for keeping quiet about it. If I'd fessed up the day they hired me, they'd have no reason to judge me a liar.

"Figured I'd light the way for ya," replied the man standing alone on the far side of the blaze. The fire cast a gleam on the oily tresses that drooped toward his shoulders. It occurred to me to drop back behind the other fellers to avoid his glance, but the colonel would surely notice. I had no choice but to stick it out.

"Good thing we been gettin' all this rain," observed the colonel, "or you'd sure enough get us broiled."

Houck disappeared into the shadows without replying. When he came back out, he was mounted on a strapping white. "Heard you was bringin' a fugitive," he said quietly as he reached out to shake Atkinson's hand.

"Some a the boys caught him on the trail to the Graham place. Said he'd come down to fetch back a horse he'd loaned out. I reckon we fetched him instead."

Both of them laughed. Then Houck spoke again. "Howdy, Jim," he called out to the prisoner. "Bet you didn't expect to see me so soon after our little squabble."

"I'll gunfight ya here and now, Houck, if you'll come over and untie me," said the prisoner.

"Got no time for chitchat," interrupted Atkinson. "Got to get on over to Mott's place and make our arrests."

"Imagine I'll be runnin' my sheep on his spread when all this is over," said Houck in a low tone, looking at the colonel. "Assuming he's found guilty, of course. Even a horse thief deserves a trial."

"Good Lord," said Atkinson, "thought you was a cattleman, Houck."

Houck spat a stream of tobacco juice. "There's two dollars for a shear and six dollars a mutton in them animals, Atkinson. You can buy 'em for a song and they breed like horny prairie dogs. Soon as the Republicans raise the wool tariff, I aim to be a sheep king."

Atkinson's smirk gave way to a smile. "Well I won't truck with no Mesikan sheeper, but I guess I'll tolerate the white ones."

"Watch what ya say, Atkinson. Them Mexicans are my wife's people."

The colonel's face was blank. Then it ripened with a friendly grin. "If you're married to a Mesikan, more power to ya, Houck." He leaned back on his horse and shouted out to the other men. "Get off your horses and put the fire out."

"It won't burn nothin'," said Houck. "Take half an hour to get it out. Let's get a-movin'."

Atkinson stared at him, then gave his horse a prod. "Let's move," he shouted. "Don't worry about the damn fire."

The more I reflected on my predicament, the more scared I got to feeling. So long as the darkness kept me shadowed, I figured Houck might not remember me. Only once the sun came up, he'd be certain to see my features.

Half an hour later, Atkinson reined up in a clearing. He and Houck talked quietly, then Atkinson called out to us. "It's just a couple more miles," he shouted. "Deputy Houck and me are gonna ride on ahead. If he sees us all a-comin', he's liable to think we're fixin' to lynch him. No point worryin' him. Give us 'til daylight to get him arrested. Then y'all ride on in and we'll have a parley." He cleared his throat and turned to me. "I want you to follow along behind me, Ben. Give you a chance to earn a war feather."

I glanced up the trail, then looked back at the colonel nervously. I wanted to gallop the other direction but all I could manage was an anxious nod.

"What if he ain't there?" cut in one of the Texans.

"Well hell's fire, that's why I brung ya! We'll fan out and find him. But don't you worry. He'll be there. Deputy Houck here's been keepin' track."

Houck stayed out ahead of us as he led us along the darkened trail. I kept thinking he'd turn back and catch a glimpse of me, only he was too focused on finding the way. We'd ridden about an hour when we came through an open gate into an expanse of meadow. A few piñons and junipers stood here and there like shadowy ghosts. I could make out a fettered horse grazing to the north of us. Houck put his finger over his mouth to tell us to shush. He kept his gaze on me an extra moment, like he'd suddenly remembered me.

Finally he looked ahead again. He sat silent, then dismounted, motioning us to follow suit. When we'd crept close to the fettered horse, Houck veered off a little and pointed to a man asleep in his soogans. He had a coil of wire laid beside him. Looked like he'd been working on a fence. Houck snuck up quietly and stuck his gun in the man's face. "Don't say a word," he said when the man opened his eyes. "You're Jeff Wilson, ain't ya? Mott's hired man."

The man flinched but didn't say nothing.

"Just nod your head," said Houck. "And if ya tell me a lie, you can go back to your sleeping. For a good long time."

The man nodded yes.

Houck pointed to the badge on his vest and told the man he was taking him into custody.

"What the hell fer?" he asked angrily.

"For goddamn horse stealing with your friend Mott. Now get up and put your clothes on."

The man silently obliged. All three of us had our guns on him. When he was done dressing, Houck made him lie back down on his soogans. Then we tied up his hands and feet.

"What in hell are ya tyin' me fer?"

"So's ya won't go nowheres while we get your friend Mott."

"Goddamn you!" spat the man. "We ain't done nothin'."

When I saw he was shivering, I fetched his blanket and laid it over him.

"We'll be back for ya before the sun's high," said Houck.

"Now that there is plain luck," laughed the colonel as we walked back to our horses. "Sure didn't expect to find that hired man camped all by his lonesome."

We got back on our horses and rode 'til we came to a draw. We could see his cabin and barn about a quarter mile off. It was just getting light.

"Ain't got much time," said Houck. He'll be rising here shortly." He held his gaze on me again like he'd realized who I was. He finally told us to tie up our horses behind the timber and walk the rest of the way. Had me circle around behind the cabin and come in from the east while the colonel came in from the north. Houck stayed put while we got in position.

I circled around to the far side of the cabin and ducked behind a juniper. I felt like a damn sneak thief. I waited five minutes, then stepped toward the cabin. Houck told me to have my gun in hand but I decided to leave it holstered, afraid I'd trip on some deadfall and fire a round by accident. When I got close, I saw Houck and the colonel walking slow like a couple cats. Houck motioned me to come over to where they'd hid themselves behind the barn. "He's still inside," he whispered.

I crouched there with my heart pounding. It was a good quarter hour before we heard the creak of the cabin door. Houck put his finger over his mouth again to tell us to keep quiet. Then he motioned me to go around to the other side of the barn. "Get your damn gun out," he whispered. "Soon as I say his name, you jump out from over there."

"Jayzee Mott!" I heard Houck shout a few seconds later. "We come to arrest you." I hustled out pointing my six-gun. Houck and the colonel already had their rifles on him.

Mott grinned and dusted off his hands. "Arrest?" he asked. "Shoot, Houck, I thought you were coming to run me out. But all you want to do is arrest me. It's almost a disappointment. I take it you have a warrant." Said it like that. Calm as a summer day. You'd have thought we were his range pals just a-playing a little prank.

"Not with me," said Houck. "Left it in my coat pocket back where we camped."

"No man's perfect," winked Atkinson.

"Well what the hell," answered Mott as he looked off toward the trees. "Let's get this thing done with. I'd rather spend a few nights in Lafayette's jail than live under a cloud."

"Glad to hear it. You'll get your hearing pretty quick, I imagine. Won't even need a horse. We brung one for ya."

Mott glanced around at each of us to size up the situation. "I can dish us up some oatmeal before we ride. No point heading out on an empty stomach. It'll just take a few minutes to boil some water. I'll fry some bacon to go with it."

Houck looked at Atkinson. Atkinson smiled back. "You betcha," said Atkinson. "We're awful damn hungry. We'd be much obliged for a hot meal." Then Atkinson stooped a little and whispered something to Houck.

"Uh huh," Houck muttered. "Mott," he said in a firm voice, "we got a posse on the way. Thought you oughta know. They'll likely be riding in shortly. Don't let it scare ya."

Mott's eyes twitched a couple times. "I'm a little short on bacon but I've got plenty of oats. I'll make a big batch and bring it out. If we run short, I'll make some more."

While Mott was inside, Atkinson sent me back to fetch our horses. I brung them out to Mott's corral, then hitched them to the fence. Twenty minutes later, the rest of the men rode in. They stared like they couldn't figure it. Here we was a-setting on the porch, eating breakfast with the man we'd come to arrest. "Well don't just sit there in your saddles like ya never seen a bowl of oatmeal," shouted the colonel. "Get off them horses and get yourselves fed."

They glanced at one another and muttered some jokes. Finally a couple of them tied their horses up, then fetched out their tins. The rest of them followed suit 'til the only man mounted was the prisoner.

Mott froze for a moment when he saw him. I could see his Adam's apple working. "I see they got you, too, Jim," he called out.

The prisoner forced a grin. "Told 'em I was just comin' down to fetch back that little roan I loaned out to Mr. Naegelin. No sir, they says, you're a-coming to make trouble. Well goddamn it, I says, go ahead and arrest me."

"What in the hell, Houck?" said Mott. "You've made my hired man your prisoner just on account of he backed you down in a saloon quarrel?"

"Houck didn't arrest him," answered Atkinson. "My men done that. We just brung him up here so Houck can take custody."

"Well can't you at least untie him so he can get some breakfast?"

Atkinson and Houck looked at one another. Then Atkinson called out to one of his Texans. "Let him down. Ain't no use makin' him suffer while we get our grub."

After they'd untied the prisoner, Mott went back to ladling oatmeal. I sat myself against the front of the barn and waited to see what would happen. Just then someone called out from inside the cabin. "Do you need any help, Jayzee?"

"Who in hell's that?" asked the colonel.

"I can do it myself," Mott called back to the man in the cabin. Then he turned to the colonel. "He's sick with consumption. I let him stay here for the mountain air."

"He'd better come out and make an account of himself," demanded the colonel as he clutched his rifle.

The man in the cabin pushed the door open. He stood silently in his long underwear, squinting and shivering in the rising sun. He held a pen in one of his hands, as though somehow it might protect him. He started to cough, then made an effort to stop himself.

"Who the hell are you?" demanded the colonel.

"He's got nothing to do with any of this," insisted Mott. "I told you who he is. He's a consumptive man. He's a dry goods drummer. He came out on the train from Boston."

The colonel inspected the man. "Well that ain't any particular crime." Then he spoke more loudly. "What's your name?"

I could see the man's mouth trembling. He didn't answer. I felt queasy as I watched him. I hadn't come to persecute a consumptive.

"His name is Prentiss Reeves," said Mott. "Go back to writing your letters, Prentiss," he called out. "They have no business with you."

Houck sniffed and nodded. "He's nothin'. Let him go. It's all he can do to sit a horse. Mott hauled him out in his buggy. Thought he'd be gone b'now."

The man at the door just stood there.

"Go on, Prentiss," said Mott. "I'll be back in a few days. Keep the stove warm for me."

The man closed the door slowly. That was the last I saw him.

Mott watched the door for a moment, then went back to dishing oatmeal.

Atkinson and Houck took their time eating, then got up as if on cue. The two of them walked across the barnyard to where Mott was squatted, quietly eating his oats. "Mott," began Atkinson, "we didn't come all this way just for a meal. Gonna put you on a horse and take you to trial."

Mott uttered a stiff laugh as he raised himself to a standing position. "I know what you're here for." They walked him over to one of Atkinson's spare horses and ordered him to get on it. He didn't argue. Just mounted up, then obligingly put his hands out. After they'd finished tying him they did the same to the other prisoner.

Just then Houck went over to his white horse and wrestled something heavy from the saddlebags. When he came back over, he was carrying shackles.

"Jesus Christ!" protested Mott. "You needn't put us in irons, Houck. We're glad to go to Holbrook for trial. We've got no reason to run."

Houck didn't answer. Just went over to the man called Jim and ran them shackles under his horse, then buckled them to his legs. Then he went back to his horse and fetched another pair. "Who said Holbrook?" said Houck as he hitched them to Mott's ankles. "They're gonna mosey down the trail and hold a trial this mornin'."

"What the hell?" stammered Mott. "I said I'd submit to arrest and I will! You can take us to Holbrook and give us to Lafayette!"

"Ya goddamn murdering sons of bitches!" yelled the man called Jim. "You're fixin' to lynch us!"

"I won't tolerate such outbursts," called out Atkinson. "Murder ain't got nothin' to do with the present situation. We're givin' you a trial.

How'd you come to have them Mormon horses in your herd, Mott? Houck found 'em on your range."

"You know goddamn well those horses aren't mine! I let them water their horses while they're passing through! There's nothing more to it!"

"They woulda run us out if we didn't!" yelled Jim as he twisted desperately on his saddle. "We ain't horse thieves, goddamn it!"

"Ready to ride," Houck grunted to Atkinson.

I just sat there squatted down, pretending to eat my oatmeal. "Colonel Atkinson," I called out as I finally stood, "ain't you gonna arrest these men and take 'em in?"

"Got 'em arrested right now," replied Atkinson casually.

"Thought we was taking 'em to Holbrook to put 'em in McGowan's jail."

"Oh, that's what you thought, is it?"

"You owe us a trial!" yelled Jim. "Take us to Holbrook! We ain't done nothin'!"

"Ain't done nothing, have ya?" replied Atkinson. "Nothing but run a hotel for thieves with your bosom buddy Mr. Mott."

"No one around here turns away a traveler!" shouted Mott. "None of us! Not even the Mormons! All of us take the strays!"

"You sure do take the strays alright," answered the colonel mockingly.

Mott turned his head back and forth furiously. "Range horses, Atkinson! I take the range horses! They're not anyone's property until they're caught! If you're going to give us a trial, then at least give us a fair one!"

I ambled over to Atkinson and tried to argue. "Maybe he's telling the truth, Colonel." I thought for sure I'd get to shaking but my voice was smooth as onyx.

Mott turned and looked at me, as though trying to remember who I was. I didn't meet his gaze.

"He's a thief and a liar," continued Atkinson. "We had our boys watch him. They seen him and his friends puttin' stolen horses in here. That's proof enough."

"They're bloody liars!" shouted Mott. "Houck's been running off my stock for two years! He wants my water!"

"Order in the court!" replied the colonel. "I'll have no goddamn shouting while the trial is underway. Houck, give 'em a gag."

Mott continued to protest as Houck rode over and gagged him. He repeated the performance with the other prisoner.

Right then I saw one of the Mormons come out from a knot of men who were still standing around, muttering. He walked carefully between them, touching a couple of them on the shoulder. He was a sturdy silver-haired man with a long wavy beard. Wore a thick belt to strap his paunch but it was entirely bare of any six-gun. "Colonel Atkinson," he began, "I'm Nathan Fish. I haven't had the pleasure of meeting you but I've heard of you, of course. Perhaps you've heard of me, too. I live up on Silver Creek. May I speak?"

Atkinson squinted at him. "I'll allow it," he finally said.

"I've come to arrest men, not to lynch them. Rustlers or not, they deserve a trial."

"We're givin' 'em one."

"Colonel," I called out as I walked a little closer, "begging your pardon, sir, but how do you know Mott's a-thievin'? Maybe it's like he says. He's lettin' 'em put their horses here because he got water and they don't. He don't know whether them horses are stolen." *Goddamn it*, I thought, *I've got to go against him.* Wasn't 'til then that I finally made my mind up.

"What are you, his defense attorney?"

"No sir. Don't mean no disrespect. Just telling what I heard. They say he ain't nothin' but a rich boy. His daddy runs a cotton mill in Massachusetts. Mott's a rich boy playing cowboy. He's damn near as green as I am."

The colonel calmly pulled his pipe out and tamped tobacco in the bowl. "And who in hell told you all that?" he asked as he took a draw.

"I got a notion about that," said Houck. His leaden eyes peered at me like a prairie falcon staring at prey. "I believe I know this man. Me and Lafayette ran into him and Landis Hooper back in July when we was headed down to Pleasant Valley."

The colonel narrowed his eyes as he sucked his pipe. "This is the first I heard about it."

"Me and Lafayette got in a tussle with some renegades. Hooper and this man come chargin' out of the hills to drive 'em off. Lafayette managed to shoot a couple of 'em, then the rest of 'em skedaddled."

The colonel stared at me like I was a puzzle. "How come you didn't tell me any of that, Ben?"

My heart drummed into my mouth. "I guess I was afraid you'd send me packing." No sooner had I spoken than my heart slowed to a steady pound. "I knew Hooper from the Globe livery. I bought that skinny sorrel from him. Said he was on the way to the Rim and could show me the way to the Hellsgate. I'd never rode up there before so I took him up on it."

The colonel locked his gaze on me as he took a draw. "I took you to have more sense, Ben. That Hooper ain't nothin' but a snake. He and his brothers been devilin' the Mormons for nigh on three years." He turned back to Houck with a grimace. "What in hell's any of this got to do with Mott?"

Houck grinned and chuckled. "Lafayette and me had gone up to the Navajo rez to fetch back some stolen animals. We'd brought 'em down to Mott's spread the day before them Navajo fellers caught up with us. Figured we'd leave 'em pastured there 'til the owners could fetch 'em. After Hooper and this man helped us drive off them Navajo fellers, we got to talkin' about Mr. Mott's peculiarities."

"And others have taken advantage of Mott's pastures in similar fashion," cut in Fish. "We've no right to adjudicate horse theft in the absence of court testimony!"

"The hell we don't!" exclaimed the colonel, cocking his head sideways.

"I'm a Latter-day Saint, Colonel," continued Fish, "and I live by the Lord's will. Perhaps his will isn't apparent to you, sir, but it's clear enough to those who study scripture. Mark my words, sir: He commands forbearance. Taking blood will bring his wrath."

"His wrath?" sneered the colonel. "You're about to see some of mine. Comes a time in every country when honest men sweep the dirt."

"Colonel," I cut in, "beg your pardon, but Mott's a teetotaler—a New England prohibitionist. They say he don't even go to fiddle dances. He's straighter than these Mormons."

"And he's too good to poke a whore. I know all about it."

"Is patronizing whores your yardstick for human virtue?" Fish asked icily.

"Well it sure as hell ain't sodomy," joked a cowboy in the crowd. When I looked around to see him I realized it was Horn.

"We ain't here to prosecute anyone for sodomy, Horn," continued the colonel as he relit his pipe. "The charge is horse thievery. Keep the innuendo to yourself."

"Colonel Atkinson," shouted Fish, "the only way to know the truth is to hold a trial. I mean a real trial in a court of law. Guilt must be proven."

"It is proven. Every decent cowboy in the territory knows all the brands for a hundred miles. If Mott has our horses, he's guilty as them that stole 'em. And besides, he's been palling with them Grahams. I got a strong hunch he bushwhacked a man named Lauffer here about a week ago. Shot him in the shoulder. Prob'ly crippled him for the rest of his life."

"Someone saw it?" asked Fish.

"Found tracks towards the Rim. If it wasn't Mott, it was friends of his."

"You're operating on suspicion."

"Not hardly," someone called out from about twenty yards away. When I turned my head, I saw the anvil of a man perched atop his plow horse.

"Blake Larson," called the colonel, "come over and give your statement. We've heard enough from the damn defense."

The giant rode in a little circle around all the men until he stopped directly in front of us. I figured him for a Texan judging from his tooled boots and little potmaker spurs, but he didn't have the drawl. He reached down to shake the colonel's hand without getting off his horse.

"Blake and his men rode all the way down to Phoenix here about three months ago to fetch back their stolen horses," continued the colonel. "Thirty-some-odd animals, if I recall correctly."

"Not quite thirty but twenty-eight," called out Larson as he looked out at the knot of men. "Some of my blooded animals among them. Stolen from Mormons and driven to Phoenix. They put 'em in here first, then ran 'em down through Canyon Creek and Pleasant Valley. Then they herded 'em through the Mazatzals." He turned his head and glared at Mott. "We have witnesses. I'm not at liberty to give their names, but their testimony is entirely honest."

"Their testimony is worthless unless given in a court," answered Fish. "There's no way to judge veracity if they can't be cross-examined."

Larson's horse took a couple of steps forward. He twisted the reins as he turned her back to face Atkinson. "I may not look like an old-timey Mormon like Brother Fish," he finally said, "but I can tell you with certainty he doesn't speak for the rest of us." He turned his gaze to Fish.

"Brother, we've already heard you. You know full well what this is all about. You may not agree with it, but it's time to hold your peace." He held his gaze on Fish, then swiveled to address the others. "If we let this thieving continue, we are sinning in the worst way. We'll be driven out by our enemies sure as we were driven from Missouri and Illinois."

Fish faced the ground and shook his head, then took a couple of steps toward Larson. "As for who speaks for the Saints, your handful cry for murder while tens of thousands cry for law! And as for these thieves, if that they be, God sends this plague because we sin ourselves! You heard Apostle Young. You know precisely who he meant. You gamble; you imbibe; you fraternize with the goats. Apostle Young speaks the truth, Brother Larson. I stand to affirm him. These human locusts shall continue to plague us until we admit our sin and cry reform!"

Larson sniffed loudly, then gave Fish a toothy smile. "Then perhaps you should quit your cigar smoking, Fish." He leaned over his horse and spat on the ground. "Let me explain something to you, Brother. If we bring Mott to Sheriff McGowan he'll be obliged to give him back. He's not going to allow a bunch of reprobates to set free another criminal."

"Rubbish!" barked Fish as he walked in nervous circles. "We've got a ramrod prosecutor and good Mormons on the juries! The election cleaned the slate. Escort them to Holbrook and let justice take its course!"

Larson shook his head and smirked. "No sir. Even our own men might free 'em if the prosecution's weak. Mott's daddy will pay for some silk-hatted lawyer. He'll object this way and that way until the court lets him go."

"Not if your stock detectives have the evidence against him," protested Fish.

Larson snorted. "And make themselves targets for the Grahams' assassins?"

"Meaning you ain't got no case," I muttered.

"Meaning he's guilty as hell and he'll have his reward," answered the colonel. "When the courts won't do justice, the people do it for 'em. The people are the sovereigns, Ben, not the damn courts. Let that be a lesson."

"See there, Mott," announced Houck loudly as his horse pranced back and forth, "you're gettin' a fair trial right here. You got two fine defense lawyers and you ain't even paying a cent. Now what I wanna know is how many Mexicans you and your Hashknife friends killed,

Mott. I hear you were with 'em when they drove them sheepherders off the range. Hell, I bet you was right in the thick of it when they massacred that lambing camp and raped that little girl."

"For God's sake!" cried Fish. "He can't even talk back to you. If you've got proof he raped a girl, bring it to the courts!"

"You think it's writ on some golden tablet? He rode with 'em, goddamn it!"

I felt a lump rise at the bottom of my throat. I'd never heard about the rape before.

"Objection sustained," shouted the colonel. "The defense has a valid point. A man that's too good for a whore ain't like to be a rapist. But sure as hell he's in with thieves. Let's poll the damn jury and get this thing done with. Who votes guilty? Lift your hands high."

I held out some hope when only a few hands went up.

"He's asking for a vote," called out Horn as he walked out in front of them. "If he's guilty, raise your hands." He glanced around angrily, like he was about to make a tirade. "I don't know about the rest of you, but I come to get some broncs snapped."

"Guilty as hell," called out a man in the back as he raised his hand.

A few more hands went up as the men glanced around. After that there was some mumbling, then one by one they fell in line. "Looks like 26 to 2," announced Atkinson as he knocked the ashes from his pipe. "Now let's get a-movin'."

"You're all in on this business?" I called out to them.

No one said nothing. Just a lot of coughing and throat clearing. All the while Mott kept making garbled noises through his gag and kicking at his stirrups.

"Colonel," blurted Houck, "see here! I won't allow no lynchings. Not in Apache County. 'Course if you've a mind to take 'em across the line to Yavapai, I've got no jurisdiction. Now if you'll excuse me, I've got business in Holbrook. Just make sure you bring me back them shackles when you make your next drive to the rail pens." Then he reached over to the colonel and handed him a set of keys.

The colonel tucked the keys in his pocket. "Tell that Prentiss Reeves feller we'll be comin' through here in a few days to see that he's gone. I'd advise him to throw them letters of his into the stove and catch the first train out of Holbrook."

Houck gave a little chuckle. "I don't think you got much to worry about on that account. Him and me will have a friendly chat."

"Let's mount up, boys!" cried Atkinson. "Got a party to attend." Then he looked back at me. "Shoulda invited your friend Hooper. Reckon he knows a clever trick or two. Might could show us just how far his neck can stretch."

The vigilantes quietly began marching their captives down the trail. When we got to the edge of Mott's property, Atkinson ordered a couple of them to take one of the spare horses and fetch the man we'd left tied on his soogans. We stayed put 'til they come loping back with him. Then the colonel ordered us to move out.

Fish and I rode alongside them, trying to talk them out of it. Most didn't say nothing. Some of them laughed. A couple of the Texans grimaced and spat. We rode about an hour until Atkinson halted at a ponderosa. Fish drew up beside him, then pulled out a Book of Mormon.

"Don't you wave that book at us," yelled Atkinson. Then he knocked it to the ground and slapped Fish hard with the back of his hand, causing his mouth to bleed.

"Colonel," I stammered, "this ain't right! It's a dishonor to your daughter!"

"What in hell do you know about honor, Ben? Or did ya learn it all from that womanish George Heard?" Then he turned to the knot of men. "Get to it, boys. Let's hang the sons a bitches and be done with it so's we can ride on back home."

Fish bowed his head briefly, then rode back into our midst. "Brothers," he called out, "are we wolves, at long last? Are we merely wolves in the desert wastes? You'll be denied the Celestial Kingdom! We bring righteousness to the forsaken deserts. Righteousness!"

Atkinson whirled and pulled his six-gun, then fired three shots toward Fish. Didn't hit nothing but they did what he wanted. Fish's horse reared up, then bolted toward the forest. Somehow Fish held onto the reins. I turned Percival to follow, but Atkinson stopped me. "You stay right goddamn here! I want you to see this."

I wheeled Percival to face him. "Alright," I answered as I looked him in the eye. "I'll bear witness to it. I'll do it for Luett."

"Doin' it for my daughter, are ya? Well so am I. I ain't about to let my children be bedeviled by slithering snakes. And as for you reporting back to my daughter, you breathe a single word of this and I'll make sure it'll be your last."

I stood like a deaf-mute as they put the noose around Mott's neck. Then they took off his gag and undid the shackles. Just left his hands tied. After they'd finished, Atkinson asked if he had a final statement. I reckon they thought he'd beg for his life but they were entirely mistaken. He went to shouting right off, challenging them to fight. Called them cowards and murderers. They listened a few minutes, then one of them slapped his horse. It shot out from underneath him, leaving him dangling. After his head turned purple, they finally lowered him. He floundered in the dirt for a time, struggling to get his wind. Soon as he could talk again, he went back to trying to shout.

"You're lynching me for no reason but ignorant malice," he rasped. "Because I'm a Yankee gentleman with a wealthy father! And you're a bunch of rebel scum and fanatical zealots! The twin pillars of perfect barbarism, polygamous lechers and secessionist trash!"

Then they done something strange. "Reckon you're right, Mott," answered Atkinson. "Here we are in the company of a New England gentleman and damn but we've forgot our manners." He looked around at the group. "Gather round here, fellers, and pay your respects." Then he reached into his saddlebag and plucked out a piece of fabric. "I brung a pretty silk scarf just especially for this occasion," he went on as he held it in the air. "With your permission, Mr. Mott, I'll wrap it around your gentle neck so's you won't suffer any from the burn of the rope. If a gentleman's got to be lynched, why it ain't right to make it a torment."

Mott tried to jump away when Atkinson came with the scarf, but three men went and grabbed him. Mott continued to spit his curses as Atkinson tied the scarf and lay the noose over his neck again. Then they pulled him into the air. After he kicked helplessly a couple minutes, they dropped him back to the ground. "Tell us who you was thievin' with," said the colonel. "Maybe we can arrange for clemency."

Mott squirmed and gasped in the dirt, tossing himself like a landed bass.

"Hang the other ones," cried Larson. "Let him watch 'em. Then he'll talk."

"Let them go for godsakes!" Mott called out in a hoarse whisper. "They haven't done anything!"

"Done it by yourself, did ya?" replied Atkinson.

"String me up if you're determined, but let those men go! I only hired them to build my fence! They did nothing wrong!"

"Take off their gags and shackles," commanded the colonel as he handed the keys to Horn. "Got to give 'em a chance to make their last statement, if they want. Got to make sure we do this fair."

No sooner had he spoken than Horn carried out his order. After he was done he fixed the nooses on their necks. The first man flinched and begged. He was still begging when they hoisted him. He kept squirming and kicking until he was limp. The second one died almost the same. All the while Mott was lying on his side with his hands tied. Two men grabbed him up and put the noose around him, then handed the loose end of the rope to Atkinson. He tied it around his saddle horn and rode a few paces. Mott twirled a couple times then hung like a gunny sack. Just his foot twitched.

A wayward breeze floated over the silence. Atkinson marched his horse around the lynching tree to tether the rope, then got off and tied it firmly. Then a few of them began to whisper. I saw one man retching loudly as he bent sideways on his mount. I felt myself begin to heave right after him. A load of bile exploded out of my mouth not three feet from Colonel Atkinson. He gave me a disgusted look as he got back on his horse. He called his men to gather round him, then they trotted off toward Pleasant Valley. The Mormons rode the other direction.

Atkinson stopped about fifty yards away and looked back at me, as if to ask if I was coming. I didn't budge. Then he called out to the men in front of him. I saw Horn stop his horse and turn. Atkinson pointed in my direction. Horn sat still for a moment, then started off toward me. My heart gave a desperate lurch as I looked around for Fish. I kicked Percival into a canter as I rode out to find him.

When I topped out on a little bluff, I stopped and surveyed the scene. I could see Horn down below, puffing lazily on a quirly. He'd hobbled out his horse and sat himself against the hanging tree. Then I heard a horse approaching from behind me. I pulled my gun and wheeled, then shook my head grimly when I saw it was Mr. Fish.

"What's the hell's he doin' down there?" I asked as he drew up to me.

He looked down at the hanged men then let out a sigh. "They've stationed him as a guard. They don't want us to cut the bodies down. They'll leave them there until the maggots drop as a warning to the rustlers."

A bite of fear scared me awake in the blackest pitch of a desert night. I felt my mind swimming blindly as I struggled to figure where I was. The rasps of a distant toad brought the poisoned memories stabbing back at me. Fish and I had spent the day lurking in the forest then ventured on the trail at dusk. We'd ridden through silhouetted bluffs and powdery sands 'til we'd come to our destination. After turning Percival loose in a cow pasture, I'd laid my blanket in the rear of his barn.

I made an effort to put my mind at ease, then settled in my nest of straw. When at last I fell under the spell of sleep again, I saw my pa come to give me a whipping. Every time he'd call my name, I'd run deeper into the matted woods. When finally I didn't hear him, I reclined against the trunk of a pine. Only when I looked into the branches, I got a fright. Jayzee Mott hung there with his eyes blinking. It dawned on me he was half alive. I sat mute as stone watching his suffering. When it occurred to me I was in the throes of a nightmare, I tried to pry myself back into wakefulness. Only my limbs were sand. I could feel myself desperately shouting but the sound was a stifled grunt. I finally managed to open my eyes.

I lay in the dark as my mind boiled with desperate worry. All the dime books I remembered were full of pluck and chivalry and nuggets of gold for just reward. Only what I'd found weren't any fable. I couldn't see nothing but fires of malice in every direction I turned my gaze. I guess the colonel had it right in one regard. Once the settlers had pushed out the Indians, they'd gotten to quarrelling with one another. The cattlemen smoldered at each other on account of their jealousies for range and water, only they held their choicest rage for herds of sheep. Half of them warred with the sheep barons and the men in their service whilst the rest harried the grasping Hashknife. And in case all that fury weren't enough to spark an inferno, you had the Mormon-haters, and the Mormons that hated back.

Two years of drought and a crash in the cattle markets hadn't helped any, but the fire came from something else. Plain old greed served as ready tinder, but it was winds of vengeance that gave it force. Only it weren't any Biblical eye-for-eye sort of vengeance they wanted; they'd made their pillages into a game of dare. In the thick of all those swirling flames of anger, men got free with their ropes and running irons. They'd take each other's horses and cows to spite their enemies, then they'd lash out with their burnings and bushwhackings 'til someone organized a crew to lynch.

Only I don't guess they knew who to go after. I never did know for sure whether Mr. Mott and his men were innocent of stealing or shooting someone, or raiding a sheep camp, or just generally casting their net of contempt over polygamists and Texas colonels. Alls I knew was that the vigilantes weren't any surer than Benjamin Holcomb, else they'd have brought their case before a lawful jury. They picked the targets they could find in the naked daylight instead of the shadow men in the broken hills.

And yet for all that I regretted my protest. If it hadn't been for the lynchings, I'd have stayed at the ranch forever, listening to the colonel's stories and basking in his devilish glow. Luett had no interest in me and I wasn't keen on Enna, but I'd have met his other daughters when they came back from the school in Santa Fe. They both ended up marrying his hired cowboys, and I guess one of them might have chosen me. Now and again I still find myself secretly pondering whether I'd have been happier if I'd held my tongue.

But the more that I reflected on it, the more the wistfulness turned to smoke. It was my eagerness to be a cowboy that steered me to the Atkinsons' and it was my disgust that turned me round. I was ashamed I'd failed the colonel, but there was part of me that was squarely proud. I was staking a claim to myself after the colonel tried to brand me. Only in the doing, I'd taken sides. I'd never imagined I'd be with Mormons, but there I was, cast ashore.

——•——

It was high morning when the door opened. "Time to rise," barked Fish as he stepped inside with a sloshing bucket.

"I'm awake," I answered. My voice was a muffled croak.

Fish smiled down on me like we were headed to a church social. "I didn't intend to give you a scare. I've brought a bucket and a rag. I thought you might want to give yourself a rubdown. Might want to give that black horse of yours a rubdown, too. That's a fine looking animal. Where'd you get him?"

"Belonged to Luett Atkinson," I muttered, "Colonel Atkinson's daughter. She thought my sorrel needed a rest."

"Gave him to you outright?"

I looked at him sheepishly. "Not exactly. Had to promise I'd abstain from drink."

He walked over to Percival and gave him a once over. "You'd better have a piece of paper to prove it, else people will think you're riding a stolen animal."

"And a stolen saddle to boot. I don't imagine she'll be filing charges. She was the one that made me go. She thought somehow I could talk him out of it." I propped myself on my elbows and looked at him blankly. "I don't wanna think about them Atkinsons."

"Then get yourself up so we can have some breakfast."

—————•—————

Half an hour after Fish woke me I got a glimpse of their sanctum. I found myself in a long room with an iron stove set at the far end and a sturdy supper table in the very center. At the near end of the room sprawled a brindled carpet stitched from rags. At two of the corners sat clumsy rocking chairs that they'd manufactured from ancient crates. Here and there on the walls hung illustrations from Eastern weeklies. Buckingham Palace on one wall and their Mormon temple directly across from it, plus three or four colored lithographs showing handsome women carrying striped parasols. The scenes in the pictures glowed like pious devotionals to their hopes for grace.

"This is Henrietta," announced Fish as he walked over to the plump gray-haired woman who was setting the table. "Also known as Sister Henny. We met in St. Louis when I went there on a mission. I converted her to the tenets of Mormonism and she converted me to the vows of marriage."

"Pleasure to meet you," I replied.

"Likewise, Mr. Holcomb," said Henrietta. "Why don't you take a seat while we finish the preparations. Mr. Fish says you've had a hard go."

Just as I sat down, I saw a girl approach with a bowl of beets.

"And this is my wife, Calista," said Fish.

I glanced up with a nervous grin. She had eyes black as midnight and round as moons, with a long silken braid coiled completely round her head. Tiny scars dotted her cheeks and nose like an ancient splatter from a boiling pot. A timid smile washed over her face as though she was apologizing for her blemished beauty.

"I'm pleased to meet you," I mumbled.

I had her figured for a Mexican until she greeted me in perfect English. "You're a welcome guest, Mr. Holcomb. My husband says you helped him. Not that we need to talk about it."

We bent our heads while Fish said grace, then he lifted a plate of biscuits and passed them around. It was the older wife that broke the silence. "Mr. Fish tells us that you're a connoisseur of horses."

I looked back at her with my brows raised. "I'm not sure I know the word."

"It means you appreciate things of excellence," answered Fish as he tucked a napkin under his shirt collar. "Ben tells me the gelding was a bribe of sorts."

"A bribe?" asked Calista.

"Luett Atkinson gave him the horse in exchange for a promise."

Henrietta raised her eyebrows as she filled Fish's water glass.

"I had to promise I wouldn't drink," I explained awkwardly. "At least not around her father."

"She's certainly got more sense than he does," said Henrietta as she set down the water pitcher. "I met her last year at a temperance meeting in Holbrook. Not a single church in that entire Sodom but at least a dozen foul saloons. Plus one solitary chapter of the Woman's Christian Temperance Union, of which she and I are members."

"Be thankful she didn't give you a mule," said Calista.

I swallowed some water, then looked at her.

"I have a favorite mule," chimed in Fish. "He'll do anything I want but pays no attention to Calista."

"He prefers the society of his fellow jackasses," replied Henrietta with a wry smile, "and vice versa. Place a fool on a mule and he doth think he rule."

"Henny's keen on rhymes," Fish said as he turned to me with a smile. "Much needed in my hours of despair."

I scooped potatoes on my plate, then looked up with a grin. "I'm eager for another one." I was keen to route the conversation in any direction but the Atkinsons.

"About mules or husbands?" asked Henrietta.

"Tell him about Brigham and Buchanan," said Fish.

"It's more mean than funny, but I'm obliged to do what's commanded. 'Brigham rode a fine horse, Buchanan rode a mule. Brigham was a fine man, Buchanan was a fool.'" She shook her head and smirked. "It's from a ditty they sang back when President Buchanan sent troops to Utah Territory. It has several verses that I'd rather not repeat." Then she turned again to Fish. "Of course we women have other versions. 'Henny rode a fine horse; Nathan rode a mule. Henny cooked a fine meal; Nathan did with gruel.'"

"Now you see the glorious truth behind our vaunted Mormon patriarchy," laughed Fish.

"I've heard that first verse," I replied. "Only the way the cowboys tell it, it's General Lee on the fine horse and Honest Abe stuck with the jackass."

Fish chewed nervously, then swallowed and looked at me. "And what be you, Ben? Yank or rebel?"

"Damn Yankee, I guess. My daddy fought in Sherman's army. Marched to South Carolina when he was sixteen. Shot two times but didn't lose nothin' 'cept his temper and one little finger. Voted for the party of Lincoln all his life. Prob'ly still does, though I haven't seen him in a couple years."

"Fighting to free the slaves, was he?"

"Well he sure didn't think Lincoln was no fool. The Declaration of Independence said men are created equal but I reckon Mr. Lincoln had to fight Mr. Lee to make it so."

"And the Declaration was written by Thomas Jefferson, who kept two hundred slaves," answered Fish as he fumbled with the potato bowl. "They weren't equal then, and they're certainly not now."

I was silent for a moment, taken aback by his ire. "I thought you Mormons got chased out of Missouri on account of you wanted to free the slaves." It was as if I'd siphoned the flow of cheer to a patch of barren desert.

"Indeed we were blamed for that. Wrongly, for the most part. Which only proves again the Lord's contempt for human plans."

"I don't follow your drift."

"It was a hard blow to be driven from Missouri and Illinois, but it was part of the Lord's design. He appointed these wastes to be our refuge from that senseless bloodbath you call the 'War of the Rebellion.'" He kept his gaze on his potatoes as he talked, then finally forked off a piece and thrust it in his mouth.

I furrowed my brows as I studied him. "You don't think slavery was wrong?"

"Not unless the Lord is. All the wars in the world cannot undo the stain of sin. Cain murdered his brother Abel and his descendants bear his mark." His fork chinked against his plate as he cut off a hunk of spud.

Calista smeared butter on a biscuit, then set it on her plate. "Yet those delightsome white Saints you rode with yesterday weren't overflowing with perfect righteousness."

Fish swallowed, then got silent. "My apologies for Calista's rudeness."

"This isn't proper conversation," scolded Henrietta. "I'll not allow it in my home."

Calista handed the biscuits to Henrietta, then reached for the water pitcher. "It's rumored to be both our homes. As for proper conversation, we can do better than dispute our guest."

There was a hush for a moment, then Fish went back to eating. Soon as we heard his fork clink, the rest of us took his cue. I was hungry as a feral dog but I could hardly taste my food. I kept glancing at Calista. I couldn't figure why a handsome girl would marry a man as gray as winter.

Soon as we'd finished, Fish smiled at his wives, then loudly announced that it was time for a man talk. "The church frowns on tobacco," he said as he turned to me, "but the body requires a respite."

"You need no respite," answered Henrietta as she whisked a bowl off the table.

"What I don't need is clucking. I'll get around to giving up the cigars once things get calmed down." He motioned me to follow as he stepped quickly toward the door.

———•———

"Have a seat on a hay bale," he began after he'd closed the barn door. "It's not a parlor, but it'll do."

I did as he suggested. Then he fetched a cigar thick as a pig's thigh from his pocket and handed it to me. He lit mine, then lit his own, then he sat there puffing while I coughed a fitful storm.

"Don't tug too hard! It's not a cigarette."

"Wish you'd told me from the get-go."

"I wanted to apologize for my conversation."

"I didn't take offense."

"Nor was any intended. It's my nature to argue." He made a smacking noise as he took a puff. "You know, Ben, I was a well-to-do man before I became a Mormon. Ran a nice hotel in a place called Rochester." He exhaled and watched the cloud drift.

"Erie Canal town, ain't it?"

"'The Young Lion of the West' they used to call it. Just a raw, rugged frontier sort of town when I was there. A workingman's town. Full of boatmen and roustabouts. Gamblers. Prostitutes. And not a few rich gents with flour mills and steamboats. A wonderful town for making money."

"You've come a ways from Rochester."

He was pensive for a moment. "My parents read Joseph's book and then gave it to me," he finally said. "And lo, the scales dropped from our eyes. It was glorious divine water come pouring forth on barren souls. We promptly sold our possessions and joined a caravan to Utah."

"I guess we were neighbors." I figured he'd angle to convert me if I didn't shunt the conversation. "We moved to New York when I was a button. Stayed a couple years before my pa got the itch to move us."

"Well howdy do, neighbor!"

"Howdy to you, too, neighbor."

"Us New York boys have to stick together, don't we, Ben?"

"Yes sir! Us against the world."

He studied me quietly. "This is a hard land, Ben. Shrivels everything. Including souls."

"Not yours, I reckon."

"I keep mine well watered," he mused as he propped himself on one arm and puffed out a cloud. "From the cisterns of holy scripture. That, however, does not keep me from reminiscing. My family ran a fine hotel back in Rochester. With a restaurant. Employed two chefs, both of 'em first-rate. We served veal and venison and duck and puddings and tarts and some of the most delicious brandy in the world." He puffed another cloud out, then turned back to me with a smile. "Sometimes I catch myself wishing I could go back. I'd spend all my evenings at the bar counter, sipping brandy and smoking cigars and talking politics with the barkeep. Instead of that, here I am, trying to farm a desert land that God never meant to be farmed. Not a bottle of brandy in twenty miles, and if there was, I wouldn't drink it. My faith forbids."

"You're smoking that cigar."

"The Lord winks," he answered dryly.

There was silence after that.

"How did you feel in there," he finally asked, "sharing a meal with a man and his wives?"

I sat quietly, trying to figure what to say. "I'm not used to arguing."

"Not that. About sharing a meal with a damnable polygamist."

"I'm not judging." I shifted uncomfortably, thinking of Calista.

"As well you shouldn't. You may not think so, but plural marriage is the will of God. In ancient Zion the polygamists were esteemed. What was righteous then is righteous now. Plural marriage is the church's apple orchard. When tended properly it yields abundance."

If his marriages had produced some apples, I hadn't seen any in the house.

He lit his cigar again when he discovered it was out. "The gentiles say we oppress our women," he went on, "but the truth is precisely opposite. There are at least a pair of godly women for every man of equal merit. If good men refuse plural marriage, they deny godly women a decent life."

"Seems like it's them giving you the decent life."

Fish gave a chuckle. "That they are! Though I fear Calista says more than she should."

I blinked nervously as I gazed at him.

"Strange things in the wind, Ben. If someone had foretold two days ago that I'd bring a gentile to my home, I'd have scoffed. Yet here I sit, confiding in a cowboy I barely know."

"Haven't been at it but a couple months."

"Which is probably why I trust you. You're not a hard case. Which is also why I want to make an offer. I'd like you to work for me. I can't pay much, but I can give you room and board. Maybe I can help you homestead if you decide to stay among the Mormons."

I nodded and gave a smile. "I'd like that."

"But if you choose to stay, I don't want you walking blindly." He drew a deep breath, then puffed his lips out as he exhaled. "Did the colonel acquaint you with their list?"

"What list?"

"Their death list. You realize they went to the territorial governor to get his approval? The governor promised them he wouldn't investigate."

"No sir," I said weakly. "Atkinson didn't tell me his secrets." If they'd gotten the governor's permission, it occurred to me, they sure as hell weren't going to let anyone stand them down.

I watched him puff before I spoke again. "Are the vigilantes sending death letters?" It was my turn to be the wise one.

He turned his head sideways. "What letters?"

"They say 'GO' in big letters. Written in blood, they told me. The Grahams think it's Tewksburys sending 'em, only the Tewksburys get 'em, too."

"How is it you know the Grahams?"

I felt a shiver come crawling over me as I damned myself for talking. "I met 'em a couple months back when I was on my way to the Atkinson place. Hooper was riding up the Rim to look for his lost pa, and I tagged along on account of he knew the country. I ended up spending a night at the Graham place before I headed to the Atkinsons'."

He dropped his cigar butt and stamped it out. When he looked up he had a grimace. "I have no idea who is sending the letters. Now listen closely, Ben. I'm not trying to frighten you, but I want you to understand. You've marked yourself by trying to argue against the lynchings. They're afraid of you. The fact that you rode with Hooper makes matters worse. When the moment is right, I'll lodge a protest. Until then, hold your tongue. Do I make myself abundantly clear?"

12.

After our talk in the barn, Fish took me out to meet his foreman. To give me a view of the place, we rode up the eastern slope. Looking down from the top of it, we could see the long, snaking thread of Silver Creek, its banks lined with shading cottonwoods. Green fields rolled outwards on both sides of the creek. Looked like an Ohio farm. Up higher was entirely opposite. Nothing but sere hills and stunted junipers as far as the eye could see. In the middle of the valley was where Fish had his house. About a quarter mile north of it sat a flat-roofed adobe compound.

"That's where the Mexicans live," called out Fish as he nodded toward the compound. He stopped his mule and scanned the valley while I pulled up alongside him. "*Nuevo Mexicanos*, I should say. Sheepherders. After the Texans drove them out of their pastures, they moved their flocks to Arizona." He rearranged himself in the saddle, then waved his hand to shoo the flies. "But the Texans followed. A bunch of Hashknife cowboys ran their flock into the sand bogs on the Little Colorado not long after I got here. Seven hundred sheep. We helped them save a couple dozen."

I felt my lips part with a "Jesus Christ" as I gazed at the hills.

"On the contrary. Jesus had nothing to do with it." He coughed the dust out of his throat, then looked back at me with a grin. "Or on second thought, perhaps he did. They were desperate enough to dig my irrigation ditches. Heaven knows they've got the know-how. Their people have been farming these desert wastes since before the English came to Jamestown."

I pulled Percival's reins tight as he made a start toward the compound. "I thought you Mormons kept to yourselves."

He gave me a glance, then waved again to shoo the flies. "They're not here permanently. We'll parcel all this to our colonists when the church gets around to sending them." Then he took off his hat and fanned himself. "That or I'll join the Mexicans," he chuckled. "I get quite a craving for *pozole*."

He kept gabbing about pozole as we rode toward the compound. When we got closer, two little boys burst out from behind a wall. "¡*Tio Nathan!*" one of them shouted, "¿*Trajo el caramelo?*"

"I'm the patron saint of caramel," smiled Fish as he reached into his saddle bag and pulled out some candy. The boys grabbed it from his hands then ran to get their father. "I'm the younger one's godfather," continued Fish. "His '*padrino*,' as they say. Unofficially, of course. The Catholic Church views it as a legal relationship. Infidels are ineligible. I gather Miguel's wife opposed it, but he convinced her I was different."

"Where's your own children at?" I asked blithely.

He went on like he hadn't heard. "I've been reading them a Spanish translation of the Book of Mormon. I take my suppers with them every Thursday and discuss a passage. I haven't made any converts, but I believe they're coming round."

I sat quietly as I studied him. "They're not cursed like Cain?"

"They bear Cain no relation. They're Mexican Lamanites. 'Indians' in our graceless idiom. Scripture tells us they're descended from ancient Israelites who fled to the Americas before Babylonians destroyed their temple. They were a prosperous and godly people. And so they'll be again if our prophecies bear the test of time." He turned to me and flashed a smile. "I'd like to share the book with you, too, if you'll allow it."

"I'll give it some thought," I answered politely. "Have your children flown the coop?"

He gave the reins a jerk to stop his mule from eating weeds. "The Lord never blessed us in that particular."

"I apologize. I didn't mean to pry."

"I take solace from Abraham. He walked in the ways of the Lord until he was a hundred, though his wife, Sarah, bore him no child. Yet the Lord told him he would father multitudes and finally made it so."

When we reached the compound we tied our animals to the hitching post, then sat ourselves on a splintered bench underneath a long veranda. At last we saw a bare-headed man trudging toward us from the creek. "¡*Buenas tardes!*" he called out when he reached us. "Who you got there, Nathan?" His broad smile made his wrinkles deepen.

"This is our new hired man, Ben Holcomb," answered Fish as he got to his feet. "Ben, meet Miguel Torres, my foreman. Ben will be working with us. I want you to boss him. Show him what's what." Both of them chuckled as I reached to shake his hand.

Fish lost his smile as he spoke a string of Spanish. They talked back and forth in low voices 'til I heard Fish say the word "Larson." Then they fell silent.

"If they dare show up here," Fish said in English, "send the boys to fetch me."

"If who shows up?" I asked.

"*Los vigilantes*. If one Mexican takes a horse, it's assumed the rest are somehow in on it. A week before they went for Mott they cut their teeth on two *vaqueros*."

Miguel looked me over carefully, like he wasn't sure he could trust me. "Houck ain't gonna let 'em."

Fish took his hat off again and fanned himself. "Larson doesn't take orders from Houck." Then he looked out over the valley. "It appears we'll have a handsome crop."

The three of us worked together most days, so they could instruct me on what they wanted. We threshed their little wheat field and plucked melons and dug potatoes in the October breeze. Sometimes a couple Mexicans helped us; sometimes they'd be somewhere else. They tended the cows and goats and ran a little flock of sheep, then they disappeared altogether when they'd hold their Sunday prayer meetings.

The fall days came like trickling spring water in the pine forests, clear and sweet and swirling 'til their waters became a shaded creek. And yet my mind was a nest of wasps.

I guess I'd have expired from the stings of worry if Mr. Fish hadn't pulled me out. He never talked about the lynching or the vigilantes, or anything but what was sunny. After all we'd witnessed, his cheer was a cooling balm. I got to thinking the killing season had finally ended, or at least I'd left it far away. Now and then we'd get a week-old newspaper with reports of death in Pleasant Valley. "News for Satan," Fish would mutter bleakly as he tossed it in the woodstove. "May the fire convey it hence." Then we went about our quiet labors 'til a piece of hell came whirling back.

It was a chilly Monday morning when Miguel and me followed Fish to a broken fence line that snaked across barren hills. They'd built it a few years back, Fish told me, to keep the cows from drifting northward. Looked like they'd woven it from cedars and juniper branches, except it was full of gaping holes. Some lengths were burnt to ashes; others were pulled apart. "Orders from the Hashknife," Fish said wearily. "No sooner do we repair it than their cowboys tear it down." We got off our mounts and walked along it, admiring their thorough work.

Fish figured to put up another fence and string it with barbed wire. Then once he'd got it in, he planned to enclose his winter pasture. We measured the line off carefully, piling boulders to mark the anchor posts. Once in a while we'd glimpse our strays on the Hashknife. Then we'd mount up and push the stock home. A little cattle dog by the name of Jenny tagged along to help us out. We were just about to call it quits when we saw one of them Hashknifes atop a hill.

"He's praying to Satan that we'll cross the fence line," grumbled Fish as he wiped dirty sweat from his face. "Then he'll ride down on me with a bull-whip."

"He'd think twice on it if you'd a let me bring my Sharps," said Miguel.

"*Absolutamente no.*"

Just then the cowboy began to ride forward. We'd tied our mounts half a mile down the fence line. Our only choice was to stand or run. "Keep together," commanded Fish as he bent to grab some stones.

"What good are rocks gonna do?" I asked.

"How did David dispatch Goliath?" replied Fish calmly, his beard fluttering in the breeze.

"Them rocks gonna get us killed," muttered Miguel.

By then the cowboy had pushed his horse into a lope. He was no more than a couple hundred yards away. We waited silently 'til he rode up to us. "You Nathan Fish?" he yelled out as he stopped his horse in a cloud of dust. That little Jenny dog started circling him, yipping her objections.

"I am he."

"Well you throw a rock and I'll shoot out your front teeth. I come to tell you that you got to leave. You and them cursed Mexicans you got workin' for you."

"On whose authority?"

"On the authority of the Hashknife. You know goddamn well you're tryin' to block off our range. This ain't the first time you been warned.

I give you two days, then I'll ride back with my men and burn your house."

"Unless you have a survey showing we're on Hashknife range, we're not going to budge."

"The hell you won't! You'll budge right now unless you mean to die here! Now you take them Mexicans and be gone in two days. If you so much as come back to harvest your spuds, I'll flay you alive, you polygamous bastard."

"Not unless you bring a marshal to evict us."

"I'll bring a marshal alright. You're wanted for bigamy, Fish. You got two wives. I'll testify personal to that. Then I'll drink a bottle a whiskey to celebrate you goin' to jail."

Jenny went to yipping and circling the horse again, making it prance. Before Fish could call her off, the cowboy pulled his six-gun. Thought he'd shoot us sure 'til he pointed at the dog. She yelped desperately when the bullet hit her. He fired another five before her flailing stopped.

"That what's comin'!" he snarled. Then he turned and galloped off.

13.

After that dog-killing bastard made his threats, I lay awake in my nest of straw. I listened to the screeching nighthawks as I imagined myself riding out with my .44. Only even if I got the drop on him there'd be another dozen hells to come. It was like the colonel told me: he'd have friends who'd want revenge. I kept tossing and rolling, trying to forget my rage. Only then I got to thinking about a different worry.

I kept remembering how Calista looked as she'd stooped over the stove at supper. Wayward strands from her forehead kept brushing against the pots. I'd pretended I was listening to Fish jabber about his Mormon books but I'd hardly heard a word. Then she'd turned and caught me gazing. I took a sip of milk and tilted toward Fish, then cast my eyes in her direction as soon as she wasn't looking. Only damned if she didn't turn again. I'd felt the blush come as I looked away.

It was early morning before my mind began to rest. Henrietta had given me extra blankets to keep out the autumn chill, but it reached right through regardless 'til I arose and put my coat on. Then I nestled in the straw and drew up my blankets. I'd just fallen asleep when someone pounded on the door. "You up and dressed?" called out Fish as he slipped inside.

"Working on it."

"How about some breakfast? Ham and potatoes."

"Yes sir," I answered as I threw off my blankets.

"Well go on in there, then. Henrietta will serve you up. I don't know where Calista went. Looks like she took her horse and rode out before dawn."

I walked over to the water bucket and cupped some to my face. "You think she'll be safe?" I asked as I wiped myself with a rag.

He pulled his bellows off a shelf, then set it down on a hay bale. "She knows better than to cross onto the Hashknife. She'll come back when she's ready."

I looked toward the barn door, then glanced at Percival. "You sure we shouldn't fetch her?"

He picked up the bellows again, then set it against the wall. "She does this like clockwork. I lose half a day trying to find her. I'm tired of it. Go in and get your breakfast, then you can help me with the blacksmithing. I need to hammer out some gate hinges."

I didn't waste any time carrying out his instructions. Soon as I came in, I saw Henrietta at the stove. "Good morning to ya, Yankee Ben."

"And to you, Sister Hen."

"I see you've got the rhyming curse."

"I'm afraid I'm prone to it," I answered as I sat down at the table.

She brought over a plate and set it in front of me, then sat herself in the chair beside me. "I want you to do me a favor," she said in a low voice. "Ride out and bury the dog."

I was so weary from lack of sleep that I had to think about what she was asking. "But Mr. Fish wants me to help him with his blacksmithing."

"You tell him I gave an order," she called out as she walked back to the stove. "He'll mind me. Unless of course he'd prefer a scolding." Then she came up behind me with a second slab of ham.

——◆——

If I had my life to live over, I'd have turned that errand down. For Luett I'd met the devil but for Henrietta I rode into hell. Not right away and not directly, but she set me on the path. She'd never come to terms with plural marriage, I reckon, and she saw the mischief that could make her free.

When I got out to the fence line, I rode up and down for half an hour. At last I came to the darkened patch where the dog had left her blood. I scanned the desert for the stiffened body, but there was nothing there but a quilt of prints. I followed the single line of tracks made by the cowboy's horse as he'd headed northward into the blur of sage. At last I noticed a second set of hoof prints heading east toward a chalky bluff.

I'd followed the tracks about a mile when I found Calista's horse. She'd hitched her to a twisting juniper. I dismounted and tied up Percival, then followed Calista's footsteps. I finally skirted a pile of boulders and found her staring at a tidy grave.

"Henrietta sent me out to bury her," I said quietly.

She looked up tiredly like she'd been expecting me. "I've already done it."

"Fish isn't happy about you coming out here."

"It's not his business."

By now I was standing beside her. "Seems a lot a trouble for a cattle dog."

"She wasn't just a cattle dog. She was the only constancy I've had for three-and-a-half years." I could see lines down her face where tears had streaked the dust.

I sat myself on a boulder, then looked back at her. "How come you brung her all the way up here?"

She kept staring at the grave. "We used to come here for the view. I'd sit on the rocks in the morning sun while she'd chase the jackrabbits."

"How'd she get the name Jenny?"

"Jinn," she mumbled, "not Jenny. J-I-N-N." A little breeze kicked up just then, lifting her hair across her face. She pushed the wisps behind her ear, then gathered it up and tied it.

"What kind of name is that?"

"It's from *The Arabian Nights*. It's a spirit that can take the form of an animal." She still didn't look at me.

"Did you say a prayer for her?"

"As best I could."

I watched a lizard crawl into shadow then looked over at the grave. "What do you figure happens to the souls of animals, Calista? I've been pondering on that."

"Probably the same as happens to us. They go to a more glorious home. At least I hope so."

"Gonna put a cross on her grave?"

"Not unless it's made of bones."

I responded with a chuckle. "Aren't you gonna mark it?"

"I'd like to. But the thing I want to mark it with is too big to move."

"What is it?"

"It's a rock. It's over there a ways." She pointed north.

"Maybe I can drag it."

"I'd appreciate that," she replied. Then she got up and led me a ways down the hill. I studied her closely as I walked behind. She wore a dress of faded gingham that looked like a hand-me-down from Henrietta. Too big around the waist and too short in the ankles. If it wasn't for her wedding band, I'd have taken her for a widowed pauper.

She wandered around a little, then pointed to a piece of trunk wood from a petrified tree. Maybe a foot-and-a-half across and six inches tall, with the bark all around it like it'd been sawed up half an hour ago. "That's a fine looking rock," I told her, "but you could have found a closer one."

"Not an orange and pink one," she said with a laugh.

I could just barely lift it, but I pretended it was nothing.

"Just what Jinn would want," she said as I put it down, "a pretty grave stone."

We kept our eyes on the grave as we sat ourselves on flattened boulders.

"Now that you did me that favor, maybe I can do one for you, Ben."

"Isn't a favor somethin' ya ask for?"

"Not necessarily. It might be something you don't know you can have, but you'd want it if you did." She reached into her jacket and pulled out something bound in wax paper. "It's a piece of chocolate. It comes all the way from Switzerland. One of our missionaries sent back a box of it. Sort of a thanks for all the folks that gave him money for his mission." She unfolded the paper carefully and broke the chocolate into chunks. Then she handed me the smallest.

"I thought you said you'd split it."

"I didn't say fifty-fifty."

"Oh, I see. I get the short end." I popped the chocolate in my mouth and began to roll it around. "That's better than any lemon drop."

"A lot better than a lemon drop. Here, you can have another." She shifted closer, then reached out her hand, causing me to flinch. "Hold still," she said. "I'm putting it in your mouth."

"Oh. You took me by surprise." Then I opened my mouth and she pushed in the chocolate.

After that she stood up and brushed the dirt off her dress, then sat back down a few feet away and stared at the desert. "Tell me something, Ben."

"Tell you what?"

"Who are you?"

"You know who I am. I'm Ben Holcomb. Worked in Globe City as a stock boy in George Heard's store. Then I worked for Luett Atkinson. Tried to stop her father from lynching Jayzee Mott and his hired men. Ran afoul of Colonel Atkinson and ended here."

"But before that. Where did you come from?"

I turned my head downward and spoke softly. "Born in Indiana. On a farm. My father moved us to New York for a couple years, then on to Ohio. Is that what you're wantin' to know?"

"Keep telling."

"That's all there is."

She looked at me expectantly. "But what was it like? Ohio, and your farm, and your family. And you. What were you like?"

"About like any farm boy," I answered as I stretched a leg out and propped myself on my elbows. "Caught turtles and snakes and swam in our lake in summers, and ran barefoot through the corn fields, and shot varmints when I was older."

"And your mother?"

"Plump and full of vim. Got plumper after she had my sisters. I reckon I about teased her to death sometimes. I'd bring her critters and dump them in her lap. Put pepper in her coffee. Stuff like that. She'd roll up her fists and pretend to box me. I get to missing her pretty bad."

"Did she go to church?"

"Now and then. She wasn't much a believer in it. Said to look for God where his home is. 'He dreams in stars and moons, then writes his stories in the whirling clouds.' If you could read the clouds, she'd always tell us, you could find your way through the trials of life. Only every time I try it, I wind up with something garbled."

"She must have loved you dearly."

I picked up a twig and broke it across my knee, then tossed the pieces into the desert. "'Cept she was moody as hell and she'd whip me with her shoe."

"Maybe you deserved it."

"Mostly."

She stared blankly at the dog's grave. "Is she still alive?"

"Got diphtheria when I was eleven. Didn't last a week."

"I'm sorry," she said softly. She was quiet for a time as she looked out at the desert. "What happened after that?"

"Nothin' good. My pa went right out and married a widow. She brung her two boys to live at our farm. Only they didn't take a shine to me.

Beat me pretty regular and threw me in the mud. I got it bad enough just from Pa. Soon as I was seventeen, I jumped a train and headed west."

"Just like that, you ran away?"

"It's what the clouds told me. Or so I thought. I guess I didn't read 'em right."

"Perhaps you're a better reader than you think," she said softly. She rubbed her arms and smiled, then folded her legs underneath her.

It was quiet for a spell, then I turned her questions back on her. "Who are you?" I asked.

"Mr. Fish's wife," she finally said with a shrug.

"But where'd you grow up?"

"Ben," she said without looking at me, "did you ever meet a girl you wanted to marry?"

I felt a blush wash across my face. "Who would I go to marrying? There aren't many Mormon women that want anything to do with a gentile."

"There weren't women in Globe City?"

"Not many you'd be apt to marry."

"How about in Ohio? There must have been girls."

"Guess I did have a favorite."

"Did you kiss her?"

"You're teasing me," I said curtly.

"I suppose I am. I apologize. I don't mean anything by it."

We were quiet a long time.

"How about you?" I asked again. "How'd you come to marry Mr. Fish?"

She kept her eyes on the grave. "Hard to explain. I guess because I'd be lonely without him."

"You just said that dog was your only companion for three years. Doesn't make any sense."

"My only *constancy*. There's a difference."

"What about Mr. Fish?"

"I wasn't fourteen when I married Nathan. Mormons may be polygamists, but they don't marry girls. We took our vows in August."

"If I'd met you before that, you'd have been an eligible young lady?"

"Something like."

I turned my head down and scooped some pebbles, then dribbled them on the ground. "It isn't fair," I said glumly.

"What isn't fair?"

"Polygamy. Even if I was a Mormon I wouldn't have a chance. All the older men go to collecting the women before the young bucks can even court."

"Maybe we should be getting back."

I stared off at the desert. Didn't wanna go back. I wanted to go on talking to her just as long as I could. All day and all night and all the next day, if I could. It took me years to finally figure it, but it was just what Henrietta hoped. Happened the moment Calista took that hunk of chocolate and thrust it in my mouth. I loved her. But I didn't dare to tell her. If I had, I'd have made it worse.

14.

It wasn't long after we buried the dog that Fish saddled his mule for a trip to the town of Woodruff. "I'll be meeting with Caleb Hartman," he told me as he mounted up. "He's my boss, so to speak. He's the highest ranking church official in this part of the territory, excepting of course the apostles who visit on occasion. We'll be negotiating with the Hashknife's land agent."

I bobbed my head to show I'd heard. "I don't imagine they'll make it easy on you."

"They certainly won't." His mule threw his head in the air a couple of times in protest, then turned and looked at us like he was tired of waiting. "Half a dozen New England plutocrats claim a million acres of railroad land and thirty thousand head of cows, yet they want everyone else's property, too. You saw how they treat us. Their cowboys think they have carte blanche to steal our animals and jump our claims. Only we're not budging." His mule threw his head up again, causing Fish to pull the reins tighter. "But that's not what I wanted to tell you. There's something else that you should know."

I felt my heart pound.

"After the Hashknife agent leaves, I'm going to talk to Hartman about the lynchings." He looked at me intently. "Your name may come up. With your consent of course."

I looked down and shook my head. "I'd rather not be mentioned."

"I'm afraid it's too late for that, Ben. I'm sure Larson has given a full report."

—•—

I spent half the day chopping juniper logs and the other half cleaning stables. When he came trotting back late in the evening, I met him with a haggard stare. He turned his mule out into the pasture, then motioned me into the barn. Once we'd perched ourselves on a couple straw bales,

I admitted he'd gotten me frightened. If Atkinson got word we'd talked to Hartman, he'd be sending one of his assassins.

"Trust the Saints to keep a secret," he said firmly. "Hartman will never tell him." When I protested that Larson would tell it for him, I saw his stomach go to jiggling. "Larson won't go against his stake president. Not unless he means to leave the church, in which case he'd be consigned to a rung of hell where the devil is a prohibitionist."

I bit my lip and looked downward. "You reckon you did some good?"

He lit a cigar and blew a smoke ring. "We agreed to pay the Hashknife's land agent $4.50 for every acre we occupy on the southern part of their range. The alternate sections, that is, this farm included. It's cheaper than going to court. In turn they've agreed to restrain their cowboys. Of course he denies vehemently that they told them to steal our horses and run us off."

I nodded to show I'd heard. "I guess you didn't have much choice."

He turned his face downward and rolled his head from side to side. Then he took a deep breath and pushed it out through his nose. "The land agent was a close friend of Jayzee Mott. And nephew to a Massachusetts governor, no less. Not to mention grandson of the Honorable Oakes Ames, censured for bribing his fellow congressmen. Of course the sins of our fathers—or our grandfathers—cannot be laid upon the sons." He shook his head bleakly. "He asked us if we knew anything."

I sat myself against the splintered wall and sucked my lips in.

"Hartman's been patient and gentle in all his counsels but the thieves were driving him to distraction." He sank his chin into his chest and closed his eyes. "He didn't authorize Larson but he didn't stop him. Naturally, he can't admit to anything. Our enemies would drive us from the territory if they had evidence we endorsed a lynching."

I rested my head against the wall and stared up into the rafters. "I mean no disrespect, Mr. Fish. But I don't see any saintliness in it."

"Nor do I." He reached into his coat pocket and plucked out the Book of Mormon. He opened it like it was something delicate. "'*The Lord worketh not in secret combinations*,'" he read solemnly, "'*neither doth he will that man should shed blood, but in all things hath forbidden it, from the beginning of man*.'" He snapped it shut as he caught my gaze. "I'm leaving out the context, but there be my pointed weapon, Ben. I shot it into Hartman's consciousness. He knows it well, but he required reminding. When we measure ourselves against holy scripture, we find ourselves falling short. And yet it's the measuring that makes us worthy."

"I guess Larson skipped that part," I said dryly.

"He's not entirely blind to goodness, believe it or not, but he has the piety of a feral mastiff. And about as much compassion when he decides he's in the right." He sniffed loudly, then puffed his cigar. "There's another matter of urgency, Ben. I should have seen it coming. I've been called on a mission to Mexico. They've given me three months to prepare, then we'll head down to Chihuahua."

I looked back at him, wrinkling my brows. "Mexico?" My heart thumped again.

"The church seeks to open a door to the Mexican Lamanites, and I speak enough Spanish to help put the colony on a sound footing. That's the official reason for my going. Unofficially, it's because I'm a polygamist. Hartman got word that the Republicans in the legislature are pushing for another round of prosecutions. The church has a legal fund, but it's already exhausted."

I sucked in a deep breath. "I guess I'll have to leave."

He took a drag on his cigar, then blew out another smoke ring. "Not necessarily. We'll find a way for you." Then he rose to his feet and walked toward the door. "I registered our protest, Ben. Let him cogitate upon it. If the killing train is to be brought to halt, we must prevail upon the brakeman."

———•◦•———

The skies were a perfect blue that autumn, but the winds pitched like a storm at sea. All the gates and doors would rattle in unison, then bang with fearsome claps. After I'd run the gauntlet from the barn to the house one morning, I found Calista sitting mutely in a squeaking rocker. I looked around in the shadows as I rubbed my eye sockets to get the dust out. "Where's everyone gone to?"

"I'll fetch your breakfast," she said dryly as she rose from the rocker. "They're out back having a look at the freight wagon."

"The freight wagon?"

"They're estimating how much they can carry back with them."

"From where?" One of the gates banged outside again, then went back to its steady rattling.

"You'll find out. Have a seat and I'll bring you breakfast. No ham this morning. Just boiled mush. You can pour buttermilk on it to make it edible." She grabbed a bowl from the shelf, then ladled out something gray-looking.

I sat at the table and rubbed my chin. Half of me worried about Fish's news. The other half wanted to flirt. "I wish I could get some more of that chocolate," I said as I sat back and stretched my legs.

"There's no more of it."

"Maybe I can ride into Woodruff and buy some."

"Here's your mush," she said as she put a bowl and a spoon down in front of me, then turned back toward the stove.

The conversation stopped when Fish appeared in the door with Henrietta behind him. He walked quickly toward me, his lips clenched in a frown. I thought he'd heard me flirting. "More bad tidings," he said as he approached. "Henrietta's mother is gravely ill. Henrietta and I are leaving for St. George to pay her a visit."

"I'm sorry to hear it," I said as I turned to Henrietta.

"I fear I'll never see her again," she said in a weak voice. "What with this Mexico business forced upon us." Her eyes were puffed and wrinkled. Either the flying sand had left them swollen or she'd been weeping from the bitter news.

"You'll be running the place," continued Fish. "You and Miguel. We won't be back for several weeks. Maybe more."

"I'll do whatever you want. Just tell me what it is."

"We'll be leaving as soon as we can get the wagon ready. I figure it'll take four days to make Lee's Ferry and five or six more to make St. George. Calista is going to stay with our neighbors, the Jameses. There won't be room for three in the freight wagon, not with all the supplies we'll be ferrying back here. I'll be stocking up for the Mexico trip. I'm leaving you in charge of the pigs and chickens."

The rattling stopped as the wind got quiet. "Yes sir," I said.

"After we leave, I want you to go back out there and finish taking inventory of our fence lines. You can do it alone. Miguel and his men can tend the stock and the crops. When you're done, I want you to ride into Woodruff and order the barbed wire. I'll pick it up on my way back. If you see our animals on the Hashknife, mount your horse and drive 'em home."

"I'll take care of it," I answered as the gates went back to banging.

———•———

As I worked along the fence line over the next several weeks, I went to cutting juniper branches to make sturdy posts. Then I dropped them into the rows I'd dug, anchoring each of them with a pile of rocks. I wore the thickest gloves I could find on the tool shelves, but the blisters swelled regardless.

Most evenings I'd sup alone, but some days I'd visit the compound. I could eat at the James place, if I wanted, but I preferred to sit with the Mexicans and force my tongue to say their curling words. Besides which, now that my heart had fixed on Calista, I had no idea what to say to her. Every time I stepped into a room with her, my thoughts jigged like a drunken puppet.

The third Friday after Fish and Henrietta left, I saw Calista come riding sidesaddle. Sister James rode right behind her, followed by her two little girls straddling a burro. I waved from outside the barn, then walked up to give a greeting. "Howdy," I said in my friendliest voice. "What are you lovely women doin' here at a bachelor's place?"

"Hello, Ben," said Calista with a smile and a timid wave. "We decided to come over and check on the place. I imagine Nathan and Henrietta will be back shortly. I thought I'd get the house ready. We'll make supper while we're here."

"I'd like that," I answered, feeling a wave of hope mixed with dread. If it was a sit-down sort of supper I'd be tongue-tied with the women. Wouldn't take much deducing for Sister James to diagnose my ailment.

I kept busy in the barn that afternoon hammering out a batch of nails. Fish was planning to build some shipping crates when he got back. I figured I'd surprise him and have them ready. I was still at work a few hours later when I heard the women talking on the porch step. They kept joking and laughing, like they were the gayest people in the world. Got me a little ruffled. I figured she knew full well I was in love with her but she didn't care a single whit. I went back to hammering to hide their voices, but my curiosity got the better of me. I finally lay the hammer down, then turned my head to listen. They joked and laughed a while longer, then Sister James called her little ones to mount the donkey. Half an hour later I saw Calista at the barn door. "Come and get some supper, Ben."

"Thank you," I said nervously as I set down the hammer. "I appreciate the offer. Why did Sister James and them kids go and run off?"

"She's taking care of her mother. The poor woman's so senile she can't remember how to feed herself. I told Sister James I wanted to stay here and finish cleaning. I'll do your wash for you, if you'll gather it." She gave a hurried smile, then turned toward the house.

"She's not afraid of leaving you?"

"I told her you sleep at the compound," she called back over her shoulder.

"I'll go after supper."

"You needn't. I just wanted to put her mind at ease." Then she opened the door and motioned me in. Thirty seconds later we were pulling out our chairs.

"Smells like seventh heaven," I muttered as I took off my jacket.

"I made it with you in mind," she replied as she dished out some meat pie. "It's called a pasty. It's said to be a favorite among the Cornish miners in Globe."

"Oh. I never heard of it. . . . But I'm sure them Cornish fellers have it every eve."

"I'd like you to say the blessing, Ben."

I bowed my head obediently and stammered out a prayer.

"That was lackluster," she said dryly. "If you decide to convert, you'll have to be more expansive."

"I guess you're right."

We ate quietly, shifting in our seats. "I don't want you to sleep in the barn anymore," she suddenly said as she forked off a piece of crust.

"I told you I'd go to the compound."

"They're crowded enough over there. After I leave, I want you to come in the house and sleep on the rug. It's too cold in that barn this time of year. I got out some blankets for you. They're stacked in the corner. If you double the rug over, it'll make a decent bed."

"I'll be fine in the barn," I mumbled as I scooped my fork into the pasty and watched the steam come rolling off.

"Did you ride into Woodruff to order his wire?"

"Yes m'am. Last week."

"He'll be mad as a jaybird if he doesn't get his wire."

I swallowed, then stared at her. "I don't know why he wants it."

"For his fences. Does your memory have a leak?"

I looked at my plate. "You're all going to Mexico."

She was silent a moment. "Mr. Fish won't stop improving this place just because we're moving."

"Just makin' more profit for Hartman. It's him that owns the land."

"It's not a business proposition. It's about building up a country. Making it fit to live in. When we go, some other Saints will take this place. And they'll go on improving it for the next family that moves in. It's what we do." I noticed she'd stopped eating.

"What about the Mexicans?"

"President Hartman will make arrangements."

"You suppose he'll make arrangements for me, too?"

"He will if you join the church."

I looked at her gloomily. "I doubt he can help me."

"What does that mean?"

"On account of what I want the most is something he can't provide."

She looked up for a second, then toyed with her food.

"I apologize. Just can't help my thoughts."

"I have thought of you, too, Ben Holcomb," she whispered.

I was thunderstruck. I sat quietly for a moment, then reached for her hand.

"Keep your distance please."

I pulled my hand back and turned my head down. "He can't love the both of you."

She toyed with her food a little more, then pushed her plate aside like she couldn't stand to look at it. "You may not believe in plural marriage, but you've no right to judge it."

"I'm judging Nathan."

"You judge him wrongly," she answered, her head bowed toward the table.

I stared at her. "I think I know why he married you."

She tilted up her head and looked me in the eye. "Because he wanted a whore, of course. You wouldn't be the first to spit that in our faces."

"You're the stray cat that found a milk bowl. I don't know what happened to you, but I sure as hell know it's wrong. You married him for his blasted charity."

A tear tumbled from her eye. Then she walked to the bedroom and shut the door.

———◦———

The waning moon pierced the window that night like the beam from a lighthouse. Got so bright I couldn't sleep. I twisted and tossed in my straw nest like a cork on a stormy sea. Then I heard the door squeak on the backside of the house. I lay silent for a time, listening to the night. Then I got up and cracked the barn door. She was silhouetted against the corral, all bundled up with her arms folded. I fumbled to get my clothes on, then I pulled on my boots and jacket.

"Cold out here," I said as I approached.

"It's like an embrace," she replied without taking her eyes off the stars. "Look at all that, Ben. Even with the moonlight, you can see the Milky Way, all splayed across the darkness like a bridge to a fairy kingdom."

I studied her silently, then looked at the sky. "If it's a bridge you're seeing, you might oughta cross it."

She gave a little sniff. "I doubt it would hold my weight." She embraced herself more tightly and drew a deep breath. Then she let out a long sigh. "What you said at supper was out of line, but it had a grain of truth."

"About what?"

"About why I married Nathan."

When I saw tears on her cheeks, I took her hand. Then I turned fully toward her and took her in my arms.

"You don't understand the first thing about me," she whispered.

"You're a train robber and a horse thief?"

She broke my embrace and stood with her head bent. "Nothing that exciting. I'm a Lamanite. I'm half-Lamanite, to be precise."

"With silky dark tresses and eyes black as jet." I drew a finger over her cheek.

"My mother is a Nevada Paiute," she said as she pushed my hand away. "Her grandfather sold her."

"Sold her to the Mormons?"

"They were starving. The people who bought her promised to care for her. Not just feed her, but make her radiant. Make Cousin Lemuel delightsome in the eyes of the Lord."

I stared at her. "'Cousin Lemuel'?"

"It's what they call Lamanites." She sighed and shivered as she looked at the ground. "They adopted her to have a servant. At least that's how she remembers it. I'm sure she didn't make it easy on them. They were loving people in every way apart from when it came to switchings."

I tried to touch her again but she turned away her face. "Is she alive?" I asked quietly.

"After my father died, she moved to the reservation. She sends me letters now and then."

We stood silently in the stillness.

"Just walked away and left you abandoned?"

"Of course not. She made President Hartman my guardian. I stayed with him while I attended the stake academy. Then he brought me to Salt Lake when he was sealed to his third wife. He introduced me to all manner of bearded men who hold positions in the church, his intention being betrothal. But I eloped with an army soldier."

She shivered again and rubbed her shoulders. When she looked up at me I could see her tears. She started to say something but she couldn't speak. Then she stooped her head and closed her eyes.

"What happened to you, Calista?"

She sniffed loudly and rubbed her eyes, then reached out a finger to trace the ridges on a fence post. "They banished us to Fort McDowell. We were there about a month." She was quiet again as she rested her hand atop the post. "Then he took our money and deserted."

I walked closer to touch her shoulder but she stepped out of reach.

"I let them use me," she whispered.

I felt like I'd been gut-punched with brass knuckles. My memories bent to the cribs in Globe City. I'd never had any particular objection to prostitutes, but I'd never been in love with one. I felt a surge of loathing for every man in the territory. I stood still for a time, swallowing the lump in my throat. "You had to eat," I finally muttered.

She wept quietly then looked back toward the moon. Then she took a deep breath and whirled around. "I made my choices. I'm not asking forgiveness."

I tried to touch her face again but she pushed away my hand. She rubbed the tears from her cheeks and looked at me anxiously. "I want you to stop thinking about me."

I felt my gut fill with an empty bleakness. "Will it make it better?"

"No. Only bearable. I can be his loyal wife."

We both stood motionless. "He rescued you?" I asked.

"I tired of it. That's all. I didn't want to pass my life that way." She let another sob escape, then turned to me with her jaw clenched. "I took Jinn and walked to Mesa City. It isn't far from Fort McDowell. Nathan's brother is a bishop there. I asked him to take me in. Then Nathan and Henrietta appeared on a visit." She got quiet as she looked at the moon.

"He hoped I'd bear him children."

"I can't do it," I whispered.

"You can't what?"

"I'll think about you 'til I'm dead."

"I cannot be with you, Ben Holcomb. I'd be as fallen as wicked Lucifer."

"What's wicked is him keeping you. You're no different from your mother. You're a goddamn Mormon slave!"

When I saw her eyes pool with water I took her in my arms. "I'm sorry," I whispered. "I know it isn't true." Then I couldn't help it. I pulled her close and kissed her. When our lips finally parted, we walked to the house. Then we coiled ourselves on the rug, tossing restlessly in storms of love.

———•———

Come the next morning Calista wouldn't talk. Every time I said something, she'd only turn away. She set breakfast on the table but she wouldn't sit and eat. Just got on her horse and set a course for the James place. I watched out the window as she drifted into shadow. Then she disappeared completely like the moon behind the hills.

15.

Two days later, Fish and Henrietta came rattling in the freight wagon with Calista in the back. They'd picked her up at the James place. He climbed down from the bench and clapped me on the back. I tried to put a smile up but I couldn't hardly look at him. Then he asked me about the farm as I unhitched the horses. It was everything I could do just to mumble out an answer. "Is something the matter with you?" he asked in a concerned voice.

"Comin' down with grippe."

He put his hand on my forehead and looked me in the eye. "Your eyes are red," he said softly. "But I don't feel a fever. Come in the house and we'll put you on the rug."

"I'm better off in the barn. I don't want you all to take sick." I didn't wait for him to answer. Just started walking the horses out to the corral. Truth is, I didn't wanna look at him. *Nothing but a hypocrite, I kept thinking. Him and his talk of righteousness.* When I finally turned back, I saw Calista hauling his trunks out. Damned if I was gonna help her. I walked quietly into the barn and curled tightly in my blankets.

———•———

Queer as it sounds, things got back to normal. I'd take my breakfasts in the house, then we'd fetch Miguel and ride to the fence line. We put up an endless line of posts, then strung them with Fish's barbed wire. Come evening, I'd go back and eat supper, then sleep on the rug. Sometimes Calista sat at the table, but mostly she'd find a chore.

Fish somehow ignored my frostiness. I never knew whether he was oblivious or above the noticing. Then one day he took me into the barn to make an apology for being aloof. He'd somehow decided he was at fault, ar at least that's what he pretended.

He handed me a gold piece and a shiny razor and told me he preferred me to all the barkeeps in the metropolis of Rochester. Then we smoked his cigars while he told a story. Back when he was a missionary in St.

Louis, he remembered, he'd gotten himself into a fierce debate. He'd made bold to preach on a street corner about how God had a human body. Since God made people in his image, he'd explained, God must be just like us. One of the gentiles asked whether God was clean-shaven or preferred a chin beard. Clean-shaven, said another gentile. Had to be, since he was sinless. To which Fish gave a resounding scoff. No self-respecting God would forego a chin beard, he retorted—folks would take him for a witless youth.

"Now that I'm gray-headed and in my autumn," he concluded, "I see sensibility in both positions. Our Heavenly Father might be clean shaven or prefer a chin beard, or perhaps he emulates whatever is fashionable. But he most certainly doesn't have scraggly whiskers." He looked at me sternly, then gave a wink. "You might want to think about that. In the event you marry, a beard might befit you. For the present, employ the razor."

———•———

The days drifted away like the sails of a China clipper, yet I wasn't any closer to figuring where I'd go. I guess I held some flickering hope of winning Calista, though I did my damnedest to bat it down. A week went by, then another and a couple more. Some days they'd leave me all alone when they went to visit neighbors, or off to their church meetings. Other days the neighbors came to us. They'd bring jam, or pickled vegetables, then help with a chore or two if they didn't go straight to socializing.

Then one day in late January, I heard a boom and a pair of pops. It occurred to me the Mexicans had lit some firecrackers. I'd just stood upright after hanging a corral gate when here came another burst. Half a dozen pops and a pair of booms. "Gunfire!" I shouted. Those angry booms weren't any firecrackers; they were buffalo cartridges from a .58. I rushed to get Mr. Fish but he came charging out the door.

"It's Hashknifes or it's vigilantes!" he yelled, "Satan's work either way! Let's get out there and put a stop to it!"

Henrietta swooped behind him like a hawk on a rabbit. "There's nothing you can do!" she screeched as she grabbed his elbow.

He didn't pay her heed, just beelined for the corral to saddle his mule, only the mule got scared and kicked its heels. "Son of a bitch!" he shouted.

"Hold your tongue!" yelled Henrietta.

"The hell with mules! We can run as fast as we can ride. Take that pillow case from the clothes line, Ben, so we can use it for a flag."

I grabbed it and handed it to him, then ran to the barn. When I came back I wore my gun belt.

"Leave the gun!" he called out. "It's apt to get us killed!"

I furrowed my brow then unbuckled it and set it down.

By the time we neared the compound, Fish was wheezing like a sick man. Not ten feet in front of us was a man lying on the veranda. Blood came pouring out a hole in his cheek. For a moment I didn't recognize him, then I realized it was Miguel. Just then I saw a pair of gun barrels poke from the windows, followed by booms and puffs of smoke. As we came up to Miguel's body, his wife, Estrella, came running out a side door.

Fish took her in his arms as she sobbed on his shoulder. One of her little boys ran up behind her. Fish asked him a question in Spanish but he was too scared to make an answer. She bent to pull him close, then she spoke to Fish in Spanish.

Fish glanced at the compound, then looked back at me. "Hartman sent men to evict them. Her people mistook them for vigilantes." He breathed deeply a couple times then looked toward the creek. "God only knows why Hartman didn't inform me." Then he yelled in Spanish for the Mexicans to stop their shooting. When they paid him no mind, he said to Estrella, "Tell them to hold their fire!"

She stopped sobbing long enough to shout something. Finally their guns went silent. "Larson!" yelled Fish, looking toward the men in the creek bed, "I'm coming over." He waved his pillowcase as he walked. I stood dumbly for a moment, then followed him. When we got nearer we saw Larson and two others crouched behind some boulders. "What in the devil is this about?" demanded Fish.

"You've sheltered these thieves far too long," Larson shouted as he reloaded his rifle. "We've got converts on the way. They'll need farm land."

"There are no thieves here!" exclaimed Fish as we walked closer.

"They are the line of Cain through Egyptus. They bear the mark."

"They are children of Laman!"

Larson gave a chuckle, then spat on the rocks. "They're mongrels from Mexico. The Lamanites weren't any too particular about mixing with Spanish slaves."

"Your pedigrees be damned! Their souls are sweet as honey. Instead of evicting them we should help them homestead!"

"They're obliged to leave."

Fish's hair blew backward, exposing his balding forehead. "And you've killed Miguel to make it so? Shot him in the face in front of his sons! Is that your idea of an eviction notice?"

"One of his people pulled a rifle and my men fired on him. Then all hell broke loose and Torres caught a bullet. What would you have recommended—that we offer the flesh of our breasts?" Larson pulled a folded piece of paper from his pocket. "Here's the damn lease. The lessor has the right to terminate!"

Fish grabbed the lease and tore it apart, then gave the scraps to a gust of wind. "We'll settle it anon. Right now I want your guns. Then you'll march back to Woodruff and tell President Hartman he'll have to go through me if he wants to negotiate with these people."

Just then one of Larson's men let fly a bullet. There was an answering boom from a .58, causing Fish to spin around. Blood went spraying on the ground as he fell and grabbed his stomach. He moaned and clenched his jaw, then doubled himself in agony.

Soon as he'd stopped thrashing I unbuttoned his bloody shirt. "Fetch a doctor!" I ordered Larson. He was stooping over me to get a look.

"Brother Fish," he said softly, "it seems the Lord has called you."

"Get him on a blanket," I shouted. "Got to carry him to the house."

"We don't have any blankets."

"Get one from the Mexicans!"

Larson clasped Fish's hand with one arm and put the other one atop his shoulder. "Old friend," he said in a whisper, "you'll see the Lord's mansion sooner than I will." Then he took Fish's pillowcase and waved it high as he proceeded cautiously toward the compound. I thought the Mexicans would fill him with a dozen balls but they held their fire and let him walk.

I took off Fish's shirt and wrapped it around his midsection. Larson came back a few minutes later with two of the Mexicans. Fish was passed out by then. We lifted him in a blanket and went stumbling home with him, holding on the best we could.

Soon as she saw us, Henrietta came running. When she realized it was Fish, she fell on her hands and keened.

16.

When I wake from death, I figure I'll be looking up at Nathan Fish. That or I'll be burning in perdition. The Mormons say that the decent gentiles wind up serving the godly Saints in the world beyond. If it means I'll be serving Mr. Fish, I'd be glad for the chance. A thousand men can profess a faith and only one of them makes it fully righteous. It's like the bow that belonged to Odysseus. About a dozen men tried to string it but only one of them had the might. Except Odysseus used his bow to slay his enemies. Mr. Fish used it to save their lives. At least that's what he tried to do when he bucked against the lynching. He didn't save Mott and his hired men, but his words finally hit their mark. After the Mott lynching, the Mormons quit.

I'm not saying he was sinless perfection. I'm not sure but what he'd have become a secessionist slave driver if he'd been born in one of the cotton states. The Mormons didn't invent all that poison about biblical sins and cursed lineages, but they'd chewed and swallowed it whole. Still I'll say this in Fish's favor: he died trying to spit it out.

If the rest of the Mormons had been like Mr. Fish, their tireless proselytizing might have cut deeper into the barren soils. I don't mean to lay a judgment. They paid their debts by the sweat of their labors and walked in the light of scripture. Only they'd become so certain of their blasted saintliness they'd let righteousness boil to fury. They'd let Larson take the lead in the lynchings, but some of the pious ones had cheered him on. Only not Mr. Fish. He'd stood like a wall against the flood of spite.

If I wake in the world beyond, I'll rejoice to see him. Only not if Calista stands at his side, shackled for all eternity. I'm ashamed of my adultery, but I'd make that choice to the cliffs of hell.

———•———

They held the funeral in Woodruff. Hartman sent a freight wagon to carry Fish's body. Calista and Henrietta sat in the back with the coffin while I rode a ways behind. I tied my bandana over my face to keep the dust out. When we came over a rise, I could make out a clump of people huddled amid the sagebrush. You could hardly tell one from the other the way they stood stooped and sideways against the gusts.

Hartman walked out to greet the women as they stepped from the wagon, grabbing their veils to keep them anchored. He walked them to the pit where the others were gathered. The only ones I recognized were the Jameses and Blake Larson, plus a couple of sheepish men I'd seen at the lynching.

Hartman took his place at the head of the grave, his black beard and frock coat snapping like flags in a gale. He blinked and squinted against the dust as he motioned the Saints to gather closer.

"Brother Fish came to Arizona on a mission to kindle the City of Enoch," he began, raising his voice over the flapping garments. "All was to be shared and all would be harmony. They named it 'Sunset' for the glory of the evenings, but the glory gave way to dark. For his efforts to hold the place together, Brother Fish harvested a crop of scorn." Hartman's voice trailed off until the wind buried it, then he lifted it again over the din. "With Brother Fish's reluctant blessing, the brethren divided their property. The colony dissolved and the people scattered. For the sake of earthly comity, he surrendered to selfishness, but he'll build his Sunset on a loftier plain."

When it was over they marked the grave with a marble hand pointing heavenward. Then Hartman walked the two women and me over to his place. While his wives milled around setting out dishes and filling glasses, Hartman told stories about Nathan's charity. He was trying to make the women feel better, but his words were sprays of dust.

———•———

After we'd finished eating, Hartman stepped over and put his hand on my shoulder, then told me to follow him down the street to his office at the co-op.

"I'm glad you came for the funeral," he said as we stepped inside a few minutes later.

"You thought I wouldn't?"

"No," he answered as he sat at the table and clasped his hands. "I knew you would. You're a worthy man, by all reports." He motioned me to sit, but I just stood by the door. "I hope you realize how sad I am."

I stayed silent.

"I told Larson to go see Nathan and explain everything, then take him along when he visited the Mexicans. But Larson can be a mule. He didn't listen." He massaged the side of his head a little, like he had some kind of ache. "What's done is done. I cannot undo it. The Heavenly Father has called Brother Fish. He's set his bearing for the Celestial Kingdom and there will be no turning him back."

I rubbed my hands together, then clenched them. "He wasn't planning to make the trip."

"We live a contradiction. No, he certainly wasn't. I'll carry this burden to my grave, knowing I made such a terrible mistake." He pursed his lips and stared at me. "Yet they continue their journeys. You may not believe me when I tell you this, but they are blessed. Miguel will find his way to Terrestrial, whence he may find the light of our faith. As for Nathan, I expect he shall father multitudes. Though childless on this earth, he and Henrietta shall bear in another."

"You should have told Fish what you were doing before you sent that bastard to evict them."

"I won't discuss that further except to note that Larson has been disciplined. He admits wrong and shares my anguish. Now, please, have a seat."

I nodded and pulled out a chair.

"I thought we might reach some arrangement concerning the property," he continued. "I'm not as heartless as you imagine. You'd like to stay there, would you not?"

"I'd like for the Mexicans to stay, too."

"That isn't possible."

"The compound is their home. They're the ones that built it."

"They're Mexican sheepherders. They're accustomed to moving." He looked away and gave a sigh. "I've made sure they receive an indemnity that will hold them until they've found accommodation. If I could do better, I would. But the arrangement we made with them was always temporary. Now I have a group of converts on the way. They're poor as dirt and they've gone through heartbreak. There were twenty-seven when they set out from Arkansas and now they're but seventeen. Ten died from fever. Ten Saints died to get here. I will not turn my back on them." He looked away again as his chest swelled. "Now let's change the subject. Do you or do you not want to stay?"

I gazed at the wall, then glanced back at him. "I do."

"Here's what I'm offering. You can take over Brother Fish's lease. Under the terms we arranged, he paid the Mexicans from the farm profits, and they paid me a monthly rent. The same terms will apply to you. You'll draw on Nathan's account at the cooperative to pay the converts their wages. They will in turn pay me rent until we parcel out the farm to them. There's about six months on the lease. That will keep you here through the harvest. Whatever profit you end up with should provide you with some savings. But I want to be absolutely crystal clear. After that six months is over, I'll expect you to leave."

I nodded to show I'd heard.

"Meanwhile, I'd like you to read our book."

"I will do that," I muttered.

"And talk to our home missionaries, if you're willing."

"I'm willing."

There was a silence after that. "What about the women?" I finally asked.

He pushed his brows together then gave a nod. "I'm counseling Henrietta to join her brother's family in their mission to Mexico. They'll be a blessing and a comfort as she works through her grief."

"And Calista?"

"I want you to think about what's best for her. There's a man in Mesa City who knows her from when she lived there. An older gent, a widower. Never took a second wife. Neither drinks nor gambles. Doesn't even smoke cigars. He owns a mercantile and a lot of real estate. It might be a worthy match."

"Not if she doesn't want it."

He smiled and crossed his arms. "We won't force her. While she's deciding, she can work in my house. My wives are overrun at the moment. After that, Calista may go wherever she likes."

"Except she's got nowhere to go but for an Indian reservation in Nevada."

"She can return to the farm, if that is what she wants. You'd like to marry her, would you not?"

I looked at him blankly.

"Since you did get her pregnant."

I felt my knees begin to shake. "What are you talking about?"

"She lost the baby the night he died."

My mouth worked but no sound came out. "It must have been Fish's," I managed to mumble.

"It was yours. Nathan never lay with her after he came back from St. George. She refused him. Henrietta thinks you'll make a good husband, by the way."

My face turned stony. "Will they lynch me?" I muttered.

"Why would they?"

"Because I've sinned."

"Those who mete out the death penalty to the defiler commit the same sin themselves."

I felt a bleakness wash over me.

"Had you held the Mormon priesthood, the penalty would be excommunication. You being a gentile, there is little we can do."

"What about Calista?"

"In committing adultery, she has broken her seal to Nathan. She can no longer reach Celestial. Will we excommunicate her? That is between her and us. If she repents honestly and fully, perhaps she may remain."

"Even if she marries me?"

He gave a tiny nod. "Yes, she can marry you and remain in the church, assuming she's not excommunicated."

I bowed my head and sighed. "I accept your terms," I replied quietly.

"I haven't finished. There is one other matter. It's bruited about that you're an associate of Landis Hooper."

"I rode with him by accident," I said in a shaky voice. "I was headed for the Atkinson place to take a job. Hooper was in Globe, and he knew the way. I went with him partway 'til we came to the fork to Payson. Nothing else to it."

"I believe you. But others won't. All they've heard is that you rode with him. If they hear that you're an adulterer, I'm not sure I can protect you."

I sat quietly as my heart raced. "You said they wouldn't lynch me."

"Nor will they. But they might very well attempt to drive you out." He glanced away like he was thinking, then turned back to me and nodded. "What matters is that they know you're working the farm for me. And reading our book." Then he stood stiffly and walked to the door. "So you see, it's a difficult situation for both you and for Calista. And for me, I might add. But if you'll stay on the farm and read our book, it'll turn out all right. But there is one final condition." He looked at me silently. "All this is contingent on you keeping that lynching business to yourself."

I breathed deeply as I turned to the door.

"Of course you do have another option. You can ride out of here and not come back."

———•———

Two days after Fish's funeral, I was alone in the house. Henrietta and Calista had packed everything they'd need, then had me load it on Hartman's buckboard. I couldn't meet Henrietta's eyes when it came time for her to leave. She looked forlorn as she climbed on the bench. I hefted the last crate, then walked over beside her.

"Ben Holcomb!" she exclaimed. "Don't go starving yourself with the women gone. No one wants to marry a scarecrow." She smiled weakly, then climbed down and embraced me. Then she got back up and they rolled away.

I didn't get any work done the rest of the day. I just sat in the house, alone with my thoughts. Finally in the evening I walked to the compound. One of the men came out and told me in broken English that they didn't want to see me. Said they had a priest coming from St. Johns to give a service for Miguel.

The next morning I rode out alone to the fence line and went to stringing barbed wire. Somehow it made me feel better. Like I was doing what he wanted. I threw myself into the work like a man in a race. Two weeks later I was nearly done. In the evenings I'd return to the house to make a supper of beans and bread with pickled gristle for a dose of salt.

Then one afternoon I came home to find Calista, digging a patch of dirt. "I couldn't stay there," she called out as she pushed back her hair.

"He just let you leave?"

She glanced up at me then went back to digging. "He called me a whore and a reprobate. Then he told me I could see you." Her eyes were ringed with shadow like she hadn't slept since Fish was killed.

"The son of a bitch!"

"I'm hardly sinless," she said softly as she went on with her digging. "When I rode here with Sister James, I didn't come to clean the house. I told myself I'd have your company."

I walked closer and clutched her arm. "Hartman told me you lost the baby."

"I'm planting daffodils," she murmured. "You'll have to tend them."

———•———

Later that afternoon, the two of us rode to the compound. Our horses stirred a line of dust as we skirted the wheat field and entered the peach orchard. As we came out through the trees, we could see a string of pack mules standing in front of the veranda. A couple of the young men had roped together a pair of baskets and slung them over the lead mule. They ran straps under his belly and tightened them, then walked back into the compound. A second later Estrella appeared. She stared at us from the doorway, then disappeared inside.

We stationed our horses at a water trough, then dismounted and looked around. No one greeted us. I reached both arms into my saddlebags to pluck out a big ham that Calista had baked, then we walked toward the veranda. We could hear them talking Spanish inside. There was a long silence after that, then Estrella came to the doorway. "*Buenos dias*," she said coldly.

"*Buenos dias*," I answered.

"You are packing the mules for Mexico?" asked Calista.

"*No es importante.*"

"*Es muy importante . . . nosotros*," I answered.

She raised a corner of her mouth. "We go to Colorado."

"We've brung a ham for you," I said dumbly.

"Put it there," answered Estrella, pointing to the veranda.

"You have relatives in Colorado?" asked Calista.

I could see Estrella's face stiffen. "A brother," she said. She walked to the lead burro and inspected the baskets. She was ignoring us. I glanced at Calista and nodded toward our horses. I could guess what Estrella was thinking. If the Mormons and cowboys hadn't come, she'd be the wife of a sheep boss instead of a widow. They'd be running ten thousand animals and counting a pile of gold.

"There wasn't a damn thing we could do," I called out.

"There is never a damn thing anyone can do," she answered. "God does what he wishes. God and Mormons."

We stood silently as she kept tugging the straps. Finally we began to walk back to the horses. "Don't go," she blurted. "I have something for you." She started back toward the compound, motioning us to follow.

When we came through the doorway, we saw baskets and wooden

boxes crowded against the walls. Estrella carefully opened a cedar chest and began pushing cornhusks out of the way. Finally she found what she was looking for. She picked it up and walked back to us. "*La Virgen María vino a Miguel en un sueño,*" she said softly. "*Ella dijo Miguel a tallar una estatuilla para el Sr. Fish.*"

"*Para Sr. Fish?*" I asked. I was worried I'd misunderstood her.

"*Sí.*"

"Miguel dreamed about the Virgin Mary," I told Calista. "She told him to make that doll for Mr. Fish. At least I think that's what she's saying."

Estrella came walking toward us holding a painted statuette. "*Ella preguntó Miguel convertir Sr. Fish a la fe verdadera,*" she said as she handed it to Calista.

I gave her a puzzled look.

"She tell Miguel to make Fish *Católico,*" Estrella said.

"Who's the doll supposed to be?"

"*San Isidro. Patrona de la conversión.*"

"She's sayin' somethin' about the doll being a saint," I told Calista.

Calista stood there mutely, then touched Estrella's arm.

"Pray to God for my children," replied Estrella. She turned back around and picked up a loaded basket, then headed toward the door. When she got there, she glanced back at us. "I tell Miguel not to give it to him. Mormon infidels go straight to hell."

17.

Calista couldn't see me but for visits, at least not straightaway. She was staying with the Jameses until she knew what lay ahead.

At first it was plenty awkward. I guess Hartman kept his promise of silence, but it didn't stop the tide of rumors. Though I was supposed to work with the Arkansans, most of them kept their distance. Then a few of them came visiting with a plucked chicken and a berry pie. It was altogether sinful, they kept whispering, for that old man to wed the girl. They were steadfast in their religious convictions except for that trash about plural marriage.

I didn't see Calista most days, but other days I did. I'd venture to the Jameses' place and sit with her on their porch. Then I'd take my supper at their table, if Sister James came and asked. Generally she was friendly, though her husband was frigid cold. But it wasn't long before he thawed. He'd ride to Fish's every Thursday with the Book of Mormon in his bags. Then he'd seat himself at the table and explain carefully what it said.

Only by spring I'd got so busy I almost forgot about the book. I fixed the plow cart to Fish's work horses and steered it through the fields. I had the Arkansas men to help me, but it was me that did the work. Most of them were too weak to do much except drop seeds in all the furrows. Not that I minded. I'd steer the horses back and forth while a batch of children tagged behind, shouting and throwing dirt clods and tumbling in the pebbled muck.

At the end of all that planting, Calista and Sister James came to Fish's to fix a supper. They'd invited women from far and wide to give those Arkansas bachelors some hope. Brother James and me had built a ten-foot table and nailed together sturdy benches. No sooner did we have them finished than our guests came pouring in. They put away half a hog and three bread loaves and finished with a row of pies. The girls would roll up old newspapers to shoo away the bugs. Sometimes they'd swat the boys, then hoot with guilty pleasure.

After we'd had our fill, I told the boys to wash the dishes. Then I took

Calista to the porch stoop and held out a little ring. I'd paid a gunsmith I knew in Globe to trim a stone of icy silica as blue as far-off mountains. He'd set it in a posie ring with a band of flowery gold. Probably sounds strange, but I'd yet to ask her hand.

I thought she'd grin and make a joke but instead she pursed her lips. She turned her face downward as she silently shook her head. Then she looked up smiling. "Just giving you a scare."

I tried to force a laugh but it sounded like a horses' snort.

"I do think about you, Ben Holcomb," she finally whispered.

"You'd marry me if I'm not converted?"

She nodded her head slowly, then gave a gentle smile. "I'd marry you if you were Hindu."

I floated like a summer cloud.

———•———

When I took stock of where I'd been, it was like George Heard had said. I'd drifted here and there and ended where I belonged. Only it wasn't exactly drifting. I was like a rock in a string of flash floods. I'd come to rest one place, then tumble to another. After I'd come to rest with George, I'd got pushed to Landy Hooper. That took me to the Graham place and almost to a gunfight. Then the colonel took me in, only the current kept a-pushing. I didn't know where I belonged, to tell the truth, 'til I'd found a home with Nathan Fish. Only I'd been set on abandoning him, too, on account of I loved Calista.

People say I lacked loyalty, and there are times I've thought it so. Only the more that I've reflected on it, the more I see it from a different angle. All my tumbling hither and yonder was on account of I'd tried to be a decent feller. I'd tried to make peace between the Grahams and the Tewksburys, though I didn't do an ounce of good. Then I'd argued against Atkinson when he'd rode to lynch Jayzee Mott. Even after I'd found Fish, I'd kicked against polygamy.

I was a pilgrim and a misfit, adrift without a sail. Then Calista said she'd marry me and I thought I'd reached my port.

———•———

It was only a couple nights later when the gales pushed me out to sea. I was reading about Odysseus taking his vengeance when I heard the faint nicker of a horse. I got up from the rocker and glanced out the window, only the lamp's reflection blocked my view. I waited a couple minutes but I didn't hear another sound. Just as I was about to go back to reading, someone pounded on the door. I ducked down and snuffed the lamp, then grabbed for my pistol.

"Lemme in, Ben!" called out the man at the door. "It's Landy Hooper."

My heart sank like a scuttled ship. I put my gun on the table, then lit the lantern again. Then I walked to the door and held it open. "You've goddamn found me."

He stood motionless for a moment staring at me, then walked in without a word. He kept shivering and blinking like he couldn't keep his eyes open. He had my haversack strapped across his shoulder. "I'm apt to get kilt unless you can help me," he said in a thick voice. His breath was ripe with whiskey. "They're sayin' I killed a Tewksbury."

"Jesus Christ," I said as I shook my head.

He walked to the table and lay the haversack atop it, then sat himself down and dropped his head into his hands. "Tom Graham asked me and some cowboys to go with him so he could avenge his brother," he mumbled. He kept rubbing himself like he was freezing cold.

"Which brother?"

"That boy from Des Moines. Billy. Jeremy Houck's been tellin' folks he'd set a trap for Tom Graham, only little Billy fell into it. Claims Billy pulled on him. Billy wasn't but sixteen."

"Houck," I murmured. *That deputized son of a bitch that helped lynch Jayzee Mott.* "What do you mean 'Houck's tellin' folks'? Did he do it, or didn't he?"

"I don't know. Billy thought it was a bunch of Tewksbury men. Only they shot him from afar. I don't reckon he saw 'em good. He lived a couple days with his guts hangin' open."

"How come Houck's sayin' he did it?"

He sniffed loudly a couple of times. "On account of he's in with 'em. He's a sheeper, same as them."

"Ain't no reason for him to say he killed someone."

"He's Lafayette's deputy. If he says he shot Billy in the line of duty, ain't no one gonna say otherwise. Won't be no investigation. You savvy?"

"Lafayette knows about it?"

"Hell yes he knows! What the hell you think he was down there in Yavapai County fer when we run into him? He was meetin' with the goddamn vigilance committee! They're all of 'em against us! The

Tewksburys threw in with Colonel Atkinson and the Mormons are with 'em, too."

"Good lord, Hooper. Every time I see you, three hells open up."

He managed a shaky grin. "They sure come along regular." He sucked his lips in and shook his head, then bent his face toward the table. "Been killin' each other back and forth since you rode off for the Atkinsons'. The Grahams recruited a bunch a Hashknives, only the Tewksburys went and matched 'em. Like Jayhawkers fightin' border ruffians. There was a lull for a while . . . only Tom Graham went and started it up again."

"So you all went out and killed a Tewksbury to get revenge."

"I didn't kill no goddamn Tewksbury! It was Tom Graham and them Hashknifes!"

I shook my head in disgust. "I reckon you were getting even with 'em for killing your brother Champ."

He rolled his eyes toward the ceiling then looked back with a grimace. "Wasn't like that. I spent the whole goddamn night trying to talk 'em out of it. Only right about first light here comes John Tewksbury and his sheepin' partner, walkin' straight down the creek a-carrying grain bags across their shoulders. Guess they'd turned loose their horses the night before and they was come out to fetch 'em. Then Tom Graham and them Hashknives jumped up and shot 'em."

"And you didn't?" I felt the anger rise inside of me but somehow it wasn't a boil. He was lying his head off I halfway figured, but I felt obliged to hear him out. He'd saved me once from getting drawn into the feuding, and I owed it to him to try to help. Or at least that's how it seemed to me, though looking back I wish it hadn't.

"Hell no! Just fired over their heads. Didn't wanna 'em to think I was some bally damn Judas."

The lamp flickered and danced as we studied one another's faces.

"Then how come the Mormons are saying it was you?"

"On account of every time somethin' bad happens, they lay it to me."

"Rightly, from what I'm told."

"Wrongly God blast it! But that ain't why they're comin'. Ain't had time to issue no warrant fer that. Alls they got is a warrant fer the horse theft. But Lafayette's fixin' to pin that Navajo killing on me, too. I guess you remember that feller that Lafayette shot to shreds after we got 'em in a crossfire. He went and died, just like I figured. If they catch me, they'll make me answer fer killing that Navajo and John Tewksbury, too. Only they ain't gonna give me no day in court. Gonna goddamn string me up."

"We helped Lafayette out of that Indian mess and he's blaming you for murder?"

He didn't answer at first. Just brushed a hand over his nose and sniffed. "I need you to go with me to Holbrook. I know an old judge there. Maybe he can help us. I've gone and got myself into this mess by talkin' too much in a saloon. Got to braggin' about how you and me kilt that Indian."

I shot out of my chair and threw it sideways. "What the blessed hell did you bring *me* into it for?!"

"On account of I wobble my mouth too much! I got drunk and went to bragging."

"Hell's bells, there was three other Indians that saw it happen and an army man to boot. They knew damn well who shot that man."

Hooper bowed his head again. "That army feller got sent to Washington Territory and no one cares what the injuns say. Lafayette's tellin' 'em you and me stole the horses."

"But he stole the goddamn horses! Him and Jeremy Houck!"

He looked down at the table and gave a snort. "Says he'd tracked us down the Rim, only them Indians went to shootin' at us before he could get us arrested. Says we fogged that Navajo feller and grazed a second one, then hightailed it fer the Graham place. I reckon Houck's gonna back him."

"Son of a bitch!" I shouted as I paced to the stove and back. "Here I am fixing to be married and you come dragging in with all this trouble!"

He closed his eyes and threw his head back, then brought it back down and sighed. "I might not be worth a damn but I sure as hell ain't a murderer."

"Well sure as hell you're a horse thief."

He looked at the floor and folded his arms. "I'll be honest with you, Ben. Thought we were doing something great by driving out the damn polygamists. If I could make it up to 'em, I'd surely do it. But not if I'm in the ground."

"Goddamn it, Hooper! What in the blast do you want me to do? You've jumped down a goddamn stinking privy hole and you expect me to haul you out. What the hell is it you want? I got no way to goddamn help."

He squinched his face into a pleading look. "Yes you do, Ben! You're a respected man around here now that you're makin' a go of this farm. These Mormons like you. Hell, I hear you went and got yourself engaged to one. Prob'ly marry in the temple."

"I ain't a Mormon, Hoop. But I'm sure gonna marry Calista soon as we can see the justice of the peace."

"Don't matter whether you're Mormon. This judge I know would believe you. All you got to do is tell him what happened when we saved Lafayette from the Navajos. He helped me once before a couple years back, but he ain't apt to do it again unless I got someone to back me."

I clenched my jaw like a pair of pliers. "I can only tell him what we did together. I don't know nothin' about whatever else you done."

"That's enough! Else I'm a dead man."

"If Lafayette catches us in Holbrook, he'll throw us in the hoosegow."

"My brother got word to me that Lafayette's in Flagstaff. We could ride to Holbrook in a day."

"How the hell would he know?"

"He's staying in Holbrook with my ma and sister. They got a little house right near the depot." Then he grabbed up my haversack and handed it to me. "Thought I'd better bring this back. There's somethin' in there fer ya. Doubt I'll have use fer it."

"What is it?"

"Open it."

I gave it a glance, then turned back the flap and reached inside. I pulled out a little paper box covered with scrolls. "It's my card deck," said Hooper. "Somethin' else in there, too."

I reached back inside and grabbed out a book. *Magic No Mystery*," I read out. "*Conjuring Tricks with Cards, Balls & Dice, Magic Writing, Performing Animals etc. etc.*"

"I promised I'd show you some card tricks, only I never got a chance. Figure I'd give ya my book so's you can learn 'em on your own."

I sat in silence as I stared into the lantern flame. "Son of a bitch."

———— • ————

Next morning I tacked a note on the front door telling the converts I'd be in Holbrook. Then I threw a saddle over Percival and headed for the James place. I made Hooper stay in the barn 'til I got back. I didn't want anyone to see us riding together.

I found Calista in the chicken coop, gathering a load of eggs. She lit up like a firefly soon as she saw me. She asked if I'd come for breakfast. I shook my head no, then got off Percival. "Goin' to Holbrook for a couple days. Figured you might want me to fetch somethin' for ya while I'm there. Maybe I can stop at the mercantile and pick up some chocolate."

"Holbrook? Why don't you ride to Woodruff and shop at the co-op?"

I looked at the ground for a second, unsure what to say. "It's for Landis Hooper," I finally blurted. "He's got himself in trouble."

"Hooper?" she shot back. "That wretched felon who steals our horses?"

"I know," I answered softly. "But I still gotta do it." I walked over to Percival, then came back with my haversack and held it out. "There's almost a hundred dollars in there. It's everything I've got. If for some reason I don't come back right away, I want you to have it."

She opened the sack and glanced inside. When she looked up at me her eyes were narrowed. "You're giving me your Book of Mormon?"

I was dumbfounded for a moment until I realized it was Hooper's magic book. "It's something Hooper gave me. Can't explain it exactly, but I'm obliged to help."

"He's playing you for a fool!"

"Maybe, but I gotta go. He's got me on the hook for killing an Indian. I told you about it. We ran into Lafayette McGowan when I was on my way to the Atkinson ranch. He and his deputy were about to get killed by some Navajos, and we ducked in to help 'em. Turned out Lafayette had took their horses."

"But you only tried to scare them!"

"That's the God's truth, but Lafayette is sayin' different. I got to go. Be back in two days."

"No, Ben. Go see President Hartman and ask his counsel!"

"Hartman don't like me, Calista. He ain't gonna understand." I reached out and grabbed her hand lightly, then turned silently and mounted up.

18.

All that breezy morning on the trail to Holbrook, I studied the swirls above us. Long lines of lace and patchwork, washing slow across the blue. They twisted into downy feathers, then hardened into runes. Only try as I might I couldn't tell their meaning.

When we came to our destination, it was just like Henrietta said. Not a single church in thirty miles but at least a dozen rank saloons. We rode by them all slumped and silent, like a couple soldiers after a bloody battle. "You sure that judge'll be here?" I asked Hooper.

"It's Sunday, ain't it?"

"I reckon."

"Then he'll be here. Won't be no court days 'til next week anyway."

We stopped off at the livery to give our horses some rest, then Hooper led me across the tracks toward the Atlantic & Pacific depot. That's when it hit me that those cloud runes were a warning.

As we stepped onto the street, we saw a tall feller wave us over. Even fifty feet away I could see the badge on his striped vest. "It's just Wattron," whispered Hooper. "He's town constable. I'll handle him. He won't make a move unless Lafayette tells him."

Wattron was standing alongside a spindly looking boy with pimples on his cheeks. "Pleasure to see you, Landy," he called out in a droll voice.

"Howdy, Frank. How's commerce at the drugstore?"

Wattron gave a chuckle. "More money in selling Injun pots, but the laudanum trade's been pretty brisk. Where you headed?"

"Just vis'tin' with my ma."

Wattron studied me closely, then looked back at Hooper. "Who's your sidekick?"

Hooper glanced at me nervously. "He's a friend a mine from Globe City."

"Ain't he got a name?" asked Wattron as he stared at me.

I hesitated a moment, then reached out my hand. "My name's Holcomb. Pleased to meet you."

"Holcomb, is it?" he said without returning my handshake. "Well it's nice you could come together. There's a warrant for the both of you."

Hooper blinked again. "That so? I hadn't heard about it. What's it fer?"

"Oh, I reckon you heard alright. Listen here, you bragging son of a bitch. You and your friend aren't welcome in this town." Then he glanced at the boy. "Run across to the sheriff's place. Tell that long-haired womanly son of a bitch shacking up with that Mexican whore that Hooper's in town. Ask him what he wants to do."

"Lafayette's in Flag," blurted Hooper as we watched the boy go trotting off.

"Came yesterday on the four o'clock train. Been tipplin' ever since. If he's too drunk to take you, I'll be vis'ting you by myself."

"Lafayette can burn in hell," spat Hooper. "I'm willin' to stand trial if it comes to it, but I damn sure ain't gonna wait around in that jail for any noose mob." Then he turned toward the tracks. "It's just yonder," he called back to me.

A couple hundred yards down the road we came to a white house behind a picket fence. Hooper hopped the fence while I went through the gate. He was already knocking by the time I caught up. We waited a couple minutes, then Hoop knocked again, only louder. We stared at the door 'til I finally glanced at Hooper. "I don't think he's home."

Hooper walked to a shuttered window and tried to look inside. "Can't see nothin'." He rapped on the glass and stood silently. "Goddamn!" he shouted. "Where the blast is he?" Then he stepped back to the door and jiggled the handle. "Got a damn lock on it." He stood there dumbly, then gave the door a couple kicks.

"I ain't got time for foolishness," I said angrily. Then I turned and walked away.

"Wait up a minute!" he called out as he came jogging after me. "Jesus Christ, Ben, where the hell ya goin'?"

"Back home."

"And they'll come marchin' over there and take you. We got to get the hell out a here. And I don't mean tomorrow."

"They can do whatever they want. I'll take my chances at the trial."

"You might not get no trial."

I wheeled and jabbed my fist in his mouth. He stumbled back a couple steps, then straightened up and shook his head. "That ain't gonna help us," he said quietly as a line of blood spilled down his chin.

"What the hell am I supposed to do?"

He wiped his mouth with his sleeve, then squinted at me. "I'm sorry I got us into this, Ben, but sure as hell I'll get us out. Just need to lay low for a while. I got a place we can hide at 'til we can send word to the judge. It's down along the Rim. I'll take you there. Got a month of provisions in a little cave and ain't no one gonna find us."

"Then let's get a-movin'."

"Not just yet."

"What's that mean?"

"Got to stop at the house and see my mother and them. Gotta tell her where I'll be." He pointed eastward. "It's that little clapboard just yonder. Come over and I'll introduce you."

"Goddamnit, we ain't got time for that."

"Won't be but a few minutes."

"I ain't meetin' no family!"

He looked around for a second, then nodded toward the livery. "Then ya may as well fetch our horses. Just walk 'em over to the house. I'll be ready when you get there."

I didn't answer. Just headed for the livery. Ten minutes later, I brought around the horses. I waited a couple minutes until the door opened. "Be right out," said Hooper. Back behind him I could see a couple boys crouched on the floor, playing a game of marbles.

"I'll take Percival and wait yonder," I answered, pointing to a crumbling adobe place about fifty yards away. "If you don't come in five minutes, I'm riding alone."

I tied Hooper's horse to the hitching post in front of his house, then led Percival down the street. After I'd stationed us behind the adobe place, I rolled a skinny quirly. I peeked my head out and scanned for Lafayette, but I didn't see any sign of him. Only I saw something else queer. Half a dozen men in suits were stepping onto the depot platform. Seemed like all the storekeepers were gathering themselves for a meeting. Thought they might be waiting for a train except they faced the wrong direction. Just talking and milling, like they were expecting to hear a speech.

I kept turning back and forth from the house to the depot, then moved back into shadow. When I peeked again, I saw Hooper emerge to check his horse. He tightened the cinches, then went back inside. He disappeared for a minute, then I saw him at the window. As I followed his line of sight, I saw a man with a stubby rifle. It was Lafayette. He marched up to the porch and pounded. A woman carrying a baby opened the door halfway and said something, then disappeared into the house. Next thing I saw was Hoop standing at the door.

"Hooper, I want you," bellowed Lafayette, as though Hoop was a hundred feet away. "Come now."

Hooper said something back to him but I couldn't hear the words. Then a gun boomed. The woman started screaming as Hooper tumbled backwards.

A blink later came a different feller—Hooper's older brother, they told me later. He swung open a second door at the far end of the porch and stuck a gun out, only the door frame clipped the back of his hand. His ball smashed into the eye of the horse. She snapped her tether and galloped blindly as Lafayette returned a shot, hitting the man in the shoulder. The man lurched back into the house. Fifty yards up the road the horse dropped to the dust and died.

Lafayette retreated to the far side of the street. He stood about thirty yards from where I was crouched, watching for any movement. Ten seconds later he fired a pair of slugs into the wall, like he was aiming for targets in the white of the paint. Just then a third man came leaping out a side window, trying to make a run for it. Lafayette shot him square in the back. I figured it for a death wound but he managed to crawl to cover. I never did find out who he was.

Lafayette reloaded as he watched the house. I couldn't hear nothing except the screams of a couple women. Then one of the boys who'd been playing marbles came lurching out with a six-gun. Held that gun with his right hand while his mother tried to grab his left. Lafayette fired once and snapped his spine. His mother caught him as he reeled backward, but it was a dead boy in her arms. She kept screaming as she dragged him into the house. Then I heard a different scream. "Aw, Jesus, Jesus, Jesus! Kill me! Someone finish me! He's blasted half my guts out!"

A wintry shiver blew across me when I realized it was Landy Hooper.

19.

Iopened my eyes in a sandy draw. About an hour before dawn I pushed off my blanket and climbed to my feet. I clutched hard at my neck, rubbing to get a knot out. Then I headed down the slope to where I'd seen a seep. I dipped a hand into it and rubbed water over my face, then kneeled down and dug the mud out. When I'd finally made a basin, I cupped my hands and drank. I kept thinking of old George all the while. I hadn't seen him in a year. I'd let him down, I reflected. I'd let down every one of them. Every one that tried to help me on my twisted path to Hades.

After Percival drank his fill, I tossed on the saddle and headed out. If Lafayette had found my track, he wasn't far behind. No more than a few hours. But if I goaded Percival any harder, he was apt to give out. He'd made a long ride to Holbrook, then we'd come another thirty miles.

I decided to follow the seep, figuring it'd lead us to a creek. Then I'd ride in the water to avoid making tracks. But the farther we drifted, the more I realized there weren't a creek. The little flow from the seep dried up altogether. All I could see was boulders in all directions. Like tombstones strewn around all sideways and helter skelter.

I headed us to Phoenix Park, hoping to find water. I kept looking back over my shoulder expecting to see Lafayette. When I at last reached the pines, I knew the Rim wasn't far. I felt a little safer once I was screened by the ponderosas. I finally took a rest at a pond fringed with aspens. I had a night of broken sleep, then started out before the dawn. Rode down into the Indian reservation, then hooked onto the Verde Road where it crosses Canyon Creek. When I saw Catholic Peak, I steered us south along the ridge.

I had one place in mind where I hoped I'd find a refuge. I figured it was just about the only goddamn place Lafayette wouldn't find me. He'd expect me to head for Snowflake or maybe Globe, but not to Pleasant Valley.

It was six o'clock in the evening when we came down into desert. I figured another three or four hours and I'd make it to the Tewksbury cabin. I'd have kept on riding 'til I got there, but I wasn't completely sure where it was. The only time I'd laid eyes on it was on my wretched ride to the Atkinson place. Besides which, I got to figuring, I'd be safer to arrive in day. They were apt to think I was a Graham assassin if I came riding up at night.

After I'd searched around a little, I found a spot between some junipers where I could bed for the night. Wasn't any water, but we'd got our fill along the way. I set the saddle on a boulder, then turned Percival loose to graze. Then I carried my soogans over to the junipers, searching for a flat stretch. I finally went to hefting boulders to clear out my spot.

I was rassling a rock about as big as my hat when something lashed like the tip of a whip. Didn't so much as rattle. Wished I'd done the same to Hooper when he'd come knocking. Before I'd pulled my gun out, it slithered under another boulder.

Got me on my wrist pretty close to the artery. Wasn't much bleeding. Just a pair of fang-marks like oozing freckles. I sat still a couple minutes waiting for the pain. When I still didn't feel it I figured it for a dry bite. They're loathe to waste their poison on shambling critters they can't devour. I sucked on the wound anyway, then sat back on a rocky ledge. That's when the pain came.

Just about then I felt the fog. I knew I had to get to shelter or sure enough I'd prob'ly die. If the venom didn't kill me, the sun would lend a hand. I managed to toss the saddle back over Percival and get myself mounted, then turned down the hill so's we'd hit Cherry Creek. Once we got to the water, I headed directly south.

———•———

I hadn't ridden but half a mile when I vomited. Then my skin went to crawling like I was covered with angry ants. By nightfall I could barely breathe. My hand had turned scorching red but somehow it didn't swell much.

I slumped over Percival's neck and rode through the night. My heart went to racing and my chest was like a fire. I felt my mouth fall every once in a while like a toothless duffer in a frown. Except I wasn't frowning. Not on purpose. Must have been ten at night when we finally made Ed's.

When I went to dismount, I lost my balance and collapsed. I struggled to shout, but my voice was a hollow whisper. Couldn't see much, either;

my eyelids weren't but slits. I must have passed out after that. When finally I awoke, I was blinded by a lantern.

"Jesus Christ!" yelled a man standing over me. I could barely see his face but I knew the voice regardless. It was Ed. "Get out here, Sax! It's Ben Holcomb and he's bad hurt!"

Next thing I remember is getting dragged through the door. Guess I'd gone out again. Somehow or other they got me in a bed.

"What the hell happened?" asked Ed as he felt my forehead. His hired hand with the bushy side chops was hunched over right beside him.

I did my best to answer only my mouth kept a-twitching. I tried to say "snake" but the word came out a garble. Ed was already holding up my swollen hand, looking at the wound.

"You're gonna be okay, Ben, just don't try to move." Then he stood up and spoke softly to a woman in the doorway. "I'm gonna hunt up some herbs. I'll be gone at least an hour. Soak his hand in Epsom salts and keep another pot a-boilin'."

———•—•———

It was three days before I managed to stay awake. "Howdy Ed," I called out when he came in from tending stock.

"Howdy back at ya, Lazarus! Ya come back from the dead!"

"I reckon."

"What in the hell?" he asked as he crouched beside me.

"Rattler got me," I answered as I fingered the poultice on my wound.

"I know that. But how is it you rode all the way to Pleasant Valley? Didn't it occur to you there's a war?"

"I didn't have nowheres to go."

As I looked around the room, I saw another bedstead. Whoever had slept on it hadn't bothered to fold the blankets. Right above it was an open window with a little breeze coming through. Every time it blew, I got a whiff of the outhouse.

"You wantin' some stew?" Ed asked. "Ain't had nothin' but broth since ya landed in bed."

"Ain't hungry. But thank you."

Then I heard someone else open the door and walk in. It was a big-boned man with a thick mustache and a tinge of gray. The feller with the bushy side chops came behind him. They were both wearing their dusty work clothes. "How's our boy?" asked the big one.

"Doin' better," answered Ed. "This here is John Rhodes," he said in a low tone as he nodded at the big man. "Best friend I got now that I lost my brother John." Then he turned and glanced at Side Chops. "Sax, too, when he's sober."

"You lost your brother?" It occurred to me I knew.

"Let's not talk about it. You need to lay still."

Then I heard a third voice, a woman's. Sounded far away. "You boys wantin' supper?"

"That's my brother's widow, Mary Ann," said Ed. "She's over there in the cookroom. We'll bring ya some vittles here shortly. You need to get down some grub, now that you're feelin' better."

"Musta had vinegar in your veins to survive a bite near the artery," laughed Sax. "That fool of a rattler's prob'ly still spittin' your sour blood."

"Glad you're back among the living, Ben," added Rhodes.

"Thank you, sir."

"I'm fixin' to get my supper, Ed," said Rhodes. "I'll see ya in the cookroom."

"Likewise," echoed Sax.

"I'll be there in a minute," answered Ed. I heard the sound of boots crossing the wooden porch. Then Ed stood and quietly shut the door.

"Now tell me how ya got here," he said, pulling up a chair.

Before I could answer, the door creaked open and the woman walked in. I saw she was pregnant.

"How is he?" she asked.

"Better, thank you," I answered in a weak voice. "I didn't expect to be meetin' any pretty ladies. I'd have combed my hair."

She smiled politely. "Mr. Rhodes told me to bring some stew for you." She walked up to the bed holding a steaming bowl on a pine plank. "Can you get it down?"

"Sure better try," answered Ed as he took hold of the plank and set it on my chest.

"Well, prop him up," exclaimed Mary Ann. "He can't eat lying flat on his back."

Ed handed the pine board back to her, then took two pillows from under the bed and carefully arranged them behind my head and shoulders. Then he put the board back on my lap. "That stew'll make ya strong," he said softly. "It's grizzly fricassee! Shot that cuss myself.

Warranted by Professor Tewksbury to cure every ailment known to man."

Mary Ann continued to study me like she was trying to see my fate. "I believe you're making progress," she finally said. "I'll be over in the cookroom if you need me. Just have Ed give a holler." Then she turned toward the door.

"I reckon I got plenty to tell," I said quietly to Ed.

"Shut up and eat," he answered with a smile.

I clumsily took the spoon and dipped it in the bowl. I took a few bites and realized I liked it. I polished it off quickly, then scraped the bottom to get the dregs.

"Now I know for sure you're getting better," said Ed.

"Then I better tell why I'm here."

"Yes sir, I'd like to hear."

I started with the part about Fish getting killed and my engagement to Calista. I wasn't keen to talk about abandoning Atkinson and riding with Hooper, though I knew I'd have to circle back and explain it lest he think I was spinning some gauzy deceit.

"Damn my melt!" exclaimed Ed when I got to talking about Calista. "Here I am an old bachelor and you're fixin' to get married. Jumped ahead of me in the line, ya slippery wriggling sprat."

"Ain't married yet."

"Don't worry yourself, we'll get you on your feet. Wouldn't do for you to die now that you've gone and stole a heart."

"No sir, it wouldn't do," I answered with a smile.

"Now tell me why you're here."

"Well there's somethin' I gotta say first."

"What is it?"

"Calista won't know what happened to me. You got to send word to her. Only you can't tell no one else."

"How am I gonna get word to her if I can't tell no one?"

"By sending a letter. Only not in the mail. You'd have to carry it."

"All the way to *Snowflake*?"

"I guess you can just put in the mail."

"Tell me your story, Ben. Don't wanna go sendin' no letter 'til I know what it is that brung ya."

I kept my eyes fixed on the ceiling. "I reckon I'll be straight. I'm on the lam."

"From Mormons?"

"No, from Lafayette."

"Stole his sweetheart, I reckon," he answered with a curling grin.

"I was there when he murdered them people in Holbrook. He's gonna arrest me for killing a Navajo, but it was him that done it."

Ed stared at me. "What murders in Holbrook?"

I rolled my head a little sideways like I was trying to get comfortable. Finally I sucked in a breath and continued. "Happened two days before I rode here and fell off my horse. Lafayette went over to the Blevins house in Holbrook and killed Landis Hooper and his little brother. Or at least I think he killed Hooper. Shot his guts out. Half the goddamn town gathered on the rail platform to see the show. Shot two other men that was with 'em, too. Hooper wasn't even carrying a gun. Not that I seen."

"Hosanna and praise the Lord!" he called out as he tilted up his head. "He was one of 'em that murdered John!"

I moved my eyes toward my chest, unsure what to say. "I don't think Hooper murdered your brother," I finally muttered. "He told me Tom Graham done that."

"I don't give a damn who pulled the goddamn trigger!" He shut his eyes tightly and drew in a deep breath. "Shot poor John in the back then crushed his head with a boulder. Jesus Christ, Ben. I heard you was ridin' with him."

I looked off toward the wall. "Wasn't nothin' but bluster from what I seen," I answered weakly.

"Then you underestimate his deviltry. Come to find out them murdering Grahams sent him round makin' everyone swear they'd pay a bounty on our scalps. Fifty dollars a head."

I swallowed hard and turned to the wall again. "I'm sorry for your brother," I said softly. "I didn't know none a that. I just rode with Hooper by accident. He told me he'd show me the cutoff to Payson." I felt my stomach turn into a square knot.

"I'm sorry, too. Sorry I didn't kill him when I caught sight of him back in Globe." He bowed his head toward the floor and got quiet. Then he rose from his chair and strode to a cupboard. He came back with a cup and pitcher. He poured the cup full, then handed it to me carefully. "Drink it down."

I swallowed it slowly, then wiped my chin with my good arm. After I felt my composure returning, I told him about how Hooper and me had run into a party of Navajos on our ride to the Rim.

"So you goddamn saved McGowan and Houck," he said as he adjusted the pillow behind my head. "Sounds to me like McGowan owes you."

"He does. But them Navajos came with an Indian agent. They were some kind of posse. The agent brought charges against Lafayette and his deputy for horse thieving and murder."

He looked at me skeptically. "Lafayette was stealin' horses?"

I gazed at the ceiling. "I really don't know who was stealing. Maybe they both were. Hooper and me just tried to help two white men fight off some Navajos."

"I don't follow. How is it that Lafayette is comin' for ya?"

"Because he don't want to stand trial for murder and horse theft! He's saying me and Hooper killed that Navajo. And Hooper made it worse by bragging we did it. Only we didn't. Lafayette did it. With his rifle. We just had six-guns and we were a long ways away."

He held my gaze for a time like he was trying to see inside me. "I seen you came in on an Atkinson horse."

I felt my heart jump. "Luett gave him to me," I explained. "Not outright, I mean, but on the promise I wouldn't drink with the colonel." My voice shook as I told him about how I'd quit Atkinson after the lynchings. "Fish sent word to the colonel that he could fetch the horse back," I went on. "I'd take him back myself if I wasn't afraid they'd kill me."

"Judas Priest," he blurted, "if I didn't know you better I'd think you was one of the rustlers. They tell me you did your damnedest to talk 'em out of lynching those sons of bitches."

I fingered my poultice as I looked out the window. "Just tryin' to be decent." I rolled my eyes toward the wall again and studied a knot in the pine. "I wouldn't have gone but for Luett. She wanted me to talk him out of it."

Neither of us spoke for a time. I sagged down into the bed and shut my eyes tightly. I finally heard him sigh. "Jesus Christ A'mighty. You sure got a nose for trouble, Ben. Alright. I'll hide ya, goddamn it. I'll do it. But for now, get your rest. When you're back on your feet, I'll get it worked out."

"But you got to get word to Calista."

"You mean send a letter?"

"That's all you can do, ain't it?"

"Yeah. But if it gets opened on the way, Lafayette's gonna know right where you're at."

"It don't need to say where I'm at. Just that I'm hidin' 'til things get calmed down."

He shook his head again as he stared at me. "You're wantin' me to write it?"

"I'll write it myself if you'll give me a piece of paper. I ain't snakebit on my right hand."

He paused and looked around the room. "All right," he said at last. "I'll figure a way to get it to her without it goin' through the mail. Won't be quick, but I'll see that someone drops it off with her. Tell her she can write you back care of the man that delivers it." He gazed at me like he was thinking it over. "Might write her myself and send that one, too."

I squinched my face in confusion. "Why would you write her, too?"

"Figure I'll slip my picture in an envelope and make a proposal," he said with a wry smile. "I'll tell her you weren't no good anyway, ridin' with damn Landis Hooper."

20.

I'll never say Ed Tewksbury was a bad man, though he wasn't always a good one. Thirty-odd years after I found myself in his cabin, I puzzle over why he protected me. He could as easily have put a bullet in me to put me out of misery. That or turned me in. I guess he could see I was just a windblown kid who didn't know enough to steer from trouble.

I was in his debt from the time he saved me, only it wasn't the debt that had me bound. There was something about Ed Tewksbury that made you love him. Something that gives a man the glow of nobility as he stands in the daylight but casts a shadow to match his height.

He didn't have the colonel's wry humor or Hooper's mischief, though he wasn't exactly sodden serious. He had a teasing streak that he used to keep his friends in line, only he never made you small. I never did see him treat a man poorly. He was as decent to the drunks in Globe as he was to family.

If he'd ever taken to rustling like the colonel told me, he'd done it because he was fighting a war. He wasn't mean-spirited or lacking morals. There were men who wanted to drive the half-breeds out of the valley, only Ed turned the tables and gave them hell. He made half the white men in the valley into his allies, too, on account of he protected their stock.

If you dealt fair with him, Ed dealt fair with you. Only it was more than that. If he took a liking to you, he was your champion. He didn't speak pretty or talk principles or make courtly bows to handsome damsels. And yet he made you feel like you were riding with some long ago cavalier with a cocked hat and billowing plume.

If nobility is a saving grace, Ed surely found his way to cowboy paradise. That or it cursed him to Hades where he flits blind as a moth in the glow of flame. The men that Ed placed in his knightly circle became law in the valley, but it was a different man that became sovereign king. The colonel had figured how to maneuver Ed, and it weren't in the cause of decency. If Ed had it in him to wage rebellion, he'd have saved himself half his agonies.

Except Ed wasn't no Benjamin Holcomb. He was loyal to the noble core.

———•———

It took me a few days to get well enough to help with the house chores. About a week after that, I was back on the range. Ed had me ride out with Sax every day, moving cattle here and there and doctoring the sick ones. We hammered together a passable line shack in one of the draws. We'd take refuge in it during the twilight hours, then cook our biscuits before the dawn. Ed thought it would be a good place to hide 'til Lafayette got tired of looking.

We were just about to head out one day when here came Ed, trotting up to us with a wicked grin. "Howdy, Sax. Howdy, Ben," he called out. "Thought I'd ride over and tell the news. Blasted war's finally over."

"Jesus Christ," Sax replied. "If you weren't wearing that ten-dollar smile I'd swear you was in a fever."

"Jeremy Houck and some other fellers came in with a posse. Ambushed John Graham, that haughty Scotsman. He come ridin' in to Perkins's store yesterday with one of Hooper's brothers and they shot 'em off their horses. I hear half a dozen other fellers took fright and hightailed it. Ain't but goddamn Tom Graham left, only now that he's got him a woman, he's sworn off of fighting."

"Killed John goddamn Graham?" asked Sax excitedly. "And Charlie Blevins to boot?"

"I believe that's the last of them blasted Blevinses unless their whorin' mother makes another."

Sax gave a whoop and threw his hat in the air, then put his pony on her heels like she was bucking. He rode around in figure eights and came back all a-smiling. "Praise the Lord! I reckon we can finally have that fandango you been blusterin' about. Thought I'd never live to see it!"

"We'll have us a little cowboy tournament and a side of beef and all the whiskey we can stomach," said Ed with a grin. "If you'll pull a bow across your fiddle we might can even dance."

"I'll fiddle a holy twister!" exclaimed Sax as he swung around on his saddle pretending he was playing.

"Can't go to no fandango," I answered in a weary voice. "Not with Lafayette after me."

"Reckon you're right," apologized Ed. "But we'll make sure ya get some whiskey. Sax can bring it up here if he ain't too hungover."

"I'll bring a bucket," replied Sax. "Might bring a woman, too, if I can rope one without her fussin'."

"Well before we do any of that, we've got some dirty business to attend," continued Ed.

"What business?" asked Sax as he shifted his weight on his saddle.

"Got to ride over to my brother John's old place and see what needs doin'. I ain't been there since they killed him. Can't bear to look at it. Only I gotta go over there so's I know what needs fixin'. Figure I oughta sell it."

"I been over there a couple times," replied Sax. "Afraid I'd see a haint but I seen somethin' more peculiar."

"What was that?"

"There was a little heifer in the cabin. Walked through the front door and made herself at home."

"How you reckon she come to do that?" I asked.

"Followin' salt. After they killed John and his partner, wasn't no one to keep the licks stocked. But they'd left a little trail a salt between the cabin and the lick. Reckon she followed it straight inside."

"That's the blam-jammedest bullshit since the costume ball in Globe," replied Ed.

"No sir. I seen it with my eyes."

"Was she sleeping in the bed?" I asked.

"Not after I come in! But she sure did stand her ground. Wouldn't budge an iota. Went to bawlin' when she seen me comin'. Tried to tie her and lead her out but she wasn't havin' none of it. I finally had to fire a round."

"Did she move?"

"Jumped right out a window. Come crashin' down and about broke her hip."

Ed grimaced and shook his head. "Was she one of ours?"

"Nope. Had an Atkinson brand. I'd a rode over and told him, only I was afraid he'd make a joke of it and forget the punch line."

"What's that supposed to mean?" asked Ed in a weary voice.

Sax arched his brows up. "He'd a prob'ly left me danglin'."

———•———

Sax kept up his joking as we rode along Cherry Creek. I guess he was trying to keep Ed's spirits from falling. At last we saw the cabin as we came around a bend. It was the usual dog-trot—cookroom on the right side, bedroom on the left, with a roofed-over breezeway joining them together. Only this one had framed windows in both rooms, one of them smashed open.

When we came up close we had to cover our noses. Smelled like a half a dozen rotting skunks all bloated up with maggots. We slowly got off our horses, then walked over to inspect the place. Ed was the first one through the door. "Son of a bitch!" he shouted. "It's that goddamn crazy heifer!"

Sax and me stayed behind him. When we looked through the doorway, we saw a dead calf with her legs splayed. She'd backed herself against a wall like she was trying to defend herself. I could make out an Atkinson brand. "Musta come back for salt," muttered Sax.

"Let's get her outta here," ordered Ed.

We dug a shallow pit, then roped her to one of the horses and dragged her into it. When we got her in the sunlight, we could see her wounds. Some lobo latched onto her nose and dragged her down, then ripped into her flanks and belly parts. We didn't try to bury her; she was too goddamn big. We just piled up some dead wood and lit her like a pyre. Thought it would stop her from stinking except that cursed smoke smelled about as bad.

Soon as we were done, Sax built a little campfire and boiled some coffee. We filled our tins, then we walked back inside.

"Look at that damn floor," said Ed. She'd left a stain big as a dinner plate where her blood had soaked the wood. "Sure makes this place haunty," he added as he glanced around the empty room. Someone had already hauled away the stove and furniture. "People will think that blood came from my brother. Him or his partner, Jacobs."

"They fell way yonder, didn't they?" asked Sax as he bent himself over and took a seat on the floor. Ed and I followed suit.

"Up the creek a ways," Ed answered in a low voice. "Some a them Graham men stood guard over 'em. Wouldn't even let the women bury 'em. Laid 'em out for the hogs to eat." He looked away as he spoke.

"Reckon that's behind us," I quietly put in.

"I sure hope so," said Sax as he took another swig of coffee. "I'm about tired to death of lookin' out for bushwhackers."

Ed stayed silent, like he was thinking of something else. "I'm glad you're both here," he said at last. He walked over to inspect the broken window, then came back and crouched beside us. "Reckon this is a good place to talk. Got a favor to ask. I need you two to do somethin' unusual. I got to fetch a letter at Perkins's store tomorrow morning. If it says what I think, I'll have to ride to Tempe. Then I'll have to hurry back so's I can make it to the shindig. I'll be signing off on a cattle deal."

"I don't follow you," I responded.

"Got to get to Tempe and back in forty-eight hours. That's pretty near a two-hundred-mile ride. Maybe more. Reckon I'll do it the way them Pony Express riders done it. But I'll need you two to help." He stood up when he'd finished talking, then sat back down cross-legged.

"You're wantin' us to station horses?"

"That's it. If you do this and it works out, I'm gonna do something for you, Ben. I got possessory rights to this cabin and the land that John claimed. I'll sign it over to you for a hundred calves with seven years to pay. That's about the best terms you're like to find. You'll have to take out a mortgage to start a herd, but you'll have right of preemption on your homestead. Ain't no one can claim it, not unless you fold."

I was about cross-eyed with surprise when it sunk in what he'd said. Calista and me were beholden to Hartman, at least for a couple months. That's when the lease ran out on Fish's farm. But that hardly mattered anyway, since I'd gone and run away. Lease or no lease, I'd need a place for Calista and me to live on.

After that ride to Holbrook with Landis Hooper, I'd got to wondering if I'd have a respite. I'd lurched hither and yon since I'd run from my father. God had finally smiled when he put me with Calista, then frowned and sent me lurching again. Only now God was smiling bigger. "Be a pleasure to help ya, Ed," I replied as I reached for more coffee.

"What's in it for me?" protested Sax.

"You ain't got no fiancé," answered Ed, arms crossed over his chest. "You don't need a place like Ben does. But I got something in mind for you, too. Gonna set aside some cattle. It's time you started a herd, Sax. You can keep 'em on my range 'til we work somethin' out. We'll figure a better arrangement later on. Just don't go losin' 'em in a spree."

Sax scoffed and looked at the floor. "Ain't fixin' to kill Tom Graham, is ya?"

Ed shook his head disgustedly. "Jesus Christ, Sax. It's a straight-up cattle deal. There's a feller in Tempe that wants me to bring him 1,500 head. We'd be cuttin' 'em from every little herd up here and payin' ten dollars for the choice ones. You two would be my top hands. It'd be the biggest drive since the prices crashed. There'd be money jinglin' in a hundred pockets."

"I don't see how he's any danger," Sax continued. "He wouldn't a moved to Tempe with his wife and baby if he'd wanted to keep the fight up."

"I've goddamn told you for the last time!" exclaimed Ed. "It's a cattle deal. I ain't gonna tell you again. Either you can believe me, or you can shut that prattling mouth."

"I'd station them horses for free," I said loudly. "You don't owe me nothin'. Hell's fire, it's me that owes you."

"Don't go gettin' between a man and his generosity," answered Ed. "Only thing is, I don't want you to tell no one. If someone asks where we were, just tell 'em we were huntin' strays. There's two or three men that won't want this to work out. I want your promise to keep mum 'til we organize the drive. You *comprende*?"

"Won't say a word, Ed, but can you do me another favor?"

"What's that, Ben?"

"I need to get another note to Calista. I never did hear nothin' after you sent that first one."

"I guess I should tell ya. I never did send it. Couldn't figure a way to get it to her without Lafayette sniffing it out."

"Never sent it?"

"Nope. I'm sorry."

"Goddamn it to hell, Ed!"

———◦—◦———

The morning we begun our errand bloomed blue and cool like early spring. Ed, Sax, and me met up on the trail, then rode over to Perkins's store trailing a string of horses. Soon as we got inside, Ed gave a little whoop, then walked to the counter. "Reckon ya lost some customers here lately," he said in a wry voice. "Looks like their creditors finally caught 'em."

"Not apt to miss 'em," chirped Perkins as he wiped the counter.

"I hope you'll be celebrating at my hoopla," said Ed. "I know you're a teetotaler, but you can waltz with the females. Might be half a dozen if they know we'll be a-dancin'. Sax here is gonna break his fiddle out."

"Long as they don't mind getting their feet stepped on," said Perkins with a smile.

Ed smiled back, then spoke in a hushed tone as he handed him an envelope addressed to Calista. "She'll have it in a week," Perkins called out to me. "I'll make sure it's confidential."

I grinned and nodded, then felt my eyes fill with water. I guess it sounds ridiculous, but I kept picturing her opening it with tearful joy. I'd wrote it pretty as I could. Told her how I'd been forced to run on account of a crime I'd had nothing to do with, and how God had finally smiled again and made amends. I'd poured it on a trifle thick, my mind being glazed with honey. I wiped my sleeve across my eyes as I watched him carry it to his desk and stick it in a slot marked "outbound." Then I saw him pull out a different envelope and march it over to Ed. Only Ed didn't open it. Just uttered a weary thanks.

"Care to buy supplies?" Perkins asked as he walked behind the counter. "Beans? Flour? Pint of laudanum?"

"Hell's fire, Perkins," called out Ed. "I get that stuff from George Heard same as you do. His mark-up's high enough."

"I can save you some rides to Globe."

Ed gave a friendly snort as he fitted on his hat. "You mean you can truck in them pretty fat whores to go with your beans?" He paused for second, grinning. "I'll be doin' plenty a business with ya, Charlie. But right now us cowboys got to ride the range. Gotta collect them half-wild cattle for the fall drive to Holbrook." He tipped his hat, then headed for the door.

Once we were outside, Ed walked to his horse and ripped the envelope open. He glanced at the note inside, then wadded it up and thrust into his saddle bags. "It's a go," he called back in a voice dark as death.

———•———

Sending the letter had put my mind at ease. I knew it wouldn't be a Sunday ride, but I figured I could go forever. A couple cotton balls loafed across the blue, their shadows floating on the sweeping pastures. If my mother had read the clouds, she'd have seen an invitation to a splendrous journey. Only the farther we traveled, the more the worrying filled my head again.

We kept the horses at a trot until thc trail headed up the Sierra Ancha. Ed reined up at the first steep climb and turned himself to face us. "We'll cross over to Gun Creek then follow it down to where it flows into the Tonto. You and me'll leave Sax at the confluence, Ben, then head toward Reno Mountain. I got a spot picked out near Sugarloaf where I'll leave you and the horses."

"Don't have to shout," said Sax as he took off his hat and fanned himself. It was already getting hot. Then he reached down and plucked a bottle of whiskey from his saddlebags. He grinned big as he held it out. Then he popped off the cork and passed it to Ed.

"Put that stuff away," Ed scolded after he'd taken a long swig and handed me the bottle. "Got a hell of a ride ahead of us."

"Yes sir, boss!" said Sax as he watched me take a couple sips. Soon as I handed it back, he tilted up the bottle and swallowed greedily. "Now that's all I'm gonna have," he added as he corked it up and thrust it in his bag. "At least 'til tonight."

Ed went on ahead while Sax took off his gun belt, then folded it into his saddlebag. "Feels like a goddamn anvil," he cursed. I watched him fasten the buckle, then I stripped off my own gun belt and tucked it in my bags. Then we goaded our horses into a lope to catch up with Ed.

After that we were silent. Just lost in our laments. My mind wandered to Calista again, following its customary path. She was probably gathering eggs, I got to thinking, or hanging wash. Or sitting on the Jameses' porch, searching the desert in hopes she'd glimpse me. Then I went to studying Ed as he rode out ahead. He'd put his shirt in his saddlebags. His dirty striped vest hung over a back bare as a chicken carcass. Reckon he was keeping cool but it made him look like a bally renegade.

A goddamn cattle deal, I thought bitterly. *Horseshit. Sax was right. He's ridin' off to kill a Graham.* I began to drop back a little, half thinking I'd break for Snowflake. When he looked over his shoulder and saw me lagging, he turned his horse and cantered over, trailing his second horse behind him.

"You think this is some pleasure ride?" he shouted. "I need you to keep up with us, goddamn it. I don't have time to fool around."

I pushed my horse into a trot as I followed him. Then I went to reproaching myself. He might not be a saint, but I'd never known him to dissemble. I went back and forth like that—damning Ed and second guessing—'til at last we saw the thread of green that snaked along Tonto Creek. We rode in among some cottonwoods and dismounted. Ed told us to pull the saddles off our mounts and turn them loose to drink.

After we'd fed them from our grain bags, I grabbed my saddle to throw it atop Percival. "Not just yet," said Ed, "we'll take a little rest." He pulled out his pocket watch and glanced at it. "We'll head out in fifteen minutes. Sax can stay here with the spent ones." He walked to the creek and dipped his hat in. After he'd filled the brim, he slung it over his head again, letting the water run onto his shoulders. Then he headed into the trees to do his business.

No sooner had Ed disappeared than Sax pulled out his whiskey bottle. "If you're wantin' a goddamn drink," I scolded, "just walk over and get some creek water." I stepped over and grabbed the bottle from him, then tucked it in my saddlebags. He didn't protest. Just marched to the creek and peeled his boots off. Next thing I knew, he'd walked into a pool and gone to splashing.

"Get the hell out of there!" blurted Ed as he came back from the trees. "We didn't goddamn come here to go swimming in the creek!"

"Ben told me to get a drink," Sax said dryly. He dipped his face down into the water, then turned up and spat a stream.

"Goddamn you!" Ed exclaimed as he backed away a couple steps.

"You been crosser than bearcat hell," whined Sax as he ducked again. "Oughta jump in the creek and cool yourself." What happened next seems strange even now. They were like soldiers before a battle, I reckoned, playing pranks to raise their spirits. Only it took a different turn.

Ed threw his hat on the ground then stripped off his belt and pants. Half a second later he jumped in and tackled Sax. I thought he was gonna give Sax a whipping 'til he came bobbing up like a grinning catfish. "Grab him and throw him in!" exclaimed Ed.

"You're slow as mud turtles!" I pulled off my boots and stockings then flopped in right beside them. Only soon as I was in the water, I felt Sax's hands on my back. He pushed my face down hard against the gravel, then put a knee between my shoulders. I thought it was only horseplay only he kept his hold 'til I was desperate. Finally he pulled me up by my hair.

"Jesus Christ," I gasped. "What the hell was that for?"

"Did you goddamn tell Graham who killed that bastard Mott?!"

I kept gasping and coughing water out.

"You goddamn heard me! You cursed goddamn spy! You sent him a letter with all the names, goddamn it!"

"I didn't send no goddamn names!" I sputtered. "I don't even know 'em!"

Sax grabbed my hair again and shoved me down to the gravel. I shook my head trying to free myself and started scrabbling with my legs. I finally managed to get loose of him then lurched out of the water and lay a fist into his nose.

By then Ed was on the bank with his six-gun in his hand. He raised it up and pointed it, then fired over our heads. "Lay off him, Sax!" he shouted. "Goddamn it, I told you he didn't have nothin' to do with it."

Sax stood there with his nose bloodied, then waded back over to the bank.

"Come on out, Ben," Ed said quietly. "Sax ain't gonna do nothin'."

I sloshed onto the bank with my clothes sopping. I had blood running from an eyebrow where the rocks had cut.

"Keep my horse in the shade here," Ed called out to Sax. "Hobble her out and keep a watch on her. Give her all the oats she wants and keep her near the water. I want her fresh when I get back tomorrow. Don't let her wander. If she ain't here when I need her, I'll flay you alive. Now go over and tell Ben you're a sorry son of a bitch."

Sax finished wringing his shirt out. He put it on without buttoning it, then walked over with his head stooped. "I guess I'm a damn fool," he said quietly.

"Now let's get a-movin'," said Ed.

"Workin' on it," I responded as I saddled up Percival.

———◆———

Ed put his horse in a trot and headed toward Reno Mountain. After we'd got out of sight of Sax, he stopped and turned. I felt my heart race as I drew up to him. I was scared as a hunted rabbit.

"Come up close," called out Ed as he saw me rein up twenty yards behind him. I urged Percival into a slow walk 'til we came up beside his stirrup. Then he reached an arm over and grabbed my shoulder. "If he'd pushed you down again back there, I swear to God I'd have shot him. But I'm askin' you to forget it. You hear me? Don't try to get even with him. Just leave it alone. He's riding around half-cocked on account of the fix we're in. I'll see to it he don't go off again. But I don't want you to start nothin'." He looked me with his brows furrowed. "Do you hear me or are ya deaf?"

I nodded and looked away. "What in the goddamn hell?" I muttered.

His horse bent her neck to glance at me then started off toward the mountain. Ed pulled the reins to stop her then jerked her back around. "Goddamn Atkinson put him up to it. Someone told him you'd come riding in here atop one of Luett's horses. He tracked down Sax and poured him whiskey until he blabbed I was hidin' you." He tugged the reins again to keep his mount still. "Atkinson don't care any about the horse. Luett told him she gave him to you. Only he's somehow got the idea that you gave Graham the names of his vigilantes."

I felt my face turn ashy.

"I know what you're thinkin', Ben. Atkinson's told Lafayette where you're hidin' and he'll be marchin' down to take you. Only that ain't gonna happen. When I say a man's my friend, then damn sure no one better come for him. Not if they wanna live." He reached his arm out for a handshake, then clapped me on the shoulder again. "I imagine ol' Sax will have some time today for reflection. By the time we get back there, it'll all be okay. Just don't try anything on him. I won't tolerate my men fighting."

I nodded again and swallowed a lump back. "I hear ya."

We put the horses into a trot and headed up the slope of Reno. I figured we'd stop for supper on the far side, only Ed kept a-going. We headed right into the setting sun as we came down into Sunflower Valley. Then we followed a desert creek as the purple evening turned to blackness. A little quarter moon crossed in front of us, turning the saguaros into looming shadows. He finally stopped and pointed as we came out into bouldered foothills. "That's Sugarloaf," said Ed. Just off to the north I could make out the silhouette of a desert mesa.

He threw a leg over his horse and stepped to the ground, then put the saddle on his fresh one. I dismounted right behind him, then turned Percival loose to drink. He walked straight over to the cobbled creek bed and put his nose into a stagnant puddle.

"Wait here 'til noon," called out Ed. "If for some reason I don't show by then, you go back and fetch Sax, then ride to the ranch. Tell Mary Ann I might be gone a few days more than expected. You hear me?"

"A few days? I thought this was a cattle deal." I noticed his voice sounded funny.

"It sure as hell is, Ben," he chuckled. "It's a goddamn big one. I'm pretty sure I'll be back by noon tomorrow. If I ain't, I want you to get word to Mary Ann that I've been delayed. Pronto. Don't take any detours."

I saw him dip a little to the side as he trotted off, then pull on the reins. His horse turned so fast he almost fell. He'd been quietly tippling, I realized, though he'd forbidden Sax to have a drop.

By the time he'd disappeared, I was sprawled on the ground. Then I got back on my feet and hobbled out the horses. I took out a canteen and drank, then rested my back against the flank of a sycamore.

I dozed off a couple times but I couldn't stay asleep. Kept picturing Mr. Fish as he waved his pillowcase at Larson. I'd wake with a start, like I somehow had to help him. Then I pictured Calista a-staring at the Milky Way. "Sure as hell better be a cattle deal," I heard myself whisper. "If she gets wind I've helped kill a man, she'll dump me like rancid milk." Right then was when the fear came. *Goddamn it,* I thought. *He's gone to kill a Graham and I'll be hanged in the blasted bargain.*

It was pretty near noon when Ed came loping back. Only instead of the bay he'd rode out on, he was mounted on a frothy blue.

"You dodgy son of a bitch," I shouted as soon as he'd dismounted. "You went and killed Tom Graham and you lied to get me in on it."

He looked at me intently, then took off his scarf and wiped his face.

"You went and killed him, didn't you?"

"You think I had any goddamn choice?" he replied angrily. "If I hadn't a gone after him, he'd be up here pickin' us off from behind the boulders. Ten more men woulda died before it was over. Maybe you included."

"You told me it was a cattle deal. You wanted to get it done fast so's you could make it to your shindig. Now I'm a goddamn accessory!"

"Wasn't no cattle deal brung us here and you knew it full well!"

"No sir! I did not!"

"Well if you hadn't a goddamn asked, you'd a had your blasted alibi!"

21.

Two weeks later, Sax came trotting into camp at sunset. I glowered as he rode toward me. We'd finally got into a tangle while we were dredging out a stock pond. We'd fought like a couple stud bulls until I knocked him into a prickly pear. After I'd picked about hundred thorns out of him, we went back to our joking banter. But the surliness still came over me when I was wrung out from a day of work.

"Got some good news for ya, Ben," he called out without smiling. "I was just over at Perkins's store. He says they've dropped the charges about that Navajo killing. That horse stealin' thing got dropped, too. You're a free man. Don't have to hide no more. Ed got word to Lafayette that you's on our side and Lafayette changed his story. He's puttin' it out that it was Hooper's brother that was with him when they shot the Navajo. Lafayette says he owes you an apology for thinkin' it was you. I guess none of them Blevins boys are like to dispute him now that they're in the dirt."

At first I stood there dumbly. "You're sure of that?"

"Sure as my name's Sax," he said flatly as he dismounted and reached into his saddlebags.

"Hosanna and hallelujah!" I shouted as I jumped and kicked a foot out. "I'll be settin' a course for Snowflake before the sun shows its merry face!"

"Don't know if I'd do that," he said gravely as he handed me an envelope. It was the letter I'd sent Calista, unopened. Someone had scrawled "return to Perkins" on the front. "She went and married some rich Mormon feller down in Mesa City. Perkins seen the announcement in one of them Phoenix papers. Thought you might oughta see it yourself." He reached in his hip pocket and pulled out a folded-up piece of newspaper. "Reckon she thought you'd run off on her."

I took the newspaper with trembling hands and glanced over it, then handed it back. I had to look away to hide the tears.

"Might as well take a few days and ride down to Globe," he went on as he presented me a bottle. "Have you a good long bender and some fun with the women."

I threw the bottle on the ground then stalked off toward the trees. Reckon I'd known my share of shadows, but I'd never known the night. It was as though all I'd done, all my running and hiding and my attempts to be decent, were nothing but a line of tortures on the trail to a bitter hermit's cabin. The only future I could see was herding cattle and drinking whiskey and visiting the whores in Globe. I'd tried to keep the peace and stop the lynchings. Even tried to help Hooper, though I knew him for a snake. But God only smiled so he could trick me all the worse. I slammed my fists against a ponderosa until they were shredded into crimson pulps.

The next couple weeks wasn't nothing but a drunken blur. I stayed in the line shack like usual, but I wasn't much help to Sax. I'd get up in the morning like a dead man, then fill myself with booze. Then my luck changed. Only not for the better.

⸻·⸻

When Sax and me came trotting into camp one afternoon, we saw two deputies stepping out of our shack. "I'm Theo Burris," announced a stocky man with an ear missing, "and this is Deputy Jed Flowers. We come all the way up from Maricopa County to see you two gents. Maybe we can have some drinks. Get to know each other a little better."

"We don't have no whiskey," answered Sax.

"Don't have no whiskey?" said the one called Flowers. "They don't have no whiskey," he repeated blandly as he turned his face to Burris.

"No goddamn whiskey," said Burris. "What kinda line shack don't have no goddamn whiskey? Are you two a couple cowboys or are you a couple a short-haired old temperance women?"

"Ben drank it up," answered Sax as he nodded toward me. "Whatcha wanna ask us about?"

"Bout a killin', Pork Chops."

"What killin'?"

"We reckon you know what killin'."

"We don't know about no killin'."

"Hold on there, cowboy," said Burris as he rubbed his sweaty hair back. "We ain't sayin' you know nothin'." He smiled at his partner. "Let's just all march down to that little store over the hill. He can pour us all some whiskey while we play a game of cards."

"No sir," answered Sax. "Ain't got time for that. We're working men. We come in to get some provisions and then we got to get back on the range."

"That right?"

"Yes sir."

"Hard workers, are ya?"

"Yes sir."

"Glad to hear it. You'll do good at breakin' rocks."

"We'll go with you," I said, giving Sax a stern look.

The four of us rode about an hour until we came to Perkins's store. Flowers led the way inside. Perkins was putting a pinch of tobacco in his mouth when we came through the door.

"Mr. Perkins, can you bring us a bottle of whiskey and four glasses?" asked Flowers as he walked over to a little table. "Perkins and us are pretty good friends," he said to Sax and me. "We had a talk just this morning. In fact he was kind enough to give directions to that rat's nest you call a line shack." He looked over at Perkins and tipped his hat. "Much obliged for that, Perkins."

Perkins stared at the deputies with his brows all knitted up. Then he reached under the counter and pulled out a whiskey bottle.

"I reckon make it two bottles," added Burris, "just in case we get to celebratin'."

"You got any pork rinds?" asked Flowers. "Need some sustenance to go with my medicine."

"Howdy Ben. Howdy Sax," said Perkins quietly as he brought over a couple bottles. Then he went back to his counter and bent down for some glasses. After he'd wiped them with a rag, he set them in front of us.

"Drink up, boys," said Burris. Then he swiveled back toward Perkins. "Storekeep," he called out, "I reckon you oughta go over there in your back room and work on your bookkeeping. This here is a private conversation."

Perkins shook his head tiredly, then disappeared through the door. After he'd shut it tight, Burris poured Sax's glass full. He curled his lips in a grin as Sax gulped it down. He filled Sax's glass a second time, then reached over and filled mine.

"Slow down," I warned Sax.

After Burris poured whiskey for Flowers and himself, he set the bottle on the table.

"I know we promised a game of cards," said Flowers wryly, "only now I'm thinking of a different game. It starts kinda slow but it'll get fun before you know it. I'll start first and show you how to play. You boys ready?"

Sax and I didn't answer.

"I'll take that for a yes. Now here's my first gambit. According to what Perkins told us, you two showed up at the store with Mr. Ed Tewksbury on the mornin' of August 1. Is that right?"

"I don't recollect the days," I answered quietly.

"You ain't played this game before," answered Burris as he hunched forward, "so I'll give you a little help. The first of August would coincide exactly with when Mr. Tewksbury claims you and him went out to collect his strays. He's already on his way to Phoenix for a pleasant stay in the county jail." He gave me a wink, then settled back in his chair.

"'Salutary,'" mused Flowers as he lifted his brows, "ain't that the word they use? That desert air is salutary. Just the thing for a man in a lot of trouble. Keeps his lungs healthy 'til his execution."

Sax glanced over at me, then turned up his whiskey glass. "I reckon you're right," he said. "August the first. We came in here to the store that morning before we went out after strays. I saw the date on Perkins's calendar."

"And you're a pair of bloody liars. Is that right?"

"No sir," said Sax before downing his whiskey. "We were out there a couple days, then we drove 'em over to Cherry Creek."

"Have another drink, Pork Chops," said Flowers as he poured another round into Sax's glass. "Might improve your memory." He set the bottle down carefully, then took a deep breath. "I'll just be straight with ya. I think you two are bluffin' us. That might be to your advantage in a game of poker, but this game is different. So here's my next gambit. We just happen to be apprised that a certain half-breed feller that employs you rode straight into Tempe at the dawn of August 2. Snatched a drink at a bar then went off somewhere and hooked up with another feller. John Rhodes is his name. I guess he's a breed, too. I ain't sure. They being best friends, you'd a thought they'd gone to gabbin'. Only that ain't what they done. They hid themselves on a street corner 'til Mr. Thomas

Graham came driving by in his grain wagon. Then they rode up right behind and shot him in the goddamn neck. My point bein', we know you boys wasn't chasing strays with Tewksbury unless he floated down there like a turkey vulture."

"Mr. Tewksbury got separated," said Sax.

Flowers shook his head. "We don't have an honest man between ya. Care for another, Pork Chops?"

Sax glanced at me nervously. "Yes sir, believe I will." Sax turned up his glass and swallowed the dregs, then held it out to Flowers.

"No reason we can't be sociable," continued Flowers as he filled Sax's glass. "How about you, Ben? Have another?"

"Guess one more won't hurt."

Flowers poured the last thread from the first bottle, then pulled the cork on the second one. "Now ordinarily," he continued, "one of you would make your gambit, and then one of us would follow, and so on and so on, 'til someone finally wins. Only here's a rule you might not be familiar with. If a man stays mum after we fill his whiskey glass, he loses his turn. Which means it's my turn to go again. I hope you two don't mind. Here's my play. Unless this booze loosens your tongues pretty quick, we're gonna take you down to Phoenix. Stick you in the county jail 'til we can try you for conspiracy."

"Take another drink, Pork Chops," cut in Burris. "It'll help ya tell the truth. We got statements from eye witnesses, so I'd advise you not to fib. If ya do, though, that's alright. Might can dance us an Irish jig when they drop you through the trap door. We'll ask 'em not to tie no string around your legs so's you can kick up your heels good."

"I ain't much of a dancer," replied Sax. He picked up his drink and slugged it down. "Reckon I could stand another."

Burris quickly poured Sax another whiskey, then refilled his own glass along with Flowers's.

"Drink up and enjoy, Pork Chops," said Burris, "'cause even if they don't hang ya, they sure won't be givin' ya no booze at the Yuma pen. Likely get a good taste of your sweat most days, but not a single drop of booze."

Sax gave me a quick glance then turned back to Burris. "How you gonna put me in the pen for somethin' I didn't know I was doin'?"

"I believe you're catchin' on!" answered Flowers. "Just needed a little tutoring! Now what is it you didn't know you was doin', Sax? We'll start

with that. And then you can tell us why you didn't know you was doin'
it. Might be we can save your stinking ass if you can see your way to
helping us."

There was a long silence as Sax stared at the table. I stayed completely
mum, arms clasped across my chest. I hadn't touched the last drink they'd
poured. "Didn't know we was helpin' Mr. Tewksbury shoot Graham,"
Sax finally mumbled.

"Didn't know, did ya?" bellowed Burris, slamming his glass on the
table. "Then pray go ahead and tell us how it is ya didn't know!"

"All we knew was what Mr. Tewksbury said."

"And what the hell did Mr. Tewksbury say?"

"Just that he wanted us to station some horses between here and
Tempe. Said he needed to get down there for a big cattle deal, then get
back to Pleasant Valley in time for a shindig he'd been plannin'."

Flowers leaned forward and scowled. "Just some damn cattle deal,
and he needed to get down and back in forty-eight hours? And you had
no idea?"

"We all figured Graham was harmless since he'd moved down to
Tempe and commenced to farmin'. Sure didn't think Ed was gonna kill
him."

Flowers asked Sax to repeat what he'd said, then started scrawling
on a piece of parchment. "What's your full name?" said Flowers as he
finished writing.

"Sax Benton."

"That's your Christian name?"

"Saxton. Saxton Benton. They call me Sax."

"No middle name?"

"Nope."

"It ain't Pork Chops?"

"Nope."

"Alright, Saxton Benton. This is your statement. Read it and sign,
and we'll be done with ya. At least 'til trial."

"I can't read."

"The hell you can't!"

"He can't," I cut in. "Can't even write his name."

"Then he can make his mark." Burris read the statement aloud, then
handed it to Sax along with a pencil. Sax drew an S with a circle around
it. It was the brand he'd been planning to use when he started his herd.

Burris took it back and wrote "Saxton Benton, His Mark" under the S. Then he scrawled another copy and pushed it over to me. "Now you sign it, too. I expect you'll be telling us the same goddamn thing."

"Not signin' nothin'," I mumbled. Just then Sax laid his head down. Hadn't so much as slurred a word before he passed out like a dead man.

Burris gave a snort, then turned back to me and winked again. "It don't matter. We got what we come for. Just one last word of advice. If you lie up there on the witness stand, we'll be swingin' you with Mr. Tewksbury."

22.

They scheduled the trial for late October. Sax and me rode down to Tempe following the same route Ed took when he'd gone to kill Graham. Only we didn't station horses. We picked our way through the desert until we came out to the Verde, then followed it a couple miles where it dumps into the Salt. Kept just far enough from the riverbed to stay clear of the sand bogs and tree thickets.

We finally came to a wide place where we figured we could cross. That old Salt River don't usually come up higher than a horse's belly. Only now it was different. One of those big Pacific storms had come through, dumping rain in all the mountains. The horses were treading water almost as soon as we plunged. Sax finally got across after floating fifty or sixty yards downstream, but I wasn't so lucky. I had to jump off Percival when the current took him sideways. I flailed 'til I come near to drowning before I felt my boots hitting the gravel. I did a walk-swim into waist-deep water, then slogged to the bank. When I got back on Percival, Sax was laughing his head off.

"Well hell's bells if it ain't Ben Holcomb," he called out. "Thought an ol' toad-frog had stole your boots."

After he'd stopped his guffaws, we steered south toward the irrigation canals. It was just getting evening when we reached the green fields at the edge of town.

"You know any cheap hotels?" I asked.

"There's a flat stretch by the river with some big mesquite trees on the bank. With all this blue sky and cool weather, we can spread our soogans and shoot the bull."

"I got no bull to shoot."

Sax shook his head and grimaced. "They've got us in a hell of a pickle."

I nodded and spat. I kept picturing the piece of paper someone had tacked to the door of the line shack. We'd seen it fluttering in the breeze as we'd come back with a load of firewood. "Tell them you were hunting strays," it said, scrawled out in fat smudges like it was painted with a bloody fingertip. On the backside was a list of places with times and dates. Line corrals. Creeks. This hill, that hill. A couple cabins. Whoever wrote it wanted us to get our lies straight.

"Let's get settled in and I'll set ya up with some elixir," said Sax. "May as well have some fun."

"If we show up drunk tomorrow, they'll jail us for contempt."

He took his hat off and scratched his scalp, then turned back to me with a smile. "You don't reckon drink makes a man smarter?"

I turned my face down and spat again. "I don't think so."

"Seems like every time I have a bender, I see the world for what it is."

"Meaning what?"

"Well mostly dirt. And like as not some rocks in it."

When we got into town, we rode past Hayden's Flour Mills, then turned toward the river. The road dead-ended in a field of caliche that slanted down to roiling water. Smack in the middle sat some scraggly fellers playing a card game. They'd laid out their soogans by a clump of mesquite trees. A little farther was where the ferry crossed. It was a big square of a boat, big enough to hold a wagon. I watched it bob in the current while the crewmen smoked their quirlies.

"Think I'll take that ferry over to Phoenix when this trial's over," said Sax. "Got saloons on every street stocked with rye and pretty whores."

"And what'll you use for money?"

"Might hit ya for a loan."

"And I might hit your nose again."

Sax stopped his horse and turned to me. "And you might taste some soil, too. We got enough troubles, Ben. Ease off, cowboy."

When we reached the edge of the field we tied our horses to a Palo Verde and unpacked our blankets. After we'd finished, I walked up to the ferry.

"You fellers got a bucket I could borrow to water my horses?" I asked. "River's runnin' high. Don't want to take chances."

A big man wearing a striped shirt and baggy work pants held up his bucket and yelled. "We got one, but it ain't for loaning. Take your horses a quarter mile downstream. Let 'em wade. It's a little deep, but I reckon they can swim."

"Thanks for nothing."

"Anytime. By the way, you need a shave."

"Go to hell."

"Go to hell yourself."

I went ahead and walked the horses downstream to a shallow place. Soon as I came trudging back, I saw Sax loitering with them puffed-up ferry captains. He sawed his fiddle in a flurry, then they passed around a bottle.

I trudged over to the river bank and sprawled myself in my soogans. Figured I'd rather go to sleep with the rushing waters than listen to his blasted fiddle waltzes.

I thought the river would sooth my worries, but I kept tossing like a gasping fish. Wasn't 'til the sky was pink that I drifted into sleep. When finally I awoke, Sax was nowhere in sight. I looked around for his horse's tracks then jumped up and followed them. After I saw he'd headed for the ferry, I turned to saddle up. Only when I reached into my vest pocket, I got another surprise. The river water had gummed my pocket watch.

I jumped on Percival in a hurry then loped off toward the livery. After I'd deposited him with the livery hand, I jogged to the courthouse across the street. "Apologies for my tardiness," I said to the deputy at the door. Damned if it wasn't Flowers. "Top of the morning, Flowers," I said boldly. "I don't think I got a chance to thank you for them drinks you bought."

"Where's your other half?"

"You'll likely find him in a Phoenix whorehouse. That or he's run for Mexico. I camped with him near the ferry, only he wasn't there when I got up this morning."

"Get in there and take your seat," he answered. He rushed to fetch another deputy, then the two of them made their exit.

No sooner had I found a chair than Ed's defense lawyer called a witness. After they swore him in, they went straight to the bally alibi. On the day Graham was murdered, the man claimed, he'd seen Ed hunting strays. Said Ed had stopped at his cabin on the north side of the Sierra Anchas. Then two more witnesses took the stand and said almost the same thing. If I got up and told the truth, I'd be against every man in Pleasant Valley.

After Ed's defense witnesses had their say, the prosecutor called his own. I kept readjusting myself in my chair as I waited to hear my name. After a couple hours of testimony, the defense lawyer got up again. "If the prosecution is finished with its witnesses, Your Honor," he called out, "I'd like to bring Ed Tewksbury to the stand."

"Are you finished, Mr. Hereford?" asked the judge.

"For the time being," answered the prosecutor. "I have no objection to the defense's request."

Ed rose slowly and glanced around. He looked like a swaybacked broomtail all hunched up and shaggy headed. A couple months in the hoosegow had taken away his swagger.

Off to my right I heard someone sobbing. When I turned my head I saw a blonde woman in black damask. She sniffled behind a mourning veil as she fidgeted with a silken purse. It occurred to me she was Tom Graham's widow. Every time I'd glance at her, my heart sank with leaden guilt. Whatever sins they laid to Graham, not a single speck was her fault.

I reckon that's when it finally hit me. I'd been so torn up about losing Calista that I'd thought the world was all against me. Told myself I was entirely innocent, but all along it was a blasted lie. Ed was right. I'd known what we were doing. Knew it from when he'd asked. I'd crossed over into bally darkness like some wolf shadow on a deer's scent. Any man who'd make a widow didn't deserve to have a wife.

Just then the judge started speaking.

"Before you begin, Mr. Tewksbury, let me remind you that the charges against you are deadly serious. In the interest of proving your innocence, you and your lawyers have decided you'll testify. But please understand that, if you do, the prosecution has the right to cross-examine."

"Yes, Your Honor, I understand," said Ed.

"So be it."

Then a tall man with a small, bald head walked up to the stand carrying some papers. It was Mr. Baker, Ed's attorney. "Mr. Tewksbury," he began as he looked at his notes, "where were you on August 1 of this year?"

"Roundin' up cattle in Pleasant Valley just like those fellers told you."

"And how do you know it was August 1 when you went out after cattle?"

"I keep a calendar. The deputies took it with them after they come for me."

"All right. That certainly comports with their testimony. And what about August 2? Where were you that day?"

"Still at it. Can't get all of 'em in a day, not in Pleasant Valley. Musta rode fifty miles altogether."

"Fifty miles? In one direction?"

"No. Went back and forth through a lotta little draws. It's rough country out there. We were separated most of the time. A couple of us would ride up on the hills and drive 'em down into the draws, and someone else would be down there waitin' to head 'em off. Every time we got a few, we'd run 'em out to our line corrals, then go back into the hills and repeat the whole rigmarole. Then we ran 'em all over to the big corral. We was fixin' to drive a herd to Holbrook and put 'em on the train 'til them deputies hauled me in."

"I see. And how long did that take, altogether? Rounding them up and putting them in your corral?"

"Stayed out two whole days and part of another, but we didn't get it done. Rounded up forty-six, but there was another whole bunch still out. Damn near impossible to get 'em in a go."

"So on August 1, August 2, and again on August 3, you and your hired hands, Mr. Benton and Mr. Holcomb, were rounding up strays in Pleasant Valley."

"No."

"What do you mean, no?" Baker looked surprised.

"A stray is an animal that crosses over to another man's range. These was mostly on our range. Some was strays and some wasn't."

"I see," answered Baker, his face suddenly relaxed. "Some were strays and some weren't. Now tell me something else, Mr. Tewksbury. Did you and your hired men station horses between Pleasant Valley and Tempe on August 1?"

"I just told you. Hell no we didn't. We were rounding up cattle."

"Well supposing you did station horses. Just supposing. How far is it from Pleasant Valley to Tempe?"

Ed stared out at the gallery then rubbed his hand across his forehead. "Hundred miles, I reckon. Or a little more. Maybe a 110. I make that trip once or twice a year. Just didn't do it in August."

Baker walked back to his desk and picked up a big book. He brought it to the judge, who looked it over briefly. "That's an atlas," said Baker. "It has a good map of Arizona, made by government surveyors. It shows the distance between Pleasant Valley and Tempe to be about eighty miles, as the crow flies, give or take a few miles in accord with where one situates the boundaries of Pleasant Valley. Of course if you're following a trail, the distance is farther. Probably a hundred miles, as Tewksbury suggests."

Baker paced back and forth in front of Ed, then walked over to the jury. "Now we've already heard expert testimony that a horse isn't likely to cover more than thirty miles a day on rough, mountainous ground. So one hundred miles, well, that would take at least three or four days to cover, and that's just one way. Of course, if a man could switch to a fresh mount every twenty or thirty miles, he'd make it faster. But not in a day. Especially not in the summer, when it's hotter than a skillet fire. And he certainly wouldn't make it there and back in forty-eight hours." Then he pivoted back to Ed. "You say you've made that trip in the past, Mr. Tewksbury? From Pleasant Valley to Tempe?"

"Yes sir, but not in August."

"I realize that. But you have made the trip. When was that?"

"Make it once or twice a year when I got business down here."

"And when were you last here."

"January, I reckon."

"And how long did it take you to make the ride?"

"Three days. And that's ridin' hard, with fresh horses. It's a two-horse deal. Ride one and trail the other, then switch 'em up when the one you're ridin' gets tired. If you're stringin' pack mules behind ya, add an extra day. I reckon you could do it on a single horse, if you wasn't in any hurry."

"Three days one way? With two horses?"

"Yes sir. Three days. Got to cross the Sierry Anchies, then you ride into the basin. Go another thirty miles 'til you hit Old Fort Reno. Then you go on up the pass and cross on the other side. Thread through the Mazatzals another dozen miles, then you're on flat ground to Mesa City. Might do it in two days if you're real fast, but I never have. Just makes your horses lame."

"Thank you, Mr. Tewksbury," said Baker. Then he turned back to the jury. "My client, Mr. Ed Tewksbury, has testified that on the morning of August 2, 1888, he was rounding up strays in Pleasant Valley. And that is just what he was doing. Three different witnesses have told us they saw Tewksbury on the day the murder was committed. Not to mention on the days before and after. Saw him in Pleasant Valley, not Tempe. Yet the prosecution insists that Tewksbury rode to Tempe on August 1 and got back to Pleasant Valley by August 3. Not a man in the world could make that ride. Not Apollo in his chariot! 'Tis impossible." Baker gave the prosecutor a sidelong glance, then finally took his seat.

All the while he talked, Graham's widow sobbed behind her veil. "Don't matter what lies he tells, Annie," rasped a lanky man seated next to her. "They'll hang him like a sorry coward."

It was the first I'd ever seen a man with a face like a torn-up battle flag. I felt a shiver come crawling over me when I realized who he was. Ed said his name was Charlie English, but he'd changed it to Dushay. He'd had his face flayed in a knife fight when he was quarreling for a Mexican girl. Only that wasn't his last quarrel. He'd laid out three of Daggs's sheepherders when he'd run across them on Naegelin Rim.

Just then the prosecutor put on his spectacles and held his notes up to his eyes. I could see his hands tremble. He stood up slowly as he kept reading, then walked over to Ed. I noticed he had a hitch in his step. His eyes locked on Ed as he began his questioning. Made him go over all the details of his whereabouts between August 1 and August 3. Ed repeated the answers from the letter they'd left for us. Potato Butte on the first; McFadden's place on the second; and so on. "You're certainly well versed in the particulars," the prosecutor said sarcastically. Then he stuffed his papers in his pocket. "No point beating around the bush, Tewksbury. I'll ask you straight out. Did you, or did you not, shoot Mr. Thomas Graham on August 2 of this year?"

"No sir, I did not."

"Well I know you're lying and I'll prove it momentarily." Then he turned back to the judge. "No more questions, Your Honor. Witness dismissed."

Baker shot straight up and called out to the judge. "I object to Mr. Hereford's statement that my client is lying. I wonder what he would answer if I asked him about that bordello near the mill? I believe I saw him coming out of there yesterday."

"You're out of order!" shouted the prosecutor. "And you know damn well I was there to take a deposition."

"Take a deposition?" yelled a man in back. "Hell, you didn't take nothin' 'cept your pleasure." At first there was a hush, then the courtroom echoed with laughter.

"Order!" shouted the judge. "I won't tolerate your disrespectful innuendo, Mr. Baker. Mr. Hereford, who's your next witness?"

"Your Honor, I need to confer with the deputy." The prosecutor walked back to his table and motioned to Deputy Flowers. Flowers jumped up and ran over to him. I guess they were talking about Sax's whereabouts. They whispered back and forth for a moment, then the prosecutor turned to the judge.

The prosecutor scratched his forehead and looked dumbfounded. He turned and looked out over the courtroom. Then he turned back to the judge. "Your Honor, my star witness doesn't seem to be present at the moment. In his stead I'd like to call Benjamin Holcomb."

I walked briskly to the witness box and placed my hand on the bailiff's Bible.

"Mr. Holcomb," began the prosecutor as he turned back towards me, "Deputy Flowers and Deputy Burris believe that on the days of August 1 to August 3 you placed horses between Pleasant Valley and Tempe to facilitate Mr. Tewksbury's murder of Thomas Graham. Is that correct?"

"I imagine that is what they believe."

"That's not what I mean and you know it. Now let's start again. Did you, or did you not, station horses for Ed Tewksbury on the days from August 1 to August 3."

I was quiet for a moment as I wrestled with my conscience. "No, sir, I did not. Mr. Benton and I were rounding up strays with Mr., uh, Tewksbury on the days you speak of." Damn if I hadn't faltered.

An angry buzz of voices came swelling from the gallery. From the corner of my eye I could see Dushay's torn face glaring at me, but I kept my focus on the prosecutor. The judge knocked his gavel and screeched. "Order! Order in this damn court! I'll throw out every one of you!"

"Mr. Holcomb," said the prosecutor, "you are sworn to tell the whole truth and nothing but the truth, and if you do not you'll go to jail. Do you understand me sir?"

"Yes sir."

"We have a statement signed by Mr. Saxton Benton saying that you and he did indeed station horses for Tewksbury on the dates in question. Deputies Flowers and Burris took down the statement and Benton signed his mark. Now, will you please tell the court whether that statement is true? And before you answer, I want you to consider the penalties for perjury. Not to mention conspiracy to murder."

"Yes sir. I was there when they took down Sax's statement. But the truth is we were drinking. Drank two whole bottles between the four of us. The deputies kept filling our glasses and tellin' us we'd hang if we didn't tell 'em what they wanted. Get Sax drunk enough and he's like to say anything. 'Specially if he's scared."

The prosecutor sniffed loudly and clenched his jaw. "I suppose I needn't bother going over your peregrinations on the days in question. No doubt you've memorized the script."

"Objection!" yelled Baker. "If the prosecution is going to make wild implications, he needs to show his evidence."

The judge's face was stoic. "Sustained."

The prosecutor wiped the back of his hand over his nose and walked to his table. He called Flowers over again and whispered with him. Then he turned and walked halfway to the judge. "Your Honor, I'd like to request a recess of two hours. Deputy Flowers informs me that we can make Mr. Benton available for testimony, but he'll need some time."

The judge frowned. "What precisely is the situation?"

Hereford coughed into his hand. "He's, uh, he's in the Maricopa County jail."

"In jail?"

"It appears he drank himself into a stupor. Deputy Flowers assures me that he can get him sober enough to testify."

"I'll not delay these proceedings for a common drunkard," answered the judge. "You've already introduced his written statement. Either call another witness or proceed to your closing argument."

The prosecutor stared at the judge a moment, then grabbed off his spectacles and looked at the jurors. "I hope it's clear to you that the witness is lying."

"There he goes again!" yelled Baker. "It's innuendo!"

"Mr. Hereford," said the judge, "either continue with this witness or give your closing statement. Let's get this over with."

The prosecutor shook his head bleakly. "I'll need a moment to think about things, Your Honor."

"Is the witnessed excused?" asked Baker sarcastically.

"He is," said the prosecutor as he walked back to confer with his assistant.

"What's your preference, Mr. Hereford?" asked the judge in an annoyed voice. "Do you have another witness or do you want to sum up with your closing statement?"

The prosecutor whispered again to his assistant, then cleared his throat loudly and looked toward the judge. "I'll proceed with my closing statement. We've already shown Mr. Tewksbury to be guilty and I'll trust the jury to find similarly." Then he walked up to the jury box. "Gentlemen, I'll freely admit that my key witness has failed to testify. Because he's drunk. Now why is he drunk? I've got a hypothesis. Because he's scared that if he testifies, the defendant will kill him!"

"Objection!" screeched Baker. "That inference has no evidentiary basis. It's a vile lie!"

"Sustained. You haven't proven Mr. Tewksbury guilty, Hereford, and you certainly haven't proven that he'll seek retribution."

"Alright, Your Honor. I withdraw that statement. Now, gentlemen of the jury, my key witness hasn't testified. We don't know precisely why he didn't show up here today, though there is speculation he is drunk. Be that as it may, the prosecution has produced reams of evidence. I leave it to you to judge who is lying and who isn't. Now let me recapitulate, if you'll be so kind."

Hereford put his weight on his right foot as he leaned down toward his notes. Then he folded them carefully and put them in his pocket. "First we heard what Tom Graham said on his death bed," he went on. "He lived just long enough to tell his wife and some others the names of those who killed him. He saw them pull the trigger. Felt the missile hit his throat. He couldn't talk after that but he could still draw his breath. A weaker man would have died of shock, but Mr. Graham was a man of determination. No, he couldn't talk. His voice box was destroyed. Yet he mustered the strength to whisper. And who did he say his killers were?" I could see the flash of his jaw muscles as he turned his face to Ed. "That man right there. Ed Tewksbury. He and his fellow man-slayer, John Rhodes."

He paused for a time as he poured some water into a glass and sipped. Then he nodded slightly as he looked back toward the jury. "But of course Mr. Graham was not the sole witness," he went on in a gravelly voice. "Two young women—sixteen years old, they are—have been brave enough to come forward. They were in a buggy on the morning of the murder when Tewksbury and Rhodes made their appearance. Both girls saw them fire. Got a good look at the murderers at the moment of their crime. And in case that's not enough, the prosecution has produced three other witnesses who testified that they saw a man fitting Tewksbury's description that same morning. Two men saw him in a bar just before the murder, where Tewksbury stole a drink. Another man saw him twenty minutes after the murder, riding at a fast clip eastward. That's five eye witnesses, gentlemen, not including Graham, who, sadly, cannot be here."

Hereford shook his head, then stared hard at Ed. "I don't need my star witness. Tewksbury is guilty! Guiltiest man I've ever tried!"

"Is that all?" asked the judge.

"Indeed. I should think it plenty."

"How about you, Mr. Baker? What do you have to say?"

Baker rose from his chair and walked slowly toward the jurors, his eyes on the floor. Then he straightened and looked at each of them. "I have a few words," he finally began. "The defendant, Ed Tewksbury, has a record of honesty. We produced half a dozen witnesses who vouch for his sterling character. Several said they saw him in or near Pleasant Valley on the day of the murder. And the day before. And the day after. We've established that Tewksbury wasn't anywhere near Tempe on the day of the killing. So why are we here? Why must we leave our homes and our labors and spend a day in a courtroom, hearing the territory spin a gauzy web of innuendo?"

Baker looked at the floor again and sighed. Then he lifted his head back up and started again. "Their whole case rests on the testimony of a few so-called 'witnesses.' First they say the victim whispered the names of his killers to those at his death bed. A victim shot through the voice box, lying near death, yet he whispers the names of his killers. And yet alas no one thought to write down his testimony and get witnesses to sign it. Strange, that."

He paused again and shook his head. "This, gentlemen, is a case of Graham's friends putting words into the mouth of a dead man. We all regret Graham's murder, of course, but convicting another man falsely would only compound the evil. That brings us to the two men who say they saw Mr. Tewksbury in a bar before the murder."

He gave a tight-lipped smile to the jury, then went on. "I have an admission. I've been in that bar! In fact I've been there at dawn, after a long night of palaver. Some of you have been there, too. You know as well as I do that it's dark as hell, especially before sunup. Hell, I've given 'em ten dollars in gold for a twenty-five-cent tab. Why? Well, because I couldn't see my money. Money in my hand! It would be impossible to identify anyone with certainty unless they're three feet away. But those two men who claim to have seen Tewksbury weren't three feet away. They were halfway across the room! They didn't see Tewksbury. They don't know who they saw. And as for the man who claims to have seen Mr. Tewksbury riding east after the murder, well, he took Tewksbury for someone light complected! With a chin beard! You can see for yourselves that Tewksbury is dark-skinned. He has no beard. Never has. So much for that witness."

Baker paced back and forth silently. He folded his arms across his chest, then unfolded them, then finally turned to the jury again. "Now come the two young ladies who claim they saw my client murder Mr. Graham. They do claim to have seen a dark-skinned man. That's true. They also say the murderer was wearing a dark hat pulled down over his eyebrows so as to obscure his face. Of course we asked them to describe the hat: What color was it? Black? Dark gray? Dark brown? Did it have a feather? A black band? A brown band? Did it have a big brim? A medium brim? Was it a Stetson? A sombrero? It wasn't a silk top hat, at least they're certain of that. As for the rest, they can't answer. Well, what horse was he riding? A dark brown horse? A black horse? A roan horse? The girls agree it was a bluish-gray horse. But the territory's other witnesses say the horse was brown. Or roan, maybe. Hell, if I call them up here again, they're apt tell me it was Pegasus!"

He walked in a little circle, then turned again to face the jurors. "This, gentlemen, is a case of misidentification. What the witnesses saw was a dark-skinned man in a hat, riding a horse. If that man was indeed the defendant, then he must be a lightning-change artist of great renown. He must have been accompanied by a herd of horses, all different; he must have been a traveling hat and clothing store; he must have carried a razor with which to shave himself, and must have been provided with a hair invigorator with which to suddenly induce a hirsute appendage. To the territory's witnesses, one dark-skinned man in a hat is the same as another. I ask you all not to make the same mistake. Ed Tewksbury is not guilty!"

A couple of jurors shifted in their seats while a third one fired a quirly.

Baker walked over and put his hand on Ed's shoulder, then sat down next to him.

"So spoken," said the judge, "and I thank you both for being brief. I will now read instructions to the jury regarding findings of first and second degree murder, then leave them to decide. We'll reconvene at four o'clock. If the jury has no verdict, we'll meet again at ten tomorrow."

———•———

After the courtroom had emptied I saw a bald man in the gallery. He sat there staring at me, arms folded across his chest. I'll be damned if it wasn't George. He'd come down for the legislature after they'd moved the capital to Phoenix. He set his lips into a grimace as I walked over to greet him.

"I'll be goddamned," I said quietly as I reached out my hand.

"You're not off the hook, Ben," he answered as he shook my hand weakly. "Let's go outside."

He hurried out the door with me following a step behind. I thought he'd stop at one of the wooden benches but he walked to the edge of town. "This will do," he finally said as he found some shade behind an adobe wall. He kept glancing around like he was afraid someone would hear us. "What'd he do, pay you off?" he asked angrily. "Or did you do it out of friendship?"

I was too taken aback to answer.

"You don't even know what you did, do you?"

"I need a beer, if you'll excuse me," I muttered as I turned to go. I knew he wouldn't follow.

"You'll stay right here and listen. Do you even know what this was about? Hell no, you don't know. You don't know the first thing about it."

"I know more than you do. I rode with them people. You didn't do nothin' but keep a store."

"Ed Tewksbury can't afford that lawyer!"

I gave him a puzzled look. "Well someone's sure as hell paying him."

"Someone indeed! They're playing man-chess and you're a pawn!"

I stared at the ground and shook my head. "Whatever Ed did, he did it for revenge. It was Graham that killed his brother."

He unbuttoned his shirt collar and ran a hand behind his neck. "Well at least you admit he did it. And the hell it was just revenge. First, the Hashknife barons told their cowboys to push the sheep barons off the Rim, then the sheep barons told their minions to get a stranglehold on Pleasant Valley. And when that got out of hand, Atkinson decided to clean it up. Only they didn't get Tom Graham."

I bit my lip savagely as I looked down at my boots.

"They made you a witless pawn and you were too naïve to know it. Ed Tewksbury's not paying his legal fees. It's Atkinson and the Daggs brothers. They were scared to death Graham would come after them, so they told Tewksbury to get him first."

I didn't answer right away. Just kept looking at my boots. "I reckon I'm like that feller in the book you gave me."

"What's that mean?"

"He fights all the monsters 'til he becomes one hisself."

He gave me a puzzled grimace. "I didn't say you're a monster. Just a fool."

"Then what's Ed Tewksbury?"

He kept staring at me.

"He ain't no different than Odysseus. Gets dragged through a lot of hell 'til all he wants is vengeance. Only he still wouldn't a done it 'til a goddess egged him on."

"And they egged on Tewksbury in a similar fashion but that doesn't make him innocent."

"I just know he ain't a monster." I looked back at him, then dropped my gaze toward the dirt. "If they go and hang him, won't be nothing but another vengeance killing. I know you don't understand it, George, but it ain't no different from lynching Mott."

He pressed his lips together and nodded gravely. "You acted nobly in that affair, Ben. Luett told me about it. I only wish you'd been consistent."

"Then how is it right to hang Ed? The whole thing has to stop, goddamn it. The whole blasted killing train."

He took a handkerchief from his vest pocket and dabbed the sweat off his face. Then he turned to me with a little smile. "The tempest doth blow us fiercely."

"What the hell does that mean?"

"It's what Poseidon did to Odysseus. He denies him haven. He's done the same to us. He blows us to cursed shores yet we are armed with human goodness."

I stared out at the desert.

"You perjured yourself and I got hot with you, but you've caught me in my own hypocrisy." He breathed deeply a couple times, then stared back toward the courthouse. "Perhaps we're both right. It's wrong to acquit the murderers and yet hanging them is the purest barbarism."

He'd meant it for consolation, but it fell empty on a droughted heart. I looked away and wiped my face as I thought back on what I'd done. He'd set me adrift from Globe with nothing but a moral compass. He'd instructed me to help Luett, and that's exactly what I'd tried to do. I'd tried to calm things down, but I'd failed and failed again. After that I'd tossed my compass like a piece of jetsam in the stormy seas. It was just what George said it was. I'd done it for a bloody bribe. Ed had offered me a ranch and I'd happily accepted. I'd joined him in his bitter quarrel, then lied to get him off.

"By the way," added George, "I've got something for you." He groped inside his vest pocket and pulled out a paper. "It's a bill of gift. Luett figured you needed something to prove you own that gelding she gave you. She wrote in the saddle, too. She wants you to know she's sorry for how things worked out." He paused and put his hand on my shoulder. "She also told me to let you know that a sorrel horse by the name of Dorothea Dix is plump as a sausage."

I took the paper without looking at him and thrust it in my pocket.

"Let's get back there," he muttered. "If they don't have a verdict soon, I'll buy you a decent supper."

———•———

George and me walked back to the courthouse after that. We sat on one of the benches out front and waited for the verdict. Some of the onlookers had gone home, but most of them were still around. A cooling breeze swayed the palo verdes, but my sweat poured out regardless. I could see Dushay standing with Annie Graham at the far end of the veranda. He glanced at me then pointed. As the two of them stared at me, Flowers swung the door open.

"Jury's in!" he shouted. "Come on in and take a seat." Then he turned his face toward Ed's lawyer, who was chatting with one of the defense witnesses. "I'll wager we'll be gettin' together in a couple weeks to watch your client dance the gallows."

Flowers kept his position by the door as we filed in. I tried to pass without looking at him, but he put his arm across the entry. "I've sure had a good time today," he said in a sugary voice. "Hopin' to see you again if you'll grace me with your company. I think we could have some fun together."

I ducked under his arm, then took a seat next to George. I felt my knees begin to shake as we watched the judge make his entry.

"Has the jury decided?" asked the judge.

"Yes, Your Honor," said the foreman.

"Please read your verdict. On the count of murder in the first degree, how did you find?"

"Not Guilty, Your Honor. Not guilty on all charges."

Graham's supporters exploded. "I smell a bribe!" yelled a man in back. Then Annie Graham shot out of her seat, tugging desperately at her handbag. When I saw the butt end of a pistol in her hand I lurched up and tried to grab her. She stepped to the side and I missed her completely, but she tripped before she could fire. As she scrambled to get up, I heard the gun go off like a cannon. Just as she pointed the gun again, the deputies managed to tackle her.

When I looked over at Ed, I saw him lying on the floor. I thought for sure she'd killed him. Then he got up slowly and dusted himself off. He brushed his hand through his hair, then glanced at me and George.

By then the crowd's attention was focused on Annie Graham. She was curled on the floor with her hands cuffed behind her. Her big sobs echoed across the room, then turned into bitter keening. Dushay and some others kept haranguing the deputies to let her go.

"I reckon we're even, Ben," said Ed as we walked into the street and looked around at the billowing clouds and the dark, slanted rain way out over the Mazatzals. "I saved you when you was snakebit, and you saved me today. She'd a killed me sure if you hadn't made her stumble. Now all I need is your help gettin' home. I got a cattle business to run, and you got a ranch."

I didn't answer him. I couldn't. I kept hearing her keening as we slowly walked away. I never saw her again. I heard she went off with her baby to California. Dushay disappeared the way he'd come; just rode into the desert and lived under another alias. I imagine Ed would have killed him if he'd hung around. That or the other way around.

The war was over. That was sure. But it went on inside me. Killed a boy by the name of Holcomb just as sure as it killed Jayzee Mott and Tom Graham and all the rest. First it took away Calista. Then it took away that wispy web they call "hope" that got me through all the hell. I kept moving after that, mining one year and cowboying the next. Sold my ranch in '94 and spent some years in Oregon. I found a woman to keep me company, only she left the earth before her time. I finally bought my ranch back after I got tired of the Oregon rains. Been here ever since, running a few cattle.

I got word a couple years back from the postal clerk that Calista had died in Mesa City. Bilious fever, they said. You'd have thought I'd have stopped thinking about her, but the news cut a wound in my heart.

In my dreams I see the dead. I walk through a moonless night, following a man's silhouette. We head for the glow of a campfire, only when we get there it's abandoned. When I look up I see Mott in the hanging tree, his neck bent in the noose. His eyes are wide and blinking, like he's silently pleading. Other nights I see Calista. I'm hitching a team in Fish's barnyard when she opens the door and watches. When I turn to look at her, she steps into shadows.

About fifteen years back, Ed Tewksbury went the way of his brothers. He wasted away from consumption. Wasn't long after the war that Tom Horn had made him a partner in the business of bounty hunting, only Ed didn't stay long. He finally had the guts to break with a friend. Wasn't nothing but a killing deal, he told me later. He'd gone back to the cattle business and to his Mexican wife. By the time he came down with tuberculosis, he was father to a passel of children.

His partner, John Rhodes, got off the same as Ed did. The witnesses couldn't for sure identify him. As for George, he married Luett in the same year Ed went to his reward, then got himself elected governor. The colonel sold out and followed them to Phoenix. I guess it was Sax that got the worst of it. They jailed him for obstruction, but he didn't serve but a couple months. After Ed gave him a starter herd, he sold it and moved to Washington Territory. Finally drank himself to a grave in Alaska.

When the birds sing before the dawn, I make my coffee. The cowbells tinkle in the morning breezes and the jay birds squawk on the window sill, begging for peanuts. I do okay. I cook for the Flying V on the fall roundups. I go to the Fourth of July fiddle dances and spend my Christmases among the Saints. Their kids call me Uncle. There's one of them that pays me visits. A forest ranger. I make him supper and we tell our stories. He doesn't ask about the range war stuff. He don't know nothing about it except his people were sorely persecuted.

Now and again I venture to Globe. I follow Mott's advice and avoid saloons. I pass the days with a month of newspapers. Here and there I read a novel. Not any Western stories; they make me cross. In the evenings I sup with a widow friend, then I take her to see the pictures. If my arthritis gets any worse, I'll be moving down with her. I'd have married her except she loathes the ranch.

I have my good days and my bad ones, I guess. I'm not suffering. Not like that bollixed boy that rode from Heard's place. It's the live ones that are meant to suffer.

The fallen are in another land.

Character Glossary

(alphabetical by first name)

A. C. BAKER is based on the real-life A. C. Baker, one of the trial attorneys who defended Ed Tewksbury and John Rhodes.

ANNIE GRAHAM is based on the historical personage of the same name. She and Tom Graham were married in October 1887, only a few weeks after the most intense fighting in the war. The two of them operated a small farm in what is now southeast Phoenix prior to Tom Graham's assassination in 1892. She and Tom had two children, one of whom died in infancy. The other was a daughter who—at her own wish—was ultimately laid to rest next to Charlie Dushay in Tempe. It was actually John Rhodes, not Ed Tewksbury, whom Annie Graham attempted to assassinate during a court hearing. Her pistol somehow became entangled in her purse lining, giving the sheriff time to stop her.

BARTHOLOMEW "BARD" HOLLISTER HENRY is a fictional character inspired by real-life broncbusters and cowhands who, never having married, lived out their days on other men's ranches.

BENJAMIN "BEN" HOLCOMB is a fictitious character who experiences the very real events of the Pleasant Valley War. He is inspired by, though not really based on, Daniel Boone "Red" Holcomb, a Texas cowboy who worked for the Hashknife. Though no records indicate that Holcomb participated in the fighting in Pleasant Valley, Mormons suspected him of rustling (probably because he was friends with the Blevins brothers). Despite finding a note on his cabin door commanding him to leave or be killed, Holcomb remained on his homestead near the Mormon hamlet of Heber. According to one story, he was wont to seek hot meals from his Mormon neighbors, the Turleys, under the pretense that it was his birthday. In the 1910s, a Mormon forest ranger named Kenneth Kartchner made it a point to stop occasionally at the aging bachelor's cabin to make sure he had supplies. Kartchner avoided bringing up the war, knowing Holcomb would dispute him.

BILLY GRAHAM (SEE GRAHAM BROTHERS).

BLAKE LARSON, the Mormon vigilante, is a composite based on several real-life Mormons: Hook Larson, Osmer Flake, Evans Coleman, and Evans's brother, Prime. Though Mormons were typically farming people, all four became cowboys. Osmer Flake or one of his brothers—or perhaps his father, William Flake—may have been at the James Stott (Jayzee Mott in the novel) lynching. Osmer inadvertently gave evidence of his family's participation when he described the event in his brief manuscript history of the Pleasant Valley War. There, Flake claimed that his father, William Flake, had asked the vigilantes whether Stott had "shown the white feather." The vigilantes gave Flake a thorough description of the lynching, including details about tying a scarf around Stott's neck. They also testified to Stott's courage, telling Flake that he had cursed them and challenged them to fight one-on-one. Because the vigilantes were sworn to secrecy, it is highly unlikely they would have revealed such information to anyone outside their group. At the least, William Flake—and perhaps his sons—were among those who had endorsed the plan to lynch Stott. Two decades later, Osmer Flake served in the state legislature, where he helped repeal the ban on capital punishment that Governor George W. P. Hunt ("George Heard" in the novel) had supported. Flake regarded the repeal as his greatest legislative success.

Other evidence indicates that the lynching party that came for Stott and his two hired men—twenty-eight strong—originated partly in Pleasant Valley and partly in the Mormon towns on Silver Creek. Another Mormon—or, rather, what we would today call a "Jack Mormon"— who was almost undoubtedly among the lynchers was Hugo "Hook" Larson, a good friend of the Flakes who served as a paid stock detective and perhaps as an assassin. According to one settler, Larson, a giant of a man, was a coward who shot men in the back.

THE BOARDING HOUSE MISTRESS is a fictitious character who represents the isolation of older widows who often ran boarding houses to make ends meet.

CALEB HARTMAN is based on the real-life Jesse N. Smith (cousin of Joseph Smith), who served as president of the Snowflake Stake of Zion in the 1880s. Circumstantial evidence links Smith to the vigilantism of 1887–88. In concert with others—both Mormon and non-Mormon—he urged stake members to vote for the slate of candidates nominated by the pro-Mormon "People's Party" in Apache County's 1886 election, including Commodore Perry Owens for sheriff. In 1887, moreover, two Mormons asked Smith for permission to assassinate John Payne, who had attacked them and threatened to drive Mormons "out of the forest," meaning lands claimed by the Hashknife. Smith urged them to forebear, promising that Payne would soon be "out of the way." Even if he did not himself plan or endorse vigilantism, he seems to have been aware it was underway.

CALISTA FISH is a fictional character intended to offer a window into Mormon polygamy and race relations. Her Paiute mother is based on anecdotes about a real-life Paiute woman named Fanny Adair whose grandfather sold her to Mormons when she was a girl. She later married a Mormon man and lived in Snowflake, where she once chided an actor playing Simon Legree—Osmer Flake, specifically—for whipping Uncle Tom during a performance of *Uncle Tom's Cabin*. Adair enrolled herself at the Moapa reservation in Nevada after her three children were grown.

CHAMP BLEVINS is based on the real-life Hampton ("Hamp") Blevins, one of five brothers who came to Arizona from Texas in the 1880s. Hamp's father, Mart Blevins, as well as his mother and sister, joined the brothers at a homestead (taken from Mormons) on upper Canyon Creek. He was killed in the first skirmish of the Pleasant Valley War.

CHARLIE DUSHAY is based on the real Charlie Dushay (also spelled "Duesha" and "Duchet," though his birth name may have been Charles English). Dushay hired out to the Daggs brothers as a sheepherder, then changed sides after befriending Tom Graham. The long scar across his nose and face gave him a singular appearance. He claimed he'd received the wound in California in a quarrel with a rival suiter.

CHARLIE PERKINS is based on the real-life Charles "Charlie" Perkins, who opened a small, rock-walled store in Pleasant Valley. Somehow Perkins remained neutral throughout the fighting.

CLARETTA is a fictitious prostitute who works at the 16-to-1 saloon in Payson.

THE DAGGS BROTHERS are based on the real-life Daggs brothers (there were five) who owned somewhere around fifty thousand sheep in the mid-1880s. After their herders were barred from Hashknife range, they sought other pastures, including Pleasant Valley. In his old age, Peru Daggs recalled that the "Tonto Basin War" had cost him $90,000 (likely including money spent arming herders, paying lawyers, and losses incurred from stolen or killed animals).

DOROTHEA DIX, Ben's tattered sorrel, stands in for the plucky Indian ponies descended from Spanish Barbs that cowboys tended to label "scrubs." Though Dorothea Dix (at least initially) is thin from abuse and scanty provender, Indian horses tended to be stocky and short-legged. The colors of their coats varied enormously, though many were dappled or spotted. They had great powers of endurance, but their small stature made them poor choices for range work that pitted horse against cow.

EDWIN "ED" TEWKSBURY is based on the real-life person of the same name. Though initially friends, the Tewksburys and Grahams became enemies after the latter testified against the former in a rustling case brought by James Stinson (Old Man Stinson in the novel) in 1884. The judge, however, dismissed the case and charged the Grahams with perjury (those charges, too, were dropped). Subsequently, John Tewksbury contracted with the Daggs brothers to bring sheep into Pleasant Valley, thus deepening the rift with the Grahams and precipitating the war. In 1892, after a four-year hiatus in the fighting, Ed Tewksbury and his friend, John Rhodes, assassinated Tom Graham in Tempe, Arizona. Despite strong evidence of their guilt, neither man was convicted. Tewksbury endured two trials for Graham's murder. In the first, the jury found him guilty, but the decision was overturned on a technicality. The second ended in a mistrial. The territory declined to prosecute the case a third time, partly because witnesses had died or left the territory, and partly because of the expense. In the novel, Graham's widow, Annie, tries to kill Tewksbury after the jury finds him innocent. In reality, she had tried to kill John Rhodes during a preliminary hearing.

After the trial, Tewksbury married his Mexican sweetheart in Globe and started a family. For a time he partnered with Tom Horn as a range detective, though he found the business distasteful and soon quit. He died of consumption in 1904.

ESTRELLA TORRES (SEE MIGUEL AND ESTRELLA TORRES).

FRANK HEREFORD is based on the prosecuting attorney of the same name who tried Ed Tewksbury and John Rhodes for murder.

FRANK WATTRON is based on the real-life man of the same name. Wattron was an apothecary who served briefly as deputy to Sheriff Commodore Perry Owens. He was the Holbrook constable on the day that Owens killed three men at the Blevins home, including Andy Cooper (Landis Hooper in the novel). Wattron, it seems, told Cooper he was wanted, then dispatched a man to fetch Commodore Owens to make an arrest (or, perhaps, to assassinate Cooper). In addition to his drug business, Wattron exhumed and sold ancient Puebloan pottery to Eastern museums and private collectors. He was also a laudanum addict. In 1895, he presided over Arizona's last public hanging, having first sent invitations announcing that the "latest improved methods in the art of scientific strangulation will be employed and everything possible will be done to make the proceedings cheerful and the execution a success." Some ten years later, Governor George W. P. Hunt (George Heard in the novel) urged the state to abolish capital punishment altogether, which the voters accomplished by plebiscite.

GEORGE GLADDEN is based on the real-life George Gladden, a veteran of the so-called Hoodoo War of Mason County, Texas. After serving time in jail for murder, Gladden moved to Arizona's Rim Country, where he and his family took over a homestead claimed by Mormons. While visiting a Payson saloon, according to one settler, Gladden bought a round of drinks for everyone except Ed Tewksbury, saying, "Here's where I draw the line. I won't drink with no black man." Tewksbury then slapped Gladden and challenged him to a gunfight, whereupon Gladden rose to fetch his rifle. No gunfight ensued; Gladden rode away.

GEORGE HEARD, the Globe storekeeper and politician, is based on the real-life George W. P. Hunt, who ran away from his Missouri home in 1878 and ended up in Globe (after a stint in Colorado's mining camps and a prospecting venture to New Mexico and Arizona). He waited tables, briefly operated a ranch near Wild Rye, then became delivery boy, grocery clerk, and finally president and partner of the Old Dominion Commercial Company. In 1892, he became active in politics, winning election to the territorial legislature. One year earlier, he had begun a romantic relationship—largely via correspondence—with Duett Ellison, whom he finally married in 1904 (despite the fact that Hunt and Duett's father, Jesse Ellison, despised one another). In 1912, Hunt—already known for his sympathies for the downtrodden and his implacability toward enemies—became Arizona's first elected governor. He served six more two-year terms, making him the longest-serving governor in Arizona's history. Throughout his political life, he hewed to a Progressive agenda that included fighting for workers' rights and prison reform and banning liquor, gambling, prize fights, and capital punishment.

THE GLOBE COMMERCIAL COMPANY stands in for two mercantile establishments: the actual Globe Commercial Company, owned by J. K. Patton, and its competitor, the Old Dominion Commercial Company, which was owned and operated by several business partners. George Hunt (George Heard in the novel) worked for the Old Dominion.

THE GRAHAM BROTHERS, JOHN, TOM, AND BILLY, are based on their real-life counterparts. Their father—with his eldest son, John—had emigrated from Scotland. After stops in Ohio and Iowa, the brothers traveled to Alaska and California, and finally to Arizona. All three died during the war.

THE HASHKNIFE OUTFIT is based on the real-life Hashknife Outfit, officially known as the Aztec Land & Cattle Company. In 1884, Aztec investors—including elite businessmen, lawyers, and two former Massachusetts governors—purchased a million acres of alternating sections from the Atlantic & Pacific Railroad, which had received the land as a grant from Congress in 1872. The Aztec then bought a Texas operation known as the Hashknife and moved its 32,000 cows to Arizona, along with its brand; thus the Aztec's cowboys became known as "Hashknifes."

THE HASHKNIFE'S LAND AGENT is based on the real-life Frank Ames, who, as a young man, served as land manager for the Aztec Land & Cattle Company ("The Hashknife"). Ames was nephew to a Massachusetts governor and grandson to Oakes Ames, who had played a central role in the Crédit Mobilier scandal. The real Ames, like the fictional one, befriended Jamie Stott and decried his lynching, insisting that Stott was innocent.

THE HELLSGATE (ALSO CALLED "HELLGATE") TRAIL was (and is) an ancient Indian route stretching from what is now the White Mountain Apache Reservation to the town of Payson. It crosses the confluence of Tonto and Haigler Creeks at a chasm that settlers named "Hell's Gate." At the bottom, the two creeks form a deep, still pond between vertical walls of dark rock. Apaches—and likely Puebloans before them—attached spiritual significance to the place.

HENRIETTA FISH is a fictitious character who represents the subset of Mormon sister-wives who never fully accepted plural marriage.

JAMES "JAYZEE" ZEBULON MOTT, the temperance advocate and lynching victim, is based on the real-life person named James "Jamie" Warren Stott. Stott, the son of a well-to-do textile mill manager, grew up across the street from Thomas Talbot, a Massachusetts governor. After several years of boarding school, he headed west. He first journeyed to Texas, where he worked on Talbot's brother's ranch. He then moved to Arizona, where he filed a homestead claim and operated a horse ranch just south of Hashknife range. Perhaps Talbot—who sat on the Aztec (Hashknife) board of directors—recommended Arizona's Rim Country as a homestead site or, alternately, promised Stott a job with the Hashknife. Though Talbot's death in October 1886 left Stott without a patron, his wealthy father gave him capital to establish his ranch. Stott, meanwhile, befriended the Hashknife's land manager, Frank Ames (scion of a prominent Massachusetts family). In regard to the Pleasant Valley feud, he sympathized with the Grahams but stayed aloof from the fighting. Because he was associated with Hashknifes, however—including those involved in the feud—he became suspected of participating in horse theft and, in one instance, an attempted bushwhack. Those suspicions led to his lynching. Though Frank Ames and others sought to bring Stott's killers to trial, the county prosecutor could find no witnesses willing to talk. Two men boarding at Stott's ranch (a tubercular from the East and his attendant) had seen the lynchers and told their story but had subsequently left the territory. When two alleged lynchers were held for questioning by a grand jury, a "phalanx" of their allies (including Jim Houck) descended on the courthouse to guarantee "fair play."

The novel suggests that Stott's lynchers suspected him of being homosexual, though no direct evidence confirms that he was (one would be hard pressed to find evidence of same-sex relations anywhere in the 1880s West; the topic was almost never discussed in print, presumably because it might offend readers' sensibilities). In all probability, Stott was a heterosexual man who made his way west for adventure. Nevertheless there is at least the possibility that Stott was gay or bisexual.

Like the merchant marine, or the military, the West offered an all-male culture that offered opportunities for sex between men. In this regard it is worth noting that Stott was a handsome, polished, and athletic young man with promising social connections in Massachusetts, thanks to his father's wealth. Stott nevertheless severed himself from his home state, despite all the pecuniary and conjugal opportunities open to him there. To quote Will Barnes, one of the vigilante organizers, Stott preferred to live "all by his lonesome."

In fact, Stott was seldom alone. He had numerous friends, including not only Ames but also a host of cowboys, in addition to the two boarders at his ranch. Not long before the lynching, moreover, he hosted his mother and sister for a visit (he also wrote frequent letters to them, though he almost never wrote his father). Stott additionally hired people to work with him, including both former Hashknifes and a young Mormon couple.

Perhaps Barnes saw Stott as an isolate, not only because he suspected him of outlawry but also because Stott shied from fiddle dances, which offered prime opportunities to meet marriageable women. When Stott was lynched, his persecutors tied a silk scarf around his neck, suggesting they thought he had committed a gender offense, at least insofar as he was too genteel. One hastens to add, however, that scarves also seem to have been used to diminish the pain of the rope.

It would be wrong to suggest that Stott was lynched primarily because he engaged in same-sex relations, even assuming he did so. Contrary to what one might assume from the film *Brokeback Mountain*, there is no evidence suggesting that cowboys, or settlers generally, engaged in anti-gay violence, though neither is there evidence suggesting they were particularly tolerant of same-sex relationships. In the novel, I have tried to highlight the ambiguity of late nineteenth-century attitudes toward same-sex relations as well as the tenuous nature of scholarly understanding of those attitudes.

JASS ATKINSON "THE COLONEL," leader of the vigilantes, is based on the real-life Jesse Ellison. Ellison moved his large family—he had five daughters and two sons—and his stock from Shackelford County, Texas, in 1885 to escape "nesters" who were cutting his fences. En route, he lost most of his herd. With the remainder, he established a ranch (Apple Farm) just east of Payson, then later bought a tract at the west end of Pleasant Valley (the Q Ranch). As an old man, Ellison admitted that he had led the vigilantes, or at least those from the Payson and Pleasant Valley areas.

JEANY ATKINSON is based on Jesse Ellison's eldest son, Perle "Perly," who turned twenty-one in 1887. It seems the two men were at odds, causing Perle to leave the ranch.

JED FLOWERS is a fictional deputy who, with his partner, Burris, rides to Pleasant Valley to investigate the conspiracy to kill Tom Graham.

JEFF WILSON, who in the novel is lynched alongside Jayzee Mott, is based on the real-life man of the same name. We know little about him other than that he worked for the Aztec for a time. According to Charlie Dushay's brief and somewhat confusing memoir, Stott had hired both of his fellow lynching victims, Jeff Wilson and Jim Scott, to build his fences. The only known accusations against Wilson for horse theft came from Osmer Flake (who reported a charge he'd heard from another settler, Hezekiah James Ramer) and Sam Haught, who was likely reporting what the vigilantes had told him.

JEREMY HOUCK is based on the real-life James "Jim" Houck, who served both as vigilante leader and deputy to Commodore Perry Owens (Lafayette McGowan in the novel). In his old age, Houck bragged that he had been "leader" of the Tewksbury faction during the war. It was Houck, along with two other men, who had arrested Jamie Stott and handed him over to a lynching party. Houck claimed that the territorial governor had given the vigilantes the go-ahead. Though the real Houck was never accused of stealing horses, the army officer in command at Fort Defiance did accuse him, along with Owens, of murderous assaults on Navajos. According to Will Barnes, Houck's gaze was peculiarly intense and frightening. After the Pleasant Valley War ended, Houck operated a sheep station in Cave Creek that accommodated herds passing from the uplands to Phoenix. It was there that he committed suicide by swallowing strychnine in 1921.

JIM, the third in the trio of lynching victims, is based on the real-life James "Jim" Scott (not to be confused with Jamie Stott). Like Jeff Wilson, Scott had worked for the Aztec, as well as for another local cattle concern, Huning & Cooley. Jamie Stott, it seems, subsequently hired both Scott and Wilson to help build his fences. Joe McKinney, one of Commodore Owens's deputies in 1887 and a man who knew Scott well, later recalled that he "thought a great deal of Jimmy Scott and felt his death very keenly." McKinney suggested that one of Scott's lynchers, Jim Houck, had ulterior motives, Scott having backed him down in a saloon quarrel. The *St. Johns Herald*—despite its earlier calls for vigilantism—similarly reported that "those who have worked with [Scott] and know him best say that he was quiet, sober, and peaceable, and was never engaged in any questionable transactions." Scott's mother pleaded with both the territorial governor and with her brother, Briggs Goodrich—the territory's attorney general—to bring the lynchers to justice, to no avail. "Cattlemen who have money," she lamented, "buy up juries and witnesses, prove alibis, and control the courts." She was apparently referring to members of the Apache Stock Growers' Association, who seem to have both endorsed and financed the vigilante campaign.

JOHN GRAHAM ("THE SCOTSMAN") (SEE GRAHAM BROTHERS).

JOHN PAYNE, referred to by Ben as "Bowler Hat," is based on the real-life person of the same name who died in the first skirmish of the Pleasant Valley War. Payne, though a devout Methodist, had already gained a reputation for violence. After initially being hired by sheepherders to guard their herds, he soon switched sides and worked for the Hashknife. He assaulted at least four different Mormon men (whom he apparently believed to be trespassing on Hashknife range) and told others he would kill them if they refused to vacate their homesteads. The real Payne wore a narrow-brimmed "boss of the plains" hat, not a bowler.

JOHN RHODES is based on the real-life John Rhodes, who took the Tewksbury side in the Pleasant Valley War and later married John Tewksbury's widow. It was almost certainly Rhodes who, with Tewksbury, gunned down Tom Graham in Tempe in 1892, thus ending the war. Because witnesses found it difficult to identify him—and because Rhodes had a convincing alibi—he was released after a preliminary hearing, though not before Tom Graham's widow, Annie, tried to shoot him.

LAFAYETTE MARCUS McGOWAN is based on a real-life sheriff named Commodore Perry Owens. Owens was named after his father, who, in turn, had been named after Commodore Oliver Hazard Perry, noted for his victories on the Great Lakes during the War of 1812. Though elected by a constituency of Mormons and non-Mormons who sought to clean up Apache County, Owens was slow to arrest Andy Cooper. Holbrook old-timers asserted in later decades that the two men had been range pals, an assertion bolstered by reports that both men had murdered Navajos and stolen their horses. Given that the only warrant for Cooper in 1886 was for horse theft from Navajos, Owens may well have hesitated to bring in his friend. In the famous gunfight (or, perhaps more aptly, "assault") that occurred in Holbrook in September 1887, Owens killed three men: Andy Cooper; Cooper's fifteen-year-old half-brother, Sam Houston Blevins; and a man named "Mote" or "Mose" Roberts.

Owens's involvement in the war, however, went far beyond the events at Holbrook. It was Owens who deputized key members of the vigilantes who hanged Jamie Stott, including Jim Houck, Hook Larson, Tom Horn, William Flake, and perhaps William's son, James. He also seems to have made a sojourn under the Rim (in what was then Yavapai County) in summer 1887 to coordinate the vigilante effort with Jesse Ellison and the Tewksbury faction. Other deputies—including Jonas Brighton—conducted similar work in the eastern part of the county.

LANDIS HOOPER is based on the real-life Andy Cooper, who was a half-brother to Hamp, John, Charlie, and fifteen-year-old Sam Houston Blevins. (Among the five brothers, only John—though wounded in Commodore Perry Owens's attack on the Blevins home in Holbrook—survived the war.) After emigrating from Llano, Texas—perhaps to escape the law, though stories vary—Cooper took possession of a Mormon farm and cabin on Upper Canyon Creek (it is worth noting that Cooper later paid the Mormon owners, though they likely accepted the money under duress). Cooper's father, mother, brothers, and a sister followed him to Canyon Creek. Cooper was subsequently accused of stealing horses from both Navajos and from Mormons, though only the former accusation led to a warrant for his arrest.

LUETT ATKINSON is based on the real-life Helen Duett Ellison. In creating the fictional Luett, the novel draws on the real-life Duett's letters to George W. P. Hunt, which describe her chagrin about cowboying, her fraught relationship with her father, and her profound opposition to drinking. The letters also describe her memories of crying herself to sleep after finding that her favorite rings would no longer fit her fingers, which were made thick from work on the range. The real-life Duett married George W. P. Hunt in 1904 after thirteen years of romantic correspondence and occasional visits. No evidence suggests that she and her mother sought to stop Colonel Ellison from lynching Jamie Stott and his hired men. Duett's letters, however, reveal strong support for George W. P. Hunt's humanist politics, which included blanket opposition to capital punishment.

MIGUEL AND ESTRELLA TORRES are fictional characters based on the New Mexican sheepherders and farmers who colonized Arizona in the 1860s. Drawn by the rich pastures at the southern edge of the Colorado Plateau, New Mexicans came to Arizona shortly after the US incarcerated Navajos at Bosque Redondo in eastern New Mexico. They came not only in search of opportunity but also to escape the Texas cattlemen who were crowding them out of ranges east of the Sangre de Cristo Mountains. Unfortunately, other groups also sought the bounties of the Colorado Plateau, including Texas cowboys and Mormon colonists. According to Bishop David K. Udall, a war nearly broke out between New Mexicans and Mormons. A few years later, when Commodore Perry

Owens ran for sheriff in 1886, his opponents claimed that he and his allies intended to lynch New Mexicans. Though no large-scale lynching occurred, vigilantes did lynch at least some alleged "Mexican" (probably New Mexican) horse thieves.

Similar tensions seem to have arisen in the western part of the county after James Stinson sold his Silver Creek land to William Flake, who there founded the town of Snowflake. Rather than employ Stinson's corps of "Mexican" (probably New New Mexican) workers, Flake required them to vacate their adobe home in order to make way for impoverished converts. Despite Mormon proscriptions on interactions with outsiders, Flake and his business partner, Zack Decker, subsequently employed those same "Mexicans" (or perhaps others) to tend their flocks of sheep, at least until Hashknife cowboys frightened them into quitting. Much the same phenomenon occurred in southern Utah, where "Mexican" herders worked for Mormons (and built their own small communities) near Monticello.

NATHAN FISH is a composite. He is drawn principally from two real-life Mormon settlers: Nathan Tenney, a New York-born Mormon who died in St. Johns, Arizona, in 1882 while trying to break up a gunfight between New Mexicans and a mixed group of Mormons and cowboys; and Joseph Fish, a Mormon who briefly ran the Arizona Cooperative Mercantile Institution (ACMI)—a Mormon co-op—in Woodruff. It was Fish who had repeated run-ins with Hashknife cowboys, who was robbed by James Tewksbury while operating the co-op, and who fled to Mexico to escape polygamy charges. Fish's dog was shot by John Payne, who sought to drive Fish and his wives from their home. As for Tenney, it was his son, Ammon—who spoke fluent Spanish—who bought Arizona lands for Mormon settlement and who subsequently became a missionary in Mexico. The fictional Nathan Fish is also inspired by Lot Smith, the polygamous Mormon warrior and stake president who helped found the communistic town of Sunset; David K. Udall, the St. Johns bishop who adamantly opposed lynchings and who sought to heal the rift between Mormons and New Mexicans; John Hunt, the Snowflake bishop who "stood like a stone wall" against lynching; Neils Petersen, who decided to give up tobacco after a run-in with John Payne; and William Flake, who is said to have used rocks to drive off desperadoes.

PERCIVAL, Ben's black gelding, is inspired by the blooded horses that settlers in Arizona's Rim Country cherished. Among the several settler families known for their fine horses were the Tewksburys and the Flakes. Horse races—in which small cowboys served as jockeys—were a popular form of entertainment in Payson, Globe, Springerville, and elsewhere.

PRENTISS REEVES is a fictional character who stands in for two mysterious men who were in residence at Jamie Stott's ranch when vigilantes took him prisoner. One of those men, Alfred Ingham, may have been a consumptive. The other, Lamotte Clymer, seems to have been Ingham's attendant. The vigilantes, it seems, found Clymer in his bed, though they missed Ingham entirely. Though the two men reported their story through an anonymous intermediary in Holbrook (who then published a letter in the local newspaper), both fled the territory. Had they appeared at the grand jury that sought to bring the lynchers to justice, their testimony might well have led to murder convictions.

THE RATTLER is a Mojave Rattlesnake. Most rattlesnakes inject what herpetologists call "Type B venom," which eats away the tissue around the bite. Mojave Rattlesnakes inject what scientists call "Type A venom," a powerful neurotoxin (or sometimes both Type A and type B venom together). They are considered the deadliest of all rattlesnakes. Their desert range abuts the Mogollon Rim.

THE RIM refers to the Mogollon (pronounced "Muggy-own") Rim, the forested, cliff-like escarpment that separates the Sonoran Desert from the Colorado Plateau. Over a thousand feet high in places, the Rim winds across some two hundred miles from the southern peripheries of the San Francisco Peaks volcanic field to the western reaches of the White Mountains. Settlers usually called the Rim "the Mogollon Mountains," or simply "the Mogollons." Naegelin Rim is one of its spurs.

SAXTON "SAX" BENTON is a fictitious cowhand who works for Ed Tewksbury.

THE SIXTEEN-TO-ONE SALOON was a real saloon in Payson run by a man named William Hilligas. The saloon's name celebrated the famous "16-to-1" monetary policy beloved among Populists and many Democrats.

THEO BURRIS is a fictional deputy who, with his partner, Flowers, rides to Pleasant Valley to investigate the conspiracy to kill Tom Graham.

TOM GRAHAM (SEE GRAHAM BROTHERS).

TOM HORN is based on the real Tom Horn. After serving as a packer and a scout in General Crook's war against the Chiricahuas, Horn worked as an Arizona cowboy and became a master roper and rider. According to Horn's memoir, his friend John Rhodes recruited him into the Pleasant Valley War in April 1887. Horn later recalled that he had killed men in Arizona both in his capacity as stock detective and "regulator" (eyewitnesses placed him among the lynchers who killed Stott, Scott, and Wilson). In later years, Wyoming cattlemen hired him as an assassin, leading to his conviction and hanging in 1903.

WILLIAM PENDERGAST, proprietor of the 16-to-1 saloon in Payson, is a fictitious character whose name resembles that of the actual proprietor, William Hilligas.

Bibliography

Fiction vs. History

Readers familiar with the Pleasant Valley War—more properly called the "Rim Country War," given that it represented a merger of frictions below the Rim with those above—may be surprised that I include Mormons as key participants. Some will note, moreover, that I've moved the Stott lynching back a year (it occurred in August 1888, but in the novel the year is 1887). The purpose for placing the lynching in 1887 is to highlight the vigilante movement that began that spring and continued throughout the war. As I have argued elsewhere, the vast majority of murders during the war *may* have been vigilante actions. As for Mormons being key participants, the case is partly circumstantial and partly by their own testimony. Various Mormon journals and statements from the time suggest not just a renewal of an apocalyptic fervor in the 1880s due to polygamy prosecutions but also active participation in vigilantism. For a review of evidence, see Daniel Justin Herman, *Hell on the Range: A Story of Honor, Conscience, and the American West* (New Haven: Yale University Press, 2010), especially Chapter Nine; and Daniel Herman, "The Rim Country War Reconsidered: On Honor Rustling, Vigilantism, and How History Got Remembered," *Journal of Arizona History*, Spring 2017 (vol. 58, no. 1), 11–50.

To understand the broader sweep of events and those involved in them, I have also consulted Don Dedera's thorough and beautifully crafted monograph, *A Little War of Our Own: The Pleasant Valley Feud Revisited* (Flagstaff: Northland Press, 1988); three carefully researched and probing studies by Leland J. Hanchett, Jr.: *Arizona's Graham-Tewksbury Feud* (Phoenix: Pine Rim Publishing, 1994); *They Shot Billy Today* (Phoenix: Pine Rim Publishing 2006); and *Black Mesa: The Hanging of Jamie Stott* (Phoenix: Pine Rim Printery, 1996); Earl Forrest's pioneering investigation, *Arizona's Dark and Bloody Ground* (Caldwell, Idaho: The Caxton Press, 1936); and Eduardo Pagán's intriguing and handsomely crafted account, *Valley of the Guns: The Pleasant Valley War and the*

Trauma of Violence. Pagán and I offer profoundly different views on the nature and extent of vigilantism—and Mormon involvement—but we ardently agree that trauma begot additional trauma.

On Arizona's Mormon colonists more generally, I have relied on Charles S. Peterson, *Take Up Your Mission: Mormon Colonizing along the Little Colorado River, 1870–1900* (Tucson: University of Arizona Press, 1973); and George S. Tanner and J. Morris Richards, *Colonization on the Little Colorado: The Joseph City Region* (Flagstaff, AZ: Northland, 1977), in addition to *Hell on the Range*.

On the Hashknife Outfit (the Aztec Land & Cattle Company), I consulted Robert H. Carlock, *The Hashknife: The Early Days of the Aztec Land and Cattle Company, Limited* (Tucson: Westernlore Press, 1994); and Jim Bob Tinsley, *The Hashknife Brand* (Gainesville: University of Florida Press, 1993).

In addition, I have made use of Rita Ackerman, *O.K. Corral Postscript: The Death of Ike Clanton* (Honolulu: Talei Publishers, 2006); Larry Ball, "Hunting His Own Kind: Tom Horn's adventures in Arizona during the Pleasant Valley War Fueled Him for His Later Exploits," *True West*, April 22, 2014 (http://www.truewestmagazine.com/hunting-his-own-kind/); Glenn R. "Slim" Ellison, *Cowboys under the Mogollon Rim* (Tucson: University of Arizona Press, 1970) and *More Tales from Slim Ellison* (Tucson: University of Arizona Press, 1981); David Grassé, *The True, Untold Story of Commodore Perry Owens: A Sheriff of the Arizona Territory* (Santa Ana, California: Graphic Publishers, 2013); Phillip Ashton Rollins, *The Cowboy: An Unconventional History of Civilization on the Old-Time Cattle Range* (rev. and enl. edition; Norman: Univ. of Oklahoma Press, 1997); Philip Smith, *Jesse Ellison Washington* (N.P.: Xlibris, 2016); and Richard W. Slatta, *The Cowboy Encyclopedia* (Santa Barbara: ABC-CLIO, 1994).

Clearly—given that *The Feudist* is a work of fiction—I have been forced to invent dialogue, shape fictive personae, and sometimes collapse or partly imagine complex events (the more liberties I took with any particular character, the more I fictionalized the name). In three instances, however, I appropriate statements directly from primary sources. In Chapter 16, Caleb Hartman, the Snowflake stake president, tells Ben that "those who mete out the death penalty to the defiler commit the same sin themselves." The real-life Apostle Erastus Snow (for whom Snowflake was named) used similar words in 1884 to reproach Mormons who still adhered to the doctrine of blood atonement. See Jesse Nathaniel Smith, *Journal* (entry for September 25, 1884), Jesse N. Smith Papers, Harold B. Lee Library, Brigham Young University, Box 1, folder 2, 362.

In Chapter 18, Frank Wattron, the Holbrook constable, commands a teen-aged boy to fetch Sheriff Commodore Perry Owens thusly: "'Tell that long-haired womanly son of a bitch sacking up with that Mexican whore that Hooper's in town.'" According to a cowboy named Lucien Creswell, the real Frank Wattron had indeed told a man to "go across the river and tell that cowardly son of a bitch sacking up with that Mexican bitch that Cooper's in town. If he don't come over here and take care of the god damned bastard I am going to do so and then I am going to take care of that yellow bellied womanish son-of-a-bitching sheriff." See Lucien Creswell, "Statement of Lucien Creswell," Flagstaff, Arizona, June 10, 1935, typescript, Gladwell Richardson Manuscript Collection, Northern Arizona University, 9.

Finally, in Chapter 22, the defense attorney insists that "if that man [Tom Graham's murderer] was indeed the Defendant, then he must be a lightning-change artist of great renown." This line and those that follow are taken from A. C. Baker's actual statement in the Tewksbury trial, as quoted in Leland J. Hanchett, Jr., *Arizona's Graham-Tewksbury Feud* (Phoenix: Pine Rim Publishing, 1994), 118.

Acknowledgments

Though *The Feudist* emerged from years of independent research and writing, I could not have completed it without the help of others. First and foremost, I wish to thank my creative and wonderful father, Justin, who wrote a draft of a novel based on my nonfiction account of the Pleasant Valley War (*Hell on the Range*), then turned over the project to me. My father's story remains at the core of *The Feudist*, though I drew on my own expertise to manufacture characters, settings, and dialogue, as well as to make the story as historically accurate—and revealing—as I could make it.

I also wish to thank the excellent staff at TCU Press, including Dan Williams, director; Kathy Walton, editor; and Molly Spain, assistant editor. Their patient advice and painstaking readings helped me streamline the novel. Several of my historian colleagues—Andrew Graybill, Richard Slatta, John Mack Faragher, Thom Bahde, and Stephen Aron—also read the manuscript and offered feedback. I got more assistance from colleagues at my home institution, Central Washington University. Roxanne Easley commented on the entire manuscript. Others—Joe Powell, Steve Moore, and Jay Ball—commented on early drafts of preliminary chapters. Emily Wallen—then a stellar CWU English major; now an Amazon software developer—made similarly astute suggestions.

I got still more help from outside academia. Rita Ackerman, an independent historian and expert on Territorial Arizona, gave me feedback on the manuscript in one of its early incarnations. So did the talented Western novelist Melody Groves, who offered a thorough and encouraging appraisal when the project was in its youth. When I had questions about people or places, I consulted the indefatigable Joan Clark, the former state chair of the Arizona Archaeological Society. Joan and I share a fascination with the history of the Rim Country (and Arizona more broadly), which made our exchanges both voluminous and fun.

Finally, an effusive thanks goes to my dear and thoughtful wife, Margareta, who endured my struggles with the manuscript across the entire horizon of its development, never failing to offer patient counsel.

About the Author

PHOTO BY MARGARETA HERMAN

Daniel Herman became ensnared in Southwestern history as a boy as he pored over *Arizona Highways Magazine*. He is the author of three award-winning nonfiction books, including an account of Arizona's Rim Country War (usually called the Pleasant Valley War) titled *Hell on the Range: A Story of Honor, Conscience, and the American West* (New Haven: Yale University Press, 2010). He and his wife, Margareta, and daughter, Persia, live in Ellensburg, Washington, where Herman teaches history at Central Washington University.